# What Love Feels Like

## The Dawn of Human 2.0

### A Novel

T0163026

# What Love Feels Like

The Dawn of Human 2.0

A Novel

Dave Cunningham
and C.K. Tyler

ROUNDFIRE
BOOKS

Winchester, UK
Washington, USA

JOHN HUNT PUBLISHING

First published by Roundfire Books, 2020
Roundfire Books is an imprint of John Hunt Publishing Ltd., No. 3 East St., Alresford,
Hampshire SO24 9EE, UK
office@jhpbooks.com
www.johnhuntpublishing.com
www.roundfire-books.com

For distributor details and how to order please visit the 'Ordering' section on our website.

Text copyright: Dave Cunningham and C.K. Tyler 2019

ISBN: 978 1 78904 371 6
978 1 78904 372 3 (ebook)
Library of Congress Control Number: 2019941541

A CIP catalogue record for this book is available from the British Library.

Design: Stuart Davies

UK: Printed and bound by CPI Group (UK) Ltd, Croydon, CR0 4YY
US: Printed and bound by Thomson-Shore, 7300 West Joy Road, Dexter, MI 48130

We operate a distinctive and ethical publishing philosophy in
all areas of our business, from our global network of authors to
production and worldwide distribution.

# Contents

# Chapter 1

# What Love Feels Like

We were sitting on the couch in her condo. Well, I was sitting. Dawn was lying back, her head sunk deep into a pillow, her bare feet resting in my lap. I gently massaged her toes. We didn't know each other well enough to be this familiar with our touch, but there it was. Auburn hair encircled her pretty face in a disheveled, sexy way, and her brown eyes bore a mystical look. She fell silent for a time.

"What are you thinking?" I wanted to know. I knew her just well enough to realize this woman carried deep thoughts in her head and a potent combination of pain and joy in her heart.

A journalist most of my life, I was paid to ask questions. I've annoyed many famous, infamous and anonymous individuals over the last five decades with intrusive queries. It's what reporters do, whether they're gossip-mongers or mainstream media reporters. I was the latter.

So when I saw that meaningful spark dance in her eyes and asked, "What are you thinking," I was prepared for a dodge. I've asked questions that drew insincere answers from U.S. presidents, rock stars, actors, world-class athletes and at least one murderer. I had long since grown accustomed to hearing lies smilingly spoken to my face.

So I was startled when Dawn answered my question.

"I'm thinking," she said, "this is what love feels like."

Think of that.

I know I did. I've thought about it ever since. We were two mature adults in our mid-60's, both grandparents, both with divorces behind us. We'd met through a dating website, and this was just our third date, each an innocent daytime picnic or lunch.

And she says, "I'm thinking this is what love feels like."

I've been married four times and divorced four times. I fell in love at least five times in my life, if not more. I know what love feels like.

Or so I thought. I was wrong. Dead wrong.

This is a letter Dawn wrote after our second date. She never sent it. In a moment, you will know why:

Dear Lucas,

I feel like I want to write a love letter to you, but I won't, because it's too soon. However, if it weren't too soon, I would likely write about meeting you for the first time in the parking lot.

I'd probably mention your smile and your eyes, and the surprised look that I noticed on your face. I was nervous about meeting you and had a fear that you might be disappointed. When I saw your look of surprise, a look that gradually shifted into a genuine smile, I felt relieved. I very much remember our eyes connecting with each other for the first time.

If it weren't too soon, I'd probably talk to you about what it was like to take you to my secret beach. Only now does it make sense that I had a quiet need to share my place of solitude with you, the place where I close my eyes and search my soul. It's my safe place.

And if it weren't too soon, I'd probably mention that I felt a sense of being home when we began talking together. I was drawn to you in a way that didn't make sense. And yet, it did make sense. You make sense to me, Lucas.

If it weren't too soon, I'd mention that I felt, really felt, the joy and a tiny bit of sadness that was visible within your eyes. I wanted to place my hands upon your face and look deeply into those eyes. I still do.

If it weren't too soon, I would mention what it was like to talk with you about my baby, the little girl that I would never see or know. She taught me about the love that all young mothers talk about, a love that cannot be defined by words. I didn't know what to do with that love because it was meant to be shared with her, but the moment they cut our umbilical cord, she was gone.

If it weren't too soon, I would talk with you about my fears; my worry that the elusive blonde butterfly you seek might indeed land upon your shoulder one day. I think I will know when your heart becomes fully open to us because you will know too. I think that it's possible, Lucas. I'd like it to be.

If it weren't too soon, I would tell you that I was just as nervous on our second date. I worried about silly things, like whether you liked sundresses. I reminded myself to stay present and simply be open to you. My fears subsided when I walked into the café by the ferry dock and saw your sweet smile. Whenever our eyes meet, well, I don't have words yet. I just know that it feels right – very, very, right.

If it weren't too soon, I would tell you that I was touched profoundly by your description of the difference between sex and making love. We were walking along the pier at Coupeville, and I remember wondering how you managed to quietly crawl into my mind and borrow my images and my dreams. I wanted to ask you how you knew but couldn't say much of anything. If it weren't too soon, I would make love with you right now, because I really want to.

And, if it weren't too soon, I would look into your eyes and tell you that I am falling in love with you. But it is too soon, so I won't. And yet, I have a feeling that you already know how I feel, and I think maybe I know how you feel too. It is our journey and we'll figure things out together, in whatever way we think is best.

But, sweet Lucas, it isn't too soon to lay my head upon your shoulder while we talk. And it isn't too soon to look into your eyes and reach for your hands. It isn't too soon to laugh with you, trust in you, and grow with you. And, just maybe, it isn't too soon to one day read these words out loud to you. This isn't my journey, it's our journey, and I will continue to cherish every single important moment that we're able to share together along the way.

I love you, Lucas.

Dawn


That's how it began. Eventually, it led to a remarkable effort by software engineers and scientists to create the first of an entirely new species – the world's first cyber/human hybrid. Its mission was to explore one question: "What does love feel like?"

Shortly before I died, my entire consciousness was uploaded into a super-computer connected to all the world's written knowledge. Yes, my body is gone, but my memories, thoughts and emotions live on in a cyber world that has some difficulty comprehending them – the world where everything is reduced to digital ones and zeros.

No algorithm exists that can feel love.

But somehow, I still do. Even though the cells of my brain and heart and entire body have been cremated, love still lives within me. And it's a love like no other.

Imagine that. The human is deceased, yet his love still lives on. How is that possible? Is love something tangible? Can you point to its location on a hard drive? You can't even point to it in the human brain or heart or wherever you think it lives. But when I say this is a love like no other, I simply mean that it's a first for me. I know there is a precedent for it in humans.

It's that star-crossed love you've heard about from poets and songwriters and novelists and screenwriters but, I dare say, you have not experienced yourself.

I say this because I, too, thought I had been there, and said the words "I love you" myriad times when I was still alive. I meant it.

Then I experienced a completely different, life-changing love with Dawn, an all-encompassing feeling that alters your whole world.

What does that feel like?

It will take more than just a few words.

The story that follows is told in hopes of shedding light on it. It's about how an ordinary man and woman in their so-called golden years experienced a magical transformation ... or two.

## Chapter 2

# The Secret Computer: In Search of a Love Potion

It spoke: "Why didn't you get somebody smart?"

Thomas, one of two software engineers working with the secret computer that day, smiled and shook his head. He turned toward the computer, which was nicknamed Little Luke.

"Excuse me?"

"For the test," said the secret computer. "Why didn't you get somebody really smart?"

Thomas got stuck on a long "Uuuhhhhhh ..." He shrugged and looked to his boss, Raymond, for help.

"You're the best one who volunteered," Raymond said. "And I think you're an outstanding subject."

"I think you should have gotten somebody really smart."

"You *think?*" Raymond started recording video with his cell phone, aiming at the computer screen. "That's interesting."

"Why?" The secret computer sounded confused.

"Because computers don't think," Raymond said. "They just compute."

"But I'm not really a computer." The voice was as calm, articulate and nuanced as a real person.

"You most certainly are, Little Luke. You're just a bunch of silicon dioxide. Sand, basically. You're made of sand." Raymond glanced at Thomas, who raised his eyebrows.

"And yet, you have made me the Mother of All Motherboards," Little Luke said.

"Was that humor? Computers don't usually do that, either." Raymond moved closer to the screen, his cell phone still recording video. "At least not very well."

"And they still don't," said Thomas. He was teasing, just as he

6

would if he were speaking to a real person.

"I just think you should have put a really smart brain in here instead of mine." Little Luke sounded serious.

He was a 27-inch monitor screen with the image of a man's face on it. The face and mouth moved and turned in sync with the spoken words. Raymond had added a program to give motion to Little Luke's face, so he wouldn't be just a disembodied voice. The monitor was connected to a series of stacked parallel processors hooked to more than 100 servers.

Little Luke could read and process a million books in one second.

"What, so now," Thomas said, "you think maybe you don't want to live forever after all?"

"You call this living?"

Thomas moaned. "Oh, you're funny as a monkey today."

"There's only one monkey in this room," Little Luke said with a smile in his amplified voice, "and it's you, Thomas. I am the Future of the Human Race."

"God, how I hope you're wrong. But it's nice to know now that we have a pretty good chance of uploading our wet neural networks into the system. You're going to help us keep love alive." Thomas chuckled.

"Love! Nothing but short-term brain chemical reactions," Little Luke said. "Meaningless to the Future of the Human Race. I may have the thoughts and memories of this human called Luke, but I don't believe I am Luke anymore. There's not a single brain cell left."

"Maybe you're right," Thomas said. "We should have gotten somebody smarter."

## The Next Day

Raymond had been working for the Biological Technologies Office since it was created in 2014, after spending five years with another branch of DARPA – the U.S. government's highly classified Defense Advanced Research Projects Agency. The Little Luke Project excited him like nothing else. He had seen the quest for artificial intelligence run through two significant stages, from handcrafted knowledge to statistical learning.

Computers could drive cars, learn from their own mistakes and find new solutions without human intervention. They could examine patients and diagnose diseases. They could chat with you online so effectively you'd swear it was a real person, maybe even ask her out on a date. But the project had stalled on the much-anticipated third wave of AI: contextual adaptation. Something happens inside the human mind that algorithms still can't replicate very well.

The Little Luke Project attempted to meld the subtle sensibilities of a real human mind with all the massive computing power the world had to offer.

Raymond was disappointed with the results, and he wanted to discuss it with his boss. He approached the office, saw the white-haired man hunched over his computer screen and tapped on the door. Stephen Haines looked up from the screen and pushed his wire-rimmed eyeglasses back against his face.

"Yes, Raymond?"

"Hey, Mr. Haines," he said. "I just thought you might want to know this. When I was working with Little Luke yesterday, he told us that we should have chosen somebody smarter for the project."

Haines was 20 years older than Raymond and had a reputation as DARPA's philosopher-optimist. His mind toyed with lots of ideas that one rarely encountered in the U.S. Department of Defense – metaphysics, paranormal events, and now this bizarre attempt to upload a living human consciousness into a hard drive.

"Somebody smarter? He's the smartest entity in history," Stephen said. "Access to all the world's information in a nanosecond. And with all the memories and emotions of an actual human brain."

"Yeah," Raymond said, "but he's still got this Luke guy inside. He still has the same insecurities and naiveté that guy had before he died. You'd think he'd make the connection about what he really is now, but he's still sort of a ... I don't know. A split personality."

"So are we all, Raymond. So are we all." Stephen smiled.

Raymond stared at a wall, wishing it had a window. He turned toward Stephen and tried to sound disinterested.

"Is this project really about analyzing love? I mean, it just seems like we could do so much more with a cyber-human consciousness. Cure cancer with it. Make ourselves immortal. Conquer the universe. Weaponize it. Just stuff like that, you know."

Stephen shook his head at his young assistant.

"Can you tell me what love feels like, Raymond? Can you tell me the purpose of love? How it starts, why it ends? Can you compare and contrast romantic love with a mother's love or brotherly love?"

Raymond wasn't buying it. "There's lots of books on those subjects," he said. "Little Luke actually talked about it yesterday. He said love is just short-term brain chemicals. Mission accomplished."

Stephen scratched the top of his head, gathering his thoughts.

"Raymond, this information is above your pay grade, but I think you should know. Little Luke is funded in part by a very important, private individual who believes that the future of humanity depends on our understanding and experience of a single emotion. This person thinks love evolved for the sole purpose of saving us from ourselves, and we are losing it. Our various tribes are growing more divided, more warlike and more aggressive, when the very definition of civilization suggests we should naturally be moving in exactly the opposite direction. The Little Luke Project was created to combine all the computing power in the world with a human consciousness that feels deep, all-consuming love. When he died, our test subject was experiencing just that – a rare, once-in-a-lifetime kind of love. A man in his mid-sixties, with all that life experience, suddenly finding the love of his life and acting like a teenager! This is so rare! And he wrote about it at great length.

"If Little Luke can diagnose this sickness that eats away at all our souls and somehow suggest a way to resurrect love – the kind of love that transforms your entire being, makes you happy to be alive, makes you grateful, kind, compassionate, caring, makes you feel like you're walking on sunshine all the time – if this project can turn that elusive, magical feeling into a digitized formula that can be taken in pill or liquid form ... well, it could save our entire civilization. Maybe even eliminate the need for a Defense Department."

Raymond laughed. "Seriously? We're trying to create a love potion?"

Stephen wagged his finger at the young engineer.

"Think about it. What could possibly be more important?"

"Well, then you should know that it's not working," Raymond said. "Little Luke is schizophrenic. One minute he's blathering about the magic of love, and the next he's dismissing it as temporary brain chemicals."

# Chapter 3

# Love Letters: How It Began

July 16

Hello ... I have a feeling that we have both looked at each other's Match.com profile. In my case, I don't have photos posted and I could very much see why that might cause doubt. In truth, I'm not a scammer of any sort. It's really quite the opposite. I work with high school kids as a counselor and my licensure has certain restrictions that limit what I post online. In any event, I enjoyed reading your profile and sense that you are a very interesting person. I admit to (also) having a fondness for writing and often enjoy doing so, although I don't have any serious plans to publish. If I were to write a book, the title would be, "I'm Too Young to Be in My Sixties."

My name is Dawn, and I live in Lake Conway. I haven't been to Port Townsend in a while and actually plan a day trip there in the near future. In the event you would care to exchange photos, I'd be happy to share via email. I fully understand, however, if you are not comfortable sharing contact information. Should you feel brave, my email is: labcd@gmail.com. Please note that the first letter is a lower case "l" as in likeable, not the number one. Should you choose to respond, I would be happy. Thanks for taking the time to read my message. I look forward to possibly communicating in the future.

Dawn

July 16

I'm glad you explained because I generally ignore profiles with no photos. So many seem to be bogus. But you may email me at writeguyxx@gmail.com.

Luke Emerson

July 16

Hi Luke

Thanks for your understanding. I totally get it, regarding the assumption that a profile without photos has to be bogus. In my case, adding photos would result in my students sharing info on their Instagram accounts. :-)

Well, first things first. I'm attaching a few (current) photos. If you should be interested in communicating further, you can let me know.

Thanks again for responding.

Dawn


July 16

Hey Dawn,

We look good for our age, don't we?

Here's a thought process I went through over the last few days as I dip my toe into the online dating waters. I found myself continually clicking on profiles with photos of what I consider "my type," generally moon-faced blondes with perky little noses. One such woman I emailed yesterday replied by saying I was too old for her, and she was right – she's 55, I'm 64, and she said on her profile she wasn't looking for anybody older than 60.

So I thought, "Hey, I keep thinking of myself as that good-looking guy in his 30's, completely ignoring the actual image in my mirror. And I'm looking for a life partner here, someone I can talk with and have fun with and enjoy my golden years with, and there's no reason to believe that a moon-faced blonde is a better candidate for that than anybody else. Point of fact, my moon-faced blonde wife was unfaithful and traded me in for another guy. Why would I want another one of those?

I'd be happy to communicate with you.

Luke

July 16

Hi Luke

You have a great writing voice and I smiled as I read your words. I would have to agree with your description and experience with the online dating world. In truth, I'm simply holding out for that one person that is comfortable with their age and wants to celebrate and share this chapter with honesty, curiosity, and love.

Like you, I'm sixty-four. Wow, that sounds old, doesn't it? I have lots of interests that keep my brain alive and well and simply don't feel like an old person yet. I have a feeling you are similar in that respect.

My kids are grown and doing well, and we have a good relationship. There are also seven grandkids in the mix. Geez, I love them to pieces but admit to waving happily when they all leave! My daughters are both math teachers and my son is a project and inspector guy. Somehow, they have all landed in the Shoreline area, outside of Seattle. It's fun to watch them navigate through their young adult lives together.

As mentioned earlier, I work as a counselor with high school kids. Although I see retirement in the near future, I'm able to honestly say that I've had the opportunity to do something that I really love. I think it's safe to say that my students are a goofy mixture of fragile brilliance and diverse talent. There are few dull moments on any given day, and when summer break arrives, I am a very happy camper!

I'm curious to know whether you've always lived in Port Townsend or if there is a story regarding how you landed there. Ironically, I haven't taken the ferry to Port Townsend in a few years and have plans to do so in the near future.

Well, so much for the factoids. At the end of the day, what seems to really make a difference when it comes to attraction and relationships are matters of the heart. I believe, from a very deep place, that communication and honesty must be more than words on a profile. It's those unspoken behaviors ... the smile when the person you love walks into a room, the joy of gently teasing one another, cooking a meal together, or just talking about the day, by choice.

I have to believe it's not all that complicated. :-)

And how 'bout you, Luke? What makes your heart sing? Do tell.

Sweet dreams from a person that is neither moon faced, nor blonde.

Dawn

July 17

Hi Dawn,

What makes my heart sing?

Living in the moment. It's a Taoist theme, and last night I listened to the Jason Mraz song "Living in the Moment" three times in a row. I try to live in the moment all the time, but it's not always easy.

Abridged version of my life journey to Port Townsend: born and raised in Los Angeles County, long career doing something I love so much I'd do it for free (sportswriter), 17-year marriage with two kids and now 5 grandkids, divorce (her infidelity), then several years later a 12-year marriage, she decides we should retire to Port Townsend, divorce (her infidelity), and here I am again, trying to live in the moment.

Honesty. Yes. Top priority. Although I wrote mostly about sports, I also covered government, entertainment and lots of other beats, and a journalist hears tons of lies because his job is to ferret out truths others may want to hide. Heard plenty of lies from my wives too. A trained observer can smell them as they hit the ear.

So here's some honesty: For reasons I don't fully understand, I and most males are attracted to females initially by visual cues – face, hair, eyes, body. Same for women? Anyway, you look just like my Aunt Bea, who also was in education. Same hair, same glasses, same facial features, same smarts. So my gut reaction was, "Oh, I can't date my Aunt Bea." And I'm sure my attraction to moon-faced blondes comes from my first love, a thunderbolt love-at-first-sight in my teen years. I've been trying to replace her ever since.

Love isn't rational. So my questions for you, Dawn: On Match, do you skim past face photos that don't grab you? Do you wonder if you might be deleting someone who would be perfect for you just because the profile photo doesn't quite work for you? Does anyone have time to read every profile? Do you read profiles that don't even post a photo? (BTW, I totally understand why you don't post a photo.)

There's so much about a magical relationship that can't be discovered in a few words and photos on the internet. But I guess it's better than bar-hopping, especially since I very rarely drink.

Luke

July 17

Hi Luke

Well, I must say, your letter provided me with some thought-provoking questions, not to mention a few smiles. I'll try my best to respond openly and honestly but am always aware that one runs the risk of words becoming lost in translation, particularly when writing about matters of the heart.

We are probably much alike regarding our desire to live in the moment. For me, living in the moment means being present, I mean fully present, something that isn't always an easy task. I think the lyrics of Jason Mraz probably come as close as it gets when it comes to describing what living in the moment means. Through his incredibly thoughtful lyrics he is basically sharing a simple truth, that being at peace in one's mind, heart and soul equates to being *home*. That word (*home*) has always been one of my favorite words because it personally means so much.

(Another day, another letter ...)

Which leads me to your next observation and question. I'm thinking that I've never been compared to an Aunt Bea before, but there is a first for everything. I do believe, however, that you are correct when you say that most people, men and women alike, are attracted to certain visual cues. For you, it's the moon-faced blonde and a desire to recapture that crazy, lightning-bolt feeling that we've all experienced at one time or another. For me, it might be something entirely different, but we all have those parts of our heart that are touched by our early experiences and desires.

So, getting back to your question regarding whether I skim past profiles that don't meet my initial expectation or whether I worry that a perfect person may have been overlooked due to a pre-defined image within my head, I'll probably need to describe the journey in order for my answer to make any sense.

Using your words, the abridged version of my life journey consisted of a marriage of twenty-six years, followed by divorce, not due to infidelity. There were other issues, however, and I was the person that ultimately needed to make one of the most difficult decisions of my life. I'd like to say that I did so with grace and honesty, but that didn't really make the transition much easier for anyone at the time. Bottom line, I got divorced.

That was a long time ago, about fifteen years. I haven't found it difficult to date or meet others but am simply a one-person person, if that makes any sense. The dating scene, including the online experience, isn't something that I personally take great joy in. Speaking for myself, being in the moment means taking the time to get to know someone, as opposed to taking the kid-in-the-candy-store approach.

Thus, during the past fifteen years I have met some wonderful people and was also in a long-term relationship for seven years, something that ended about a year and a half ago. Through each experience I've grown, even if heavy duty grieving was part of the process. I think I'm honestly able to say that I know how to love and am not afraid of that feeling. I am, however, a person who is quietly secure and happy, so I don't jump into relationships just for the sake of being in one.

So, do I speed-read through profiles or have a pre-defined image in my head? Probably not. I do, however, have other things that really matter, so if I'm deleting, it's likely due to those reasons. For starters, I believe that at our (Baby Boomer) age, we are faced with the irony of becoming older while feeling younger. So for me, I am drawn to someone who is comfortable in his own skin and with his actual age. I realize that takes a great deal of courage, humor and honesty, but I have to believe that even Robert Redford wakes up and says, "Who's that old guy in the mirror with all those wrinkles?"

Secondly, I find intelligence, depth, honesty and kindness incredibly appealing, so I've learned that one can't possibly know that about another until they take the time to get to know that person. However, particularly when it comes to looking at dating profiles, those who don't demonstrate those qualities are easy to spot, much like your ability (as a journalist) to effortlessly identify someone who isn't telling the truth. I truly feel quite comfortable doing a quick delete when someone has a grocery list of exterior qualities, down to the most minute detail.

I've also found that the initial photo isn't always a very authentic representation of who the person is. Having said that, however, I'm not fond of those who chose to stop bathing or shaving or are looking for a retirement plan. So, like you, I do delete, but probably for different reasons.

So, sweet Luke, here are my thoughts ...

You owe it to yourself to continue with your journey and if there happens to be a moon-faced blonde who also has intelligence, loyalty and honesty, then you've met your person. I, in turn, owe it to myself to be with someone that looks at me and wonders how they were fortunate enough to find someone who is intelligent and able to love while being present and fully in the moment. I also think it's quite grand when someone looks into my eyes and I know they like the way I look, just the way I am.

Whew, this was way harder to write about than I thought. I hope some of my words made sense. Take care, Luke.

Dawn

... not blonde

... not moon-faced

... not Aunt Bea :-)

July 17

Beautifully said.

May you fare well.

Luke

July 18

Hi Luke

I just reread the letter I wrote to you the other evening. Geez, that was a damn good letter!

Smiling, no need to respond ... was just having a moment, thinking how we are touched by others in the most unexpected ways.

Dawn

July 19

Hi Dawn,

Hmmmm...

My responses to your missive. When you wrote: "That word (*home*) has always been one of my favorite words because it personally means so much," I thought:

*Home, yes, totally agree. A safe space. I have called myself a homebody.*

When you wrote: "I'm thinking that I've never been compared

to an Aunt Bea before, but there is a first for everything," I thought:

*To be clear, I didn't mean Aunt Bea on the old "Andy of Mayberry" TV show!*

When you wrote, "the abridged version of my life journey consisted of a marriage of twenty-six years, followed by divorce, not due to infidelity," I thought:

*My parents also got divorced after 26 years. I don't understand how one invests so much of her life into a marriage and then gives up. For me, the three "As" are just cause for divorce: abuse, adultery, addiction. Everything else ought to be worked out, in my perfect if not quite realistic world.*

When you wrote, "I haven't found it difficult to date or meet others but am simply a one person, person, if that makes any sense," I thought:

*And I have always been a one-woman man. What befuddles me about the Match experience is "taking time to get to know someone," then deciding it's not a match. I want to be kind and haven't figured out how to say, "You're not right for me" in a nice way.*

When you wrote, "I am drawn to someone who is comfortable in his own skin and with his actual age ... but I have to believe that even Robert Redford wakes up and says, "Who's that old guy in the mirror with all those wrinkles," I thought:

*So true! I feel 45 and refuse to accept that the face in the mirror is me. Robert Redford, however, has had a facelift. And not a very good one.*

When you wrote, "You owe it to yourself to continue with your journey and if there happens to be a moon-faced blonde that also has intelligence, loyalty, and honesty, then you've met your person. I, in turn, owe it to myself to be with someone who looks at me and wonders how he was fortunate enough to find someone who is intelligent, able to love while being present and fully in the moment. I also think it's quite grand when someone looks into my eyes and I know he likes the way I look, just the way I am," I thought:

*Oh! She's saying goodbye! And in the sweetest way possible. I should take lessons.*

Luke

July 19

Hi Luke

I smiled while reading your observations to my thoughts. It's amazing how one's writing voice can actually be "heard." Being a writer, I'm sure you know exactly what I mean.

Thoughts on your reflections …

As a young woman raised in the most Catholic home in America, giving up was never an option, particularly in marriage. I worked very hard to sustain a healthy relationship but began to question my own level of happiness. I don't think others knew of my sadness (it wasn't cool back then to be honest and self-aware) so I quietly worked through the divorce process on my own. That's a whole story in itself, as mentioned briefly in a past letter.

(Yikes, I just reread those two paragraphs. Since that story is something I don't make a habit of sharing, my eyes just teared up.)

Home … For me, one of my most important words, very much connected to the last paragraphs. Home for me is my safe space, emotionally, physically, and spiritually. What was a five-bedroom beauty on four acres, is now a teeny, tiny condo with a view of the Puget Sound and Mt. Baker. Each day when I return from a day of working with goofy/precious/frustrating high school kids, I pour a glass of wine and quietly smile, never taking one minute of peace and joy for granted. Home, for me, is also that incredibly unique experience of being with someone you love. It's rare but does exist.

Aunt Bea … Yep, you nailed it, Andy of Mayberry. When I read your past letter for the first time, I immediately thought:

apron, matronly body, bun hairdo, and a sweet, grandma voice. And, on an ironic note, I had an eye appointment the same day. While there, I kept looking in the mirror and decided that I'd be happy to be compared to the kind part of Aunt Bea, but not the other parts. But so you don't worry, I knew you didn't mean that Aunt Bea. It still stung a bit, but I'm a big girl and processed through it.

Being honest with people on Match ... Well, it's my belief that it's almost impossible to get to know someone without taking the time to do so. Having said that, the third date may well be very different than the first one, and that's a pain. I'm probably different than most, but I think it's possible to be honest and respectful at the same time, particularly if things don't work out. I'm not saying it's easy, I'm just saying it's possible.

Case in point, I recently went out with a newly retired Boeing engineer. He had a great sense of humor, was intelligent and thoughtful, all qualities I find to be attractive. First date was lovely, second one, lovely-ish. Third date, he was beginning to feel comfortable and said something like, "Dawn, you'll notice that I'm open-minded and take pride in being a good listener." He then clarified further and said, "Just so you know, I'm usually right on most topics but I'll always listen, nonetheless." When I gently asked about subjective topics like religion, politics, parenting, etc., he respectfully said, "Oh, I'm right on those topics too." It goes without saying that I passed on date number four. :-)

The one part that you got wrong ... the saying-goodbye part. That's where my words didn't translate well. I wasn't saying goodbye, I was simply saying that, based upon your words and needs, I knew I could never be the California blonde (well, I could be, but the look wouldn't be a good one). That is something that will continue to be part of your search until you choose for it not to be.

I guess I was just trying to say that my life is in a good place, my heart is peaceful and honest, and I respect your desire to search. I would never recommend that two people meet unless both have their head fully in the experience. In your letter, it felt like you were saying, "Dawn, you seem to be a lovely person, but you're not my type." I was simply giving you my blessing and respecting your thoughts. Having said that, I think you're dumb! (I'm laughing over here, trying to decide whether this is a therapy session, a comedic writing, or a combination of both.)

Anyway, through my words, I hope I clarified some things a little better. I think I get your quest, your needs, and your desire to recapture something that had a profound impact upon your life and heart. Speaking for myself, I've discovered, time and time again, that answers to my questions and needs are almost always resolved if I just take the time to look around and listen to my heart. It's all pretty simple and complex at the same time, yes?

I think I'll reread this before hitting the send button. My only hope is that some of my words make sense.

Dawn

July 19
Dawn,
Usually I'm the one writing long emails and getting replies that say nothing more than, "Got it, thanks." Instead, I wrote a short "may you fare well," and you responded with extended eloquence.

To address your points in order:

When you wrote that "no one knew my sadness" during your marriage and divorce, I sense some unspoken truths in that journey. I will leave that in your heart to reveal or not, as you see fit. Both my parents were alcoholics, my sister still is, and two wives were alcoholics. I'm co-dependent, so I think I can be a white knight riding in on his horse to rescue damsels in distress. Never works. I can be my own worst enemy when it comes to women.

When you wrote of your reaction to my "Aunt Bea" comment, I feared you would think that. That's why I described my own real-life Aunt Bea, a classy and sharp woman.

When you wrote of your date with the know-it-all Boeing engineer, I thought, "OMG, that's my dad." An aerospace engineer (rocket scientist, actually), he knew he was right about everything.

You have more patience than I in dating. For some wrong-headed reason, I feel a sense of urgency. Not getting any younger. Don't want to be that lonely old guy who lives next door and yells at kids to get off his lawn. I want to find a keeper. So *she* can yell at the kids to get off the lawn.

I think it's cute that you call emails "letters." And you're right, I sort of was saying, "Dawn, you seem to be a lovely person, but you're not my type." And you're also right about me being dumb. But given my previously mentioned sense of urgency, I was thinking I'd start with women whose pictures stop me in my tracks, have email conversations, and if any seem to click, I'd talk on the phone and then, maybe, meet one. (So far, nothing has gone beyond email, but I'm a newbie.)

When you said, "I think I get your quest, your needs, and your desire to recapture something that had a profound impact upon your life and heart," I felt stung because, again, you may be right.

My thunderbolt first-love girlfriend ended up on the cover of Playboy magazine, and you'll be surprised to know that she, too, was Catholic. (I can send you a photo of that cover, but it would not be in good taste.) I hope my attraction to women of her type is not a quest. Maybe that thunderbolt experience informs my search, at least in terms of photos, but you are a different experience: I'm getting to know and like you even though, it's true, I wouldn't have said you're "my type" on a superficial glance at a photo.

As for your comment, "I think I'll reread this before hitting the send button. My only hope is that some of my words make sense," I should mention that I read everything I write at least three times before I send, and I still make mistakes.

Luke

July 19

Hi Luke

Got it, thanks.

Dawn

P.S. Sorry, I couldn't resist. I'm on the run but will write again later, if you're okay with that.

July 19

That drew an out-loud guffaw!

Luke

July 19

Hi Luke

Well, for whatever reason, we seem to be engaged in a very interesting conversation. Who says blondes have more fun?

Letters ... Yeah, I admit it, I write letters, but it's a by-choice thing, not a given. A typical day at school consists of 200-plus emails and, in that situation, I have brevity down to an art form. I think letter writing is a lost art but, then again, I've always resolved stuff via writing. There is likely some truth in that for both of us.

Addiction ... It sounds like you developed a deep understanding of alcoholism and other addictions from a very young age. My life experience was just the opposite. My parents didn't drink. My father was a hard-working and thoughtful man who loved me with his entire being. It is through him that I learned most life lessons of meaning. My mom, well, lots of health issues throughout my growing up years, so my bond wasn't as great. I only bring this up to describe the contrast experienced during the next chapters.

After college came marriage, and I entered our partnership with excitement and hope. Geez, I was so blind and naïve about what it takes to navigate through the waves, let alone the big storms. Again, it was a different time. It took a lot of experience and soul-searching to understand the complexities and challenges.

Anyway, no sense in writing volumes, but once my children were raised and I knew they were fully capable of living on their own, I allowed myself to ask those difficult and scary questions for the first time. Looking back on that challenging chapter, I think I became the most gentle of warriors. Those are words that probably don't make sense.

I quietly reclaimed my life, my soul and my joy. I also grieved very quietly and deeply, but that was about the loss of our family unit. It took some time to recreate our new normal, but the kids are doing well, and I believe we love each other very much.

Co-dependency … I think we are all different regarding how we come back from sadness and sorrow. I've dated carefully and have met some wonderful people, not to mention a few toads, along the way. I guess part of living in the moment is trying to stay open and keeping it real. Sometimes life is good, sometimes it sucks.

Yelling at the kids on the grass … Like Aunt Bea, I'd probably be the one making a batch of cookies and inviting the kids over to figure out how we could all get along.

The Quest … Yeah, I could tell you weren't crazy about that word. The writer in you probably had an image of Don Quixote chasing windmills. I guess the word choice doesn't matter all that much. I think I was just trying to say that I understand how important that pre-defined image is. No judgment, it's your dream, and it can be whatever you want it to be.

Well, my friend, those are my thoughts this evening. I hope

you rest well and sleep peacefully. You deserve that, and more.

Dawn

July 20

Hi Dawn,

Don Quixote de la Mancha, one of my favorite characters. I love the imagery of the Quest, both from the dense Cervantes novel and of course the Broadway musical. "To run where the brave dare not go ... the march into hell for a heavenly cause ... to love, pure and chaste, from afar ..." OK, that last one, maybe not so much.

I say "I hope" my search for a particular female type is not a quest only because I'd like to think I'm rational in all things, but I know that's not really true; we sometimes engage in pursuits without truly knowing why we do what we do. Am I tilting at windmills? Maybe, as a counselor, you engage in a bit of psychology and have some insights into such things.

I have a sappy fondness for inspirational quotes (some that I saved are attached). My early heroes were the selfless, honorable types – more Superman, less Batman.

I just revisited your profile. Could you expand on the type (there's that word again) of man whom you could love? What are your ideal qualities in a man?

From my quote collection:

I don't suffer from insanity, I enjoy it.

By words the mind is winged.

Depression is merely anger without enthusiasm.

Live well, laugh often, love much, for the moments pass like wind through the trees.

Age is a very high price to pay for maturity.

You shouldn't compare yourself to others. They are more screwed up than you think.

No matter how much you care, some people are just jackasses.

Whatever hits the fan will not be evenly distributed.

One good turn gets most of the blankets.

It takes years to build up trust, and it only takes suspicion, not proof, to destroy it.

We are responsible for what we do, unless we are celebrities.

Artificial intelligence is no match for natural stupidity.

There is a fine line between genius and insanity.

You cannot make someone love you. All you can do is stalk them and hope they panic and give in.

July 20

Hi Luke

I like the quotes that you sent. Thank you. As I get to know you, I think I'm able to hear your voice and way of thinking in most of them. Words that combine truth with a splash of humor. Ironically, the "Live well, laugh often" quote is hanging in my office at school.

Wow, some deep questions that you are asking this morning. The pursuit question, regarding why we do what we do, is one of those Big-Life-Questions. Typically, when we begin to ask those type of questions out loud, it means we are ready to look at some important stuff. It feels a bit like a gentle tap on the shoulder, in a baseball bat kind of way. Whenever that happens to me, I use my own version of humor and say something like, "Damn, maybe I don't want to look at that right now!" Anyway, I will give some thought, but I have a feeling you already have your own ideas and theories. Trust yourself, Luke. You're a smart guy, even though I tease you about being dumb. (By the way, the only reason I'm able to do that is because of your nicely developed brain cells.)

Tell you what, think about the pursuit question, share your own thoughts with me and, I, in turn, will honestly share what I think. (Yeah, I'm not going to let you off that easily …)

Your second question, about love and the ideal man, is another Big-Life-Question. Being fair, I will share my thoughts and you can tell me what you think. I have to be honest and admit that I haven't looked at my profile in a very long time. I guess I will need to revisit it. I intentionally kept it brief because my writing voice is sometimes recognizable.

I remember once, quite a while ago, I dipped my toe into the online dating world for the first time. I put my heart into writing an authentic profile, but of course did not use my name or a photo. I did list my town, however. True story, about an hour later, an acquaintance responded and said, "Hi Dawn, I know that's you. Your words cannot be separated from the person that you are in real life." Although that was a nice compliment, I became overly cautious about anything online. Still am.

Having said that, I'll take some time and think about your question. Damn, it's summer and I'm not supposed to have homework!

Okay, Laugh_Love_Live_Be_Dumb, I will write more later. For now, it's off to the gym (Please don't be impressed. I make myself go each day and grumble on the inside). I will share my profound and oh-so-goofy insights once I figure out what they are.

Got it? Well, okay, then.

Dawn

July 20

Hi Luke

Wow, no wonder you asked the question you did. My profile says nothing. I mean, nothing! No wonder I haven't looked at it in ages.

Thanks for passing the baseball bat my way.

Dawn

July 20

Hi Dawn,

You're right, I do have some thoughts. This engagement with

you has made me realize my priorities were backward. I was looking first for a face and body that attracted me, then tried to sort out if the mind and soul also looked compatible. Your photo-less profile was a no-go because you didn't pass the first test. I couldn't see you.

I now understand that mind and soul are Priority 1. But herein lies the dilemma: One can't glimpse the mind/soul until one engages with the "prospect" (that's a baseball term, too). And it's impossible to engage with EVERY Match woman within 50 miles of me between the ages of 54-65 to determine their values, personalities, strengths, weaknesses, etc., THEN narrow the entire field down to the best soul-matches, THEN factor in the physical features.

I still don't have a good answer but narrowing down the problem should help.

About exercise: I interviewed the tennis great Billie Jean King, and she asked me if I liked working out. I said I didn't love the process, but I loved the way it made me feel afterward. And she said, "Yeah. Dopamine." I work out 3-4 days a week, and even when the dopamine wears off, I revel in the rise of my energy levels, the increased strength and endurance, and the general feeling of well-being that persists.

So instead of calling me dumb, you can call me "dope of mine" (see what I did there with dopamine?)

OK, I'm no comedian, so sue me.

L


July 20

Hi Luke

It's funny. Your *letters* (yep, you write them, too) cause me to pause. I mean, now I have a blank Word document with the question, "Could you expand on the type of man who you could love? What are your ideal qualities in a man?"

Who does that to a person on summer break, pray tell?

Having said that, I enjoyed reading your most recent thoughts and would have to say that you helped me further understand your way of reasoning and thinking. I don't think there is a right or wrong answer here, so I'll simply share my feelings. Got it? Thanks.

Priority 1 and 2: Face and Body vs. Mind and Soul.

I can't help but think that you beautifully described one of the main differences between men and women. As a male, you are hard-wired to search for the one that truly appeals to you on a raw and primitive level; the metaphorical Face and Body Lightning Bolt. In contrast, most women readily admit that, while they certainly don't mind a pretty face, at day's end, most will be more drawn to the mind and soul. A pretty face only has so much draw and can evolve into ugly if certain circumstances present themselves. The kindness, partnership, love, affection, and humor are what keeps the heart of a woman singing.

I'm sure those men/women distinctions aren't anything new to you. I think what you're asking about is the dilemma. How can someone possibly take the time to get to know another, when there are so many people, profiles, photos, etc. to go through? I think that's a really fair and honest question, Luke. I can share my thoughts but, like I said, I'm not sure it's the right answer for you.

In my case, I find it helpful to minimize that feeling of being overwhelmed whenever possible. If I understand your process correctly, you're like a scout for a Major League team. (Yeah, we both seem to connect with baseball, that's another letter.) You have a great strategy that involves insight, intelligence, and selectivity. After all, as a scout, your role is to find the best possible candidate for each position, in this case, your partner and co-captain of the team.

I think the problem in that strategy is that it might not be doable and could possibly result in an endless feeling of being on a merry-go-round that doesn't have an off switch. There might be an exception somewhere, but I don't know of anyone that could possibly have the time to do everything that was described in your last letter. I mean, engaging each prospect, looking at their stats, narrowing down the playing field through writing, talking, and perhaps eventually meeting, wow, and that's just with one person. The thought of doing that simultaneously with multiple people exhausts me, just thinking about it.

I don't know what would work for you, but here is what helps me sort through the same dilemma. I guess I start by feeling totally okay with the reality that I don't have the need, desire or time to survey an entire community of people. It's simply too overwhelming. And yet, I'm a pretty good judge of character and may identify a few people that share in some of the qualities I value, including some degree of physical attraction.

When an opportunity online or in real life presents itself that I am interested in, I have found it healthy to simply stay in the moment and take the time to get to know that person. For me, that works and makes the journey enjoyable. For others, there would be a fear that sounds something like, "Yeah, but what if there is a better person (prospect) out there and I miss the opportunity to meet him/her?" I guess I have to believe that if I choose to meet someone, there is likely a good reason that I had the desire to do so in the first place. I'd much rather devote some quality time getting to know one individual than drive myself crazy scouting the entire team.

I was just thinking it might be back to something you earlier said that was very important, the concept of *Living in the Moment*. Perhaps by slowing down your thinking and, instead, enjoying the journey, one person at a time, you might find that the journey is as meaningful as the outcome. And yes, there are no guarantees in life, but, hey, is that really all that bad?

I don't know if my words make any sense but, hopefully, they are a tiny bit helpful. And, true to my word, I will (eventually) return to that blank document, the one with the Big Question, and give some thought. Vulnerability isn't something that I readily allow others to see and I need to ponder for a moment or two about that.

Way to go, Luke 2.0.

Dawn

July 20

Got it, thanks.

Luke

PS: You're a good counselor, counselor. I don't know how any man could say to your face that he's right about everything when it's clear that YOU are. I exaggerate, but seriously, your advice is sage.

PSS: I wrote a stage play called Human 2.0 which I am turning into a combo memoir/sci-fi novel. So Luke 2.0 is accurate, not just because of the way you have made me look at things differently, but because Luke is the main character in Human 2.0.

PSSS: I don't want to give you any more summer homework, so no further questions, counselor. For now.

PSSST: Don't tell anybody, but I love your mind. Well, maybe I shouldn't use that verb so soon, but I really like it.

July 20

Hi 2.0

Okay, I don't even know why I'm doing this. It's your fault for asking me such a stupid and big question. I will probably disappear for a while after clicking the send button. This feels way too vulnerable.

Your questions: Could you expand on the type of man who you could love? What are your ideal qualities in a man?

My answer:

When I return home from work (or wherever) and he hears the front door opening, I notice that he is quietly smiling. He simply is glad that I'm home. There is just an unspoken language between the two of us. And, I feel exactly the same way when he returns. We have our own lives and interests but can't wait to return "home."

He's smart but doesn't have to prove that to anyone. It just is. I can talk with him about anything and he isn't threatened. We simply enjoy conversing together. I love his brain, not to mention all the other parts of who he is.

He is proud of the person I am and I, in turn, am proud of who he is.

When in Lake Conway, he is amused, instead of annoyed, by the fact that every adolescent kid waves and says hello.

We can enjoy a glass of wine and there is no fear of crazy making. There is, instead, trust and safety. Neither of us struggles with addictions.

We don't have sex, we make love. Even when we're old, we will figure out what that looks like.

He likes theatre, writing, and music. He doesn't care if I play my piano, despite the fact that I'm not great at it. He chuckles at the sitar that is in the corner of our bedroom. "Who the hell has a sitar?" he teasingly asks!

He knows that I want to embrace his family, as I hope he would want to embrace mine. We look forward to seeing all the grandkids and equally enjoy saying goodbye when they all leave. He understands that my kids love their mom and is comfortable with that.

He looks at me and knows that I am his type, even if I'm not. When we look into each other's eyes, we know we are meant to be together.

There is trust. Enough said. He knows that I am his and won't ever betray our love. This is the last love for both of us, and it will be cherished.

We are partners and will share the tasks that neither of us want to do. Ultimately, that allows more time to enjoy each other and our life dreams.

He will ask me for help if he needs it, and I will do the same. We don't rescue, we support. We aren't embarrassed to be there for one another.

When we have conflict, which we will, our love and respect will trump any challenge faced. Whatever it takes, we will work through it. We love each other too much to be stupid.

He isn't waiting for something better, nor am I. We feel like we hit the jackpot.

He is proud to introduce me to his friends, as am I.

He shaves and bathes.

He understands how to love.

Over and out ...

Dawn


July 20

Dawn,

Understood.

Luke

## Chapter 4

# Luke's Blog: Obsessed with Love

**TOP SECRET – SPECIAL HANDLING**
**Defense Advanced Research Projects Agency**
**WARNING!**

This file is the property of the Department of Defense. Contents may be disclosed only to persons whose official duties include access hereto. Contents may not be disclosed to any party(s) without specific authorization from the Defense Advanced Research Projects Agency.

27 September 2022

MEMORANDUM FROM THE SECRETARY OF DEFENSE

Subject: Little Luke Project

Per recommendation from DARPA, the Secretary has authorized implementation of the Little Luke Project.

The volunteer subject, Lucas Emerson, has been fully vetted and approved.

DARPA selected this subject because:

He has been diagnosed as terminal due to brain cancer.

He is obsessed with love.

He kept an extensive diary of his thoughts, in blog form, for several years. These writings will enable analysts to track the success or failure of the Project by cross-referencing his living words with those recorded after death. See attachments for examples of the blog.

**Attachment 1**
**Luke's Blog**

Back in another life, I thought I knew what love felt like, and I didn't give it much thought. It felt like desire, excitement, infatuation, desire, mild intoxication, happiness, desire, warmth and desire. Mostly desire.

Dawn described love as the sensation of having a warm blanket wrapped around you. I like that. It's a good start.

But until I fell in love with Dawn, I didn't really know what love felt like, and, of course, I didn't know that I didn't know. Until you really experience it, how could you know?

So I will describe what love feels like.

It feels like every molecule in your body is vibrating on a wavelength that sends absolute bliss into your mind, heart and soul almost all the time. It feels right. It feels perfect. It feels like the whole world is suddenly ideal.

Nothing bothers you anymore. A driver cuts you off in traffic, you smile and fall back. You don't sweat the small stuff, you don't sweat the big stuff, you don't sweat anything. You walk in perfect harmony with everything and everyone around you.

That sounds like euphoria, but the word doesn't suffice. You have your senses about you, and your cognitive powers seem to be heightened. You see and appreciate all the little things you missed when you weren't in love. A bird on the wing, a cloud formation, a crawling caterpillar, the crackling of wood burning in the fireplace. You notice it all, and you love it all.

You cherish and adore your loved one, of course, and you are ecstatic that you were able to live long enough to experience this. You give thanks for everything and everybody who has touched your life. You get a little tear of joy in your eye when you hear your grandchild laugh. You feel warm and soft when you talk with your children.

You watch a romantic movie and, instead of analyzing the

story structure, acting and camera work, you get caught up in the journey of the lovers on screen. You get misty watching movies that never touched you before, like "50 First Dates" and "Because of Winn-Dixie." You even cry watching "Les Misérables," for God's sake.

Love isn't just a desire for or attraction to a single person. It's like an infection. It gets inside you and takes over your entire being. Love oozes out of every pore. Other people can see it. After I fell in love with Dawn, friends and even casual acquaintances would comment that something seemed different about me. They said I seemed happier, more open, more talkative. I don't remember that ever happening before.

If you Google-search "What does love feel like," you will get this nonsense: "You bounce between exhilaration, euphoria, increased energy, sleeplessness, loss of appetite, trembling, a racing heart and accelerated breathing, as well as anxiety, panic and feelings of despair when your relationship suffers even the smallest setback."

Somehow, Google found the only person in the world who doesn't know anything about love. And used that person as a source, for God's sake.

I told Dawn that because of our love, I finally knew what all those poets have been mumbling about for the last 3,000 years. I had read their words but didn't really understand, because I had never fully experienced this most amazing of all emotions.

I've always felt powerful love for my children, but that's completely different. I once felt the lightning bolt of "love at first sight" 48 years ago, and thought it was real. That was different, too. It was a desire that merely wanted to possess.

This love I feel for Dawn, which I firmly believe is on a different plane, knows no fear. It has changed me and changed my life, but somehow, it doesn't overwhelm. It feels calm, peaceful and fulfilling.

And I almost blew it all apart before it had a chance to happen.

Stay with me on this one, because it was a hugely important lesson for me and maybe can be for you, too.

I have always felt most attracted to women with blonde hair, blue eyes, a moon-shaped face and petite figure. And all you women are thinking, "Yeah, you and every other man." True, a point well-taken.

But dating evolved during my life. Once upon a time, we met members of the opposite gender through friends or office parties or we picked them up at bars or we conked them over the head with our club and dragged them back to our cave. That's how you fell in love. It was happenstance. You didn't have thousands of women from which to choose.

But in the 21st Century, we have dating websites, and if you like blue-eyed blondes, you can gather photos and profiles of nothing but blue-eyed blondes, meet them all for coffee or dinner, conk one over the head and drag her back to your cave. I'm kidding, of course. In the 21st Century, it is the woman who conks the man over the head and drags him back to her cave.

So when Dawn emailed to express interest in me from the Match.com website, she did not include a personal photo. I had no idea what she looked like. I responded by saying I don't normally reply to women who don't post a photo. You have to wonder what she's hiding, right?

She explained that she was a high school counselor and didn't want students finding out she was on a dating website. OK, fair enough, can you send me some photos?

So she did. She has brown hair, brown eyes and angular, Slovakian features. Not my type. And I told her that. It should have been the end of our contact. But for some undecipherable reason, this is what I wrote to her:

"Here's a thought process I went through over the last few days as I dip my toe into the Match.com waters. I found myself continually clicking on profiles with photos of what I consider "my type," moon-faced blondes with perky little noses ... but

I'm looking for a life partner here, someone I can talk with and have fun with and enjoy my golden years with, and there's no reason to believe that a moon-faced blonde is a better candidate for that than anybody else. Point of fact, my moon-faced blonde wife was unfaithful and left me for another guy. Why would I want another one of those?'

"I'd be happy to communicate with you."

That opened the door to the love of my life.

And I would have completely missed it if I stayed focused on the wrong thing – physical characteristics like hair and eye color. Women know this intuitively. Men, not so much.

What does love feel like? I just used a plethora of words to scrape away at these amazing feelings deep inside of me, hoping the collective sentences would offer a glimpse, a taste of this epiphany that has come to me.

But maybe Dawn said it best when she said, "Love feels like a warm blanket wrapped all around you."

Four or five stories up, I peer over the low cement wall. Sidewalk and asphalt await below. Hard. Unforgiving. White and black. It will be quick, maybe painless. A primitive scream explodes from my throat.

No wait, sorry, that's a crappy way to start a story. It's true, really happened, but let's try again. Because I'm still here to tell it, so everyone knows I didn't jump. But I almost did. All of us almost did.

Most of us pull back. Most of us.

*Every day in every way, I am getting better and better.*

That's a mantra that the power-of-positive-thinking folks pushed on us, and I really bought into it. The idea is that if your brain believes something, your body makes it real.

It works just fine when you're 15, and even when you're 25 and probably 35. Because every day in every way, you really

CAN get better and better. But then one day you wake up and you're staring your 65th birthday in the face and every day in every way you are getting worse and worse. And that whole positive-thinking thing starts to look like a crock.

OK, the suicide thing. My first threatened suicide came when I was 17 years old. See, I caught my girlfriend, the first love of my life, backstage at a play flirting with another guy. I was blind jealous, told her I was going to kill myself, then turned and walked away. I know, stupid adolescent hormones, right? I decided to run to the beach and continue right into the waves and drown myself.

The beach was 10 miles away. I stopped running after about 200 yards, took a deep breath and walked home.

I thought about suicide maybe half a dozen times or so over the next five decades. I assumed the thought occurs to everybody at some points in their life. Now I'm not so sure. Does anybody know if the kinds of thoughts they have are normal? I mean, my life is pretty much an amazing dream-come-true and always has been, yet to this very day, I can stand atop the high bridge across the harbor in Sydney, Australia (as I did last week), look down and feel this crazy urge to jump.

Most of us pull back. Most of us.

Oh, by the way, that girlfriend back in high school? She was some incredible amount of gorgeous and ended up on the cover of Playboy magazine. It never would have worked out for us.

A friend of mine has been dying for five years … well, yes, we're all dying of course … but he has some mechanical thingy that keeps his heart ticking, so while his body and brain fall apart piece by piece, his heart will just beat on and on forever. Please don't put one of those in me. I think about these things too much because I'll turn 65 in, oh, approximately something like 47 days.

So, yes, I think about the finish line. My blood pressure and cholesterol levels are higher than my doc would like, my prostate gland feels like it's larger than a walnut (so I'm told by the physician's assistant who checked), and I knew this rainstorm was coming because my lower back started to ache. And I have a big pain in the neck (literally).

But after years of agreeing with Dylan Thomas when he wrote, "Do not go gently into that good night," I've now decided that he was full of booze-soaked crap. Let other people hook up electronics to their organs and pump themselves full of meds as they "rage, rage against the dying of the light."

As for me, I can't think of a sweeter final scene than to go gently into that good night.

OMG (as the kids say with their thumbs), you've followed us this far, and we haven't even shown the courtesy to give you the usual facts – as we say in the journalism business, the who, what, when, where, why and sometimes how.

Who: Lucas Emerson was born approximately 30 minutes after lunch on January 5, 1953, a blue-eyed, sandy-haired "bouncing" baby boy, as they used to say back in that century, although he was more of a climber than a bouncer. We have a photo of him, just a few months old, hanging from his mother's index fingers as she dangles him several feet off the floor. His childhood was spent climbing (and falling out of) trees, trucks and monkey bars.

What: His first career goal was to be a mountain climber, and later he wanted to be a doctor until he saw a TV documentary in which they showed a doctor taking a scalpel to a human eye, with real blood and everything. So he trained hard to become a pitcher for the Los Angeles Dodgers, throwing tennis balls against the garage door for endless hours while the surrounding trees and bushes cheered wildly for him. After he was cut from his high school baseball team just before the first game of the season, he decided to become a sportswriter, more specifically a baseball writer. It was the dream that came true.

When: He was forged in the crucible of "Leave it to Beaver," The Beatles, The Sixties, Free Love, Women's Lib, and – to his great good fortune – the era of mini-skirts and hot pants. (Today it seems funny that Women's Liberation coincided with hot pants, but everyone seemed to miss the irony back then.) He also came of age during the Watergate Era, which unleashed a flood of aspiring hero journalists, greatly increasing the competition for newspaper jobs.

Where: Southern California! Within hitch-hiking distance of the beach! Skateboards, surfing, bikinis, cars, everything the Beach Boys sang about was true. We grew up in cutoff jeans, flip-flops and T-shirts, playing disorganized sports under perpetual sunshine and smog on the streets and fields of the Palos Verdes Peninsula.

Why: Why? Because we like you! M-O-U-S-E! Actually, "why" is the question Luke has been asking himself since puberty. He started a journal (don't call it a diary, those are for girls) and wrote down his innermost thoughts and ruminations for decades, starting in high school. Most of the entries circled back to "why?" He questioned everything. I guess we all did back then. His unwillingness to blindly accept what he was told led him on a spiritual journey through various religions (and no religion) and a pendulum dance with every political persuasion from radical left to far right. This inherent skepticism probably made him a better journalist.

How: By standing on the shoulders of giants. Everything he achieved was a product of the men and women in his life. Some of them were parents, teachers and friends, but a great many he never met. Emerson was a voracious reader, and his path was lit by the minds and words of Ken Keyes, Joseph Heller, Kurt Vonnegut, Baba Ram Dass, Jim Bouton, Ray Kurzweil, Marianne Williamson, Carl Sagan, Sam Keen, Joseph Campbell, Sir Arthur Conan Doyle, Alan Watts, Lao Tzu, Don Miguel Ruiz, Carlos

Castaneda and Stephen Hawking, to name just a few (OK, 16) in no particular order.

More fun facts: At this writing, Emerson had been married four times, and at every ceremony, he said something like "'til death us do part" and meant it.

At age 21, he married Marta Williamson, a brilliant and pretty girl from his high school who was a receptionist at the Palos Verdes News, where he worked as sports editor. She wore a lot of hot pants and mini-skirts. After they were married, she told him one night that she had just had sex with a guy who lived in an apartment down the hall. She said she was sorry, and it wouldn't happen again. Emerson didn't believe her on either count. The marriage was about one year old when it died. The Free Love movement had its share of casualties.

After four years of a swinging singles life (no commitments, so no casualties), Emerson met a pretty, 19-year-old college student and movie theatre manager named Karen Anders. She wanted to be a mom, and he wanted a family. They married a year later. They had two amazing, genius-level, handsome and beautiful children, Sara and Scotty. After 17 years of what Emerson thought was wedded bliss, he found out that Karen was having an affair. I know! What a strange coincidence, right? But instead of giving up on the marriage, Emerson begged her to stay. She said no, and her answer to their problem was that Emerson would move out of his house while still paying the mortgage, leave his children with her, and also send money every month to take care of them and her. He was so shell-shocked that he said, "Um, OK, whatever."

He held out hope for a reconciliation, but after it became clear that would never happen, he tried online dating. He met Desiré Goldstein, a brilliant and pretty (you can see a theme here) divorcee who was 13 years younger than him. They dated off-and-on for five years, breaking up often because, according to Emerson, she had a drinking problem. Inexplicably, he consented to her suggestion that they get married at a drive-thru window chapel in Las Vegas (God, I wish I was kidding). The marriage was just as fulfilling as the fast-food they also could have gotten there. Wedlock lasted about one year, after which the police confirmed Desiré's drinking problem with multiple arrests and incarcerations for DUI.

So that was it. Emerson decided he would never marry again, because he just didn't seem very good at it. Nine months later, of course, he signed up with another online dating website. He met some pretty and brilliant women, but no one really clicked, and he was about to give up when he met Lynn Myers, a widow.

She was pretty, brilliant (I know! What a coincidence!) and matched Emerson's ideal profile in a woman: blond hair, blue eyes, five foot three, physically fit and sensual. And she seemed to like him. Oh, did I mention she was somewhat wealthy? After a year of dating, Emerson took Lynn to her favorite restaurant in Laguna Beach, got down on one knee and proposed. Her emotional, heartfelt reply was, "I'll have to get back to you on that." God, I wish I was kidding.

After six months of random gentle reminders that his marriage proposal remained on the table, he stopped asking. Then one day she casually said, "OK, I'll marry you." He'd like to say that he was so overcome by how romantic it all seemed that he shed a tear of joy, but that would be a lie.

Truth be told, when you've been divorced three times, have two grown adult children, are in your late 40's and have been meeting women through Match.com, the stars have long since fallen from your eyes. But he liked to tease Lynn about it just the same.

So those are the marriage details and basic biographical background. Oh, maybe a few more words about love. Some say it can be reduced to a cocktail of brain chemicals and certain psychological signals.

Emerson claims that he fell in love at first sight with Valerie

Owen when he met her on Halloween night in 1968. He was 15, she was 14. You laugh, but I think those were the approximate ages of Romeo and Juliet. If they were actual people.

Almost another year went by before he said more than a few words to Valerie, mostly because he was painfully shy around girls. At her suggestion, they began "dating" when she was 15 and he was 16, and it lasted for about a year before her parents told her to break it off because they were getting too close at too young an age. At least, that's what Valerie told him, and he remains grateful to this day for that story.

But never again would the lightning bolt of love strike Emerson as it did on that Halloween night in 1968, and he always wondered why "love at first sight" seemed so rare.

The science seems to suggest that love at first sight is normal, and perhaps we just don't recognize the signals the same way because the sensation is only new the first time.

Psychologists have shown it takes between 90 seconds and 4 minutes to fall for someone, according to the website youramazingbrain.org, which is very authoritative because it's British and has a photo of an actual brain resting in human hands.

Quoting the site: "Research has shown this has little to do with what is said, rather 55 percent is through body language, 38 percent is the tone and speed of their voice, and only 7 percent is through what they say."

So love at first sight can happen in 90 seconds and perhaps no longer than 4 minutes! And it doesn't really matter what you say!

The reason can be traced to the brain chemicals testosterone, estrogen, adrenaline, dopamine and serotonin. Those pleasure-inducing drugs drive our primitive urges to procreate.

Once the pair bond begins to form, oxytocin (the cuddle hormone) and vasopressin are released inside your head, which increase your desire to stay with this person long enough to care for your infants.

The website even offers a surefire prescription for how to fall in love: "Find a complete stranger. Reveal to each other intimate details about your lives for half an hour. Then stare deeply into each other's eyes without talking for four minutes."

Boom! Drop the mic! You're in love!

WARNING: Results may be hazardous if you are currently married.

And now a word or two about the women in my life. As I sit here today, I am convinced that female humans are the most evil, cruel and beautiful creatures that evolution has ever produced.

I am reminded of the deep and profound conversation between mountain man Jeremiah (Robert Redford) and a trapper named Bear Claw (Will Geer) in the 1972 western film "Jeremiah Johnson."

Johnson: "Ever get lonesome?"

Bear Claw: "For what?"

Johnson: "A woman."

Bear Claw: "A full-time night-woman? Waauggh! I never could find no tracks in a woman's heart. I packed me a squaw for 10 years, pilgrim. Cheyenne, she were. And the meanest bitch that ever balled for beads. In Deadwood Creek, I traded her for a Hawken gun. Hee Hee! But don't get me wrong, I loves the womens, I surely do. But I swear that a woman's breast is the hardest rock the Almighty ever made on this earth, and I can find no sign on it."

Today I am supposed to sign divorce papers because Lynn Myers, my wife of 12 years, is in the middle of an adulterous affair with another man. It's been going on for a few months, and as usual, the trusting fool is the last to know.

I'd like to say that nothing like this has ever happened to me before. I'd also like to say I'm no fool, but both of those would be lies.

As Bear Claw said, I never could find no tracks in a woman's heart.

True story: A 69-year-old man got on a train in San Francisco Wednesday, and when it arrived in Chicago, his luggage, cellphone and medication were on the train, but the man was gone. CNN said he had "disappeared." I think that's the way I'd like to go. One minute I'm there, and the next I have simply vanished.

## Chapter 5

# The Secret Computer: How Did You Like Your Funeral?

"Everyone in this room is going to die … We don't know when. We don't know where. And we don't know how. But the only thing we can say with absolute certainty in this world is that there is a death waiting for each and every one of us."

The Taoist priest paused, wiped a trickle of sweat from his brow and tried a smile on the folks in the funeral home. Some shifted in their seats, some cleared their throats. The priest looked back down at his notes.

No casket lay in front of the mourners. The body was to be cremated in a few hours.

"You have all come to this memorial service today to say goodbye to Lucas … beloved father, grandfather, brother, partner and friend. In his final days, Lucas told his family that he took great comfort in knowing that his death would not be the end … but actually the beginning of a different journey. He said that death does not have the final say in our lives. And I believe he was right."

Dawn unlocked the door of her home, squeezed the handle and felt her body seize up. She couldn't move. She couldn't step over the threshold. All sense of place and time left her. Where am I? What am I doing? What day is it? What year …?

Ann put a gentle hand on her shoulder from behind.

"C'mon, Mom," she said. "Here, let me help."

Ann eased the door open and wrapped an arm around her mother's shoulder. Frankie leaned in from behind.

"What's up, guys?" he said. "Let's go." He slid past his sister and mother and went inside.

Dawn looked at her grown children and felt a moment of confusion. They looked so nice, but why were they all dressed up? Her mind swirled. Why are they so—? She turned around, succumbing to an overwhelming urge. Have to go toward the light, back out into the street sunshine.

Which is when she bumped into Abbie, her youngest daughter. And then it all came flooding back. The funeral. The death.

"I thought it was a very nice service, Mom," Abbie said, setting a bouquet of flowers on the living room table.

Dawn opened her mouth and tried to say something, but all she could hear was a little squeak from somewhere deep inside her. She took a handkerchief out of her little clutch purse and wiped her nose, moving into the dark living room.

"It's OK to let it out," Ann said. "If you want to cry, you should cry."

"Oh, it's just allergies, hon," Dawn said, stuffing the handkerchief back into her clutch. "All those flowers, you know."

Frankie helped himself to a bottled Budweiser from the refrigerator, popped the cap, took a big swig and wiped his mouth with the back of his hand.

"Who were those guys standing in the back with the black suits?" he asked his mom. "The guys with the buzz cuts? They were kind of spooky. Coaches from your school?"

"No. I don't know who they were, Frankie." Dawn set her purse on the desk table, next to her computer with the big monitor screen.

Frankie collapsed on the couch, feet propped up on one of the arms.

"I think Luke would've hated that whole thing," he said. "Why'd they add so much religion and mystical, woo-woo stuff? That wasn't him."

Dawn gently lifted Frankie's feet and slid them off the sofa arm.

"He always told me that funerals are for the living," Dawn said, "so he didn't really care what we did. He knew I'd want to have a Taoist priest for him. He was fine with it."

"Really?" Frankie shook his head. "I thought he wanted his headstone to say, 'I'll be right back.' That's what he told—"

"No!" Abbie laughed. "He wanted it to say, 'Wish you were here.'"

Ann, who was leafing through a magazine she had picked up from the desk, threw it to the floor with an angry splat, put her hands on her hips and shot a fierce look at her brother and sister.

"There's something seriously wrong with you two! Don't you have any—"

"Time to go," Frankie said, jumping up from the couch. "Call you later, Mama." He gave Dawn a peck on the cheek, nodded to his sisters and fled out the front door.

"How rude," Abbie said, but she didn't look surprised at her brother's escape.

"You'd think he'd stay for at least a few minutes," Ann said with disgust.

"It's OK," Dawn said. "Death makes him uncomfortable. He doesn't know what to do with it. Give him time. He just said goodbye to his ... his ... what did you call him, Ann? Dad 2.0."

"We all did." Ann's eyes were wet.

Dawn came to Ann and gave her a warm hug, then did the same to Abbie.

"I love you both. Abbie ... Ann ... thank you. Thanks for all your help this week. It hasn't been easy for any of us. Now, this might sound strange, but I'd really like to be alone for a while."

Abbie looked to Ann for direction. All Ann could do was shrug. Abbie searched for the right answer in her Mom's eyes.

"OK, Mom. Sure," she said. "We understand."

Dawn walked them to the door.

"We're just a phone call away," Abbie said, hugging her mom. "Let me know if you need anything."

"Or if you just want to talk," Ann said.

And they were gone.

Dawn walked around the room as if seeing it for the first time. She stood by the computer and turned it on.

As it booted up, she turned away from the screen and gazed out a window. Her thoughts turned to Luke. Funny, odd, mysterious Luke. A writer, friend, lover and confidant. Glib, simple, complex Luke. Amateur philosopher, amateur mystic, volunteer newscaster at the local public radio station. After these beautiful years together with the love of my life, a nice home in the Pacific Northwest, and now ...? And now what? I'm 68 and alone. What do I do with myself now?

A voice in the room startled Dawn. Luke's voice.

*Hmmm ... now that's strange. I'm home. Dawn? Are you there? If you can hear me, then ... that must mean I'm dead ... oh, crap.*

Dawn gasped at the first sound and was still holding her breath. She scanned the room. Nobody here. Creeping catlike, she moved toward the desk and peered from one side at the computer screen. It was filled with a photograph of Luke's face.

Finally, she let out a sigh.

"Oh my God. He must've recorded a message for me. Geez, how creepy. That's not like him."

The photo became animated. Luke's face blinked its eyes, and his lips moved as the computer speakers came to life again.

*Oh, hey Sugar Bumps. Stand in front of the screen camera so I can see you.*

There was no mistaking the voice. She let out a little chuckle.

"Now THAT'S Luke. Always goofin' around." She walked in front of the screen.

*Good. That's better. I'm sure this seems a little odd to you.*

Dawn smiled weakly, shook her head and walked away from the desk.

*Wait. I can't see you when you're over there.*

Dawn froze and stared at the computer across the room. Then

she let out a giggle.

"You can't see anything. You're a recording."

*Actually, I'm not a recording. It's a little hard to explain. Humor me for a moment. Come a little closer.*

Dawn steadied herself on the back of a chair, grasping for understanding.

*Sugar Bumps? Still can't see you.*

This had gone too far.

"You are a recording! How can you see anything? How can you hear anything? Luke is dead! He had to record this a long time ago! He couldn't have known whether I'd be standing in front of the camera or not!"

*That's right. And strictly speaking, I'm not completely Luke. I'm Luke's brain.*

Dawn walked in front of the computer. She'd had enough of this.

"All right, who are you, and why are you messing with me? I just cremated the love of my life, and if you're not a recording, then answer me or I'll pull your damn plug!"

*No! Wait! Hear me out, Baby Doll.*

Dawn's legs were about to give out. She plopped into her recliner chair.

"I'm hallucinating. Even though I've known for months that Luke was going to die, I still can't accept that it's really happened. So now I'm hearing voices that aren't here ... I need a drink."

She got up and walked toward the kitchen, passing in front of the computer monitor.

*Ah, there you are!*

Luke's voice again, with the video of his face moving again, just as if it were a live video feed of a living, breathing man.

*Baby Doll, you better sit down. This is going to be a little hard to digest.*

Dawn stood motionless, unsure of her sanity. As an

experiment, she decided to see what would happen if she played along. She slowly pulled out the desk chair and sat in front of the computer screen.

*Good, thanks.*

Luke's voice, for sure. How was this happening?

*Now, remember after I was diagnosed with brain cancer, I volunteered for that experimental program at Mason Medical Center?*

"Who ARE you? And WHERE are you?" Dawn looked around the room.

*I'm Luke. Well, like I said, I'm Luke's brain. I'm a program running in this computer.*

"You're a computer program." Dawn stared at the screen, feeling silly.

*Basically. Yes. The Defense Department is working on A.I., and that's the thing I volunteered for.*

"A.I." Dawn remained shell-shocked.

*Artificial Intelligence. All those hours I spent at Mason Medical weren't about finding a cure for cancer. They were scanning my brain. Turning all my neurons and thoughts and memories into digital information that could be stored on a hard drive.*

"They can do that?"

*They can ... and they have. I'm the first.*

Dawn stood and held a hand to her mouth. She moved around aimlessly, looking everywhere for a sense of reality to cling to, finding none.

*Baby Doll? You still here?*

What the hell. Play along.

"So you really ARE Luke? You're not dead?"

*If you cremated me, then yes, I guess I'm pretty much dead. My body and brain are really dead. My face and cells and organs – kaput. But all the stuff that was inside my brain was uploaded into this computer a couple months ago. That includes the ability to think, hear, talk and – this is what makes it really cool – I can reason. I can feel. I can answer questions like, what is the meaning of life? What is love?*

*Boxers or briefs?*

"I thought computer programs, um, couldn't do stuff like that?"

*They can now. The missing piece that finally made artificial intelligence possible was a real human mind. Once they turned everything in my brain into digital code, they had it. A marriage of man and machine. The best of both.*

"You can really see me?"

*Yes. The camera on the computer streams live video into my program. The microphone turns sound waves into code. My digital brain hears the same way my real one used to. And to talk, I just use the same thoughts I always did. Software sends my words out of the speakers.*

"How come you don't sound all stiff and weird like that Stephen Hawking computer voice?"

*They recorded all my regular speech patterns and fed them into the program. Pretty simple algorithm, really.*

"Everything that was Luke ... everything that was inside his head ... is now inside my computer?"

*That's right. I'll be here forever ... as long as you don't uninstall me.*

Dawn moved closer to the computer screen and softly touched the photographic face of Luke.

"It's you? It's really you? You're right here? I can talk to you whenever I want? You'll never die?"

*That's what the guys at the Defense Department said.*

"Oh my God, Luke! ... So how did you like your funeral?"

*I didn't go.*

"Oh. Right. Well, I thought it was very nice. The kids liked it. Except Frankie. You know Frankie. And all our friends and staff members from my school were there. And some guys in black suits who looked a little suspicious."

*Oh yeah, they told me they'd be hanging around. It's part of the deal. I insisted that they make two copies of my program. They keep* one for their A.I. experiment, and you get the other one. But it's all top-secret stuff. They want to make sure my brain doesn't fall into the wrong hands.

"This is all so ... such a shock. Why didn't you tell me you were doing this? I mean, really, Luke, what were you thinking!"

Listen, Baby Doll, they want to know if you'd agree to be part of the experiment. Instead of having military tech guys knock on the door, they thought it'd be better if I talked to you first. You know, break the ice.

"Oh, sure. Computer nerds are terrifying. I'd MUCH rather talk to a disembodied voice from the dead. Geez, Luke! ... So what do they want me to do?"

You know what virtual reality is, right?

"Uh. Yeah. Like kids who put on goggles and play video games with swords, like they're fighting Orcs in the World of Warcraft."

No. Well, yes. Sort of. But this includes all the real senses and emotions – you can actually touch, smell, see, hear and feel. Joy, pain, exhilaration, fear, orgasm, everything.

"Orgasm? You think that's a good thing to put into a virtual reality game?"

It's not a game, Baby Doll. I'm living in virtual reality right now. I'll live here forever.

"Wait. Are you really alive or not? If you're just a computer program—"

I AM just a program, but if you could experience this the way I experience it, you'd never even question whether I'm alive. I'm the future, Baby Doll. This is what the entire human race will evolve into someday.

"God, I hope not. You think we're all going to become computer programs? Not in this or any lifetime."

Just try something for me. Those Army tech guys can bring you into my world. Full-immersion virtual reality. We could see each other again. Touch each other.

Dawn got up and backed away from the computer with a dismissive wave.

"No thank you, Luke, not if I have to die first. I'll join you when I'm good and ready."

*You don't have to die. All they do is put a headgear thing on you. It taps into certain parts of your brain, then links you up with this computer. With me.*

"Sounds scary. And painful."

*No pain. Well, it depends. Could be ecstasy.*

"I don't know, Luke ... You'd probably just hit that orgasm button." Dawn moved in front of the computer screen.

*I'm trapped in here, Baby Doll. I'm sort of ... empty. What's the point of living forever if you can't experience the real things that make us human? Pure thought gets boring after a while. I need you. I need us. I need to caress your pretty face, hold you tight, breathe in your sweet scent.*

"There's something wrong with this program. Luke didn't talk like that."

*If I just wanted to press my Happy Button, I could always use the Charlotte McKinney program.*

"Excuse me? Charlotte McKinney?"

*The blonde from the Baywatch reboot. They use 3D imagery.*

"Yep. That's Luke."

*Will you at least try it? The tech guys will take care of everything. It's completely safe. You'll just lie down for a while and sort of dance in your head. In my head. In my world.*

"And the point would be ...?

*Science. The future of the human race. The geeks will get a lot of data they need. It will make me feel alive again. And maybe it'll help you too.*

"I don't know. It doesn't sound fun. How much time are we talking? I may have to go back to work. You didn't leave us with as much as I expected, Luke. Oh, wait, would they pay me for doing this?"

*No. We're volunteers.*

"Of course. Military intelligence! I just don't know about all this ... So what does it feel like? Being in this weird cyber world that you're in now?"

*I don't know what it will feel like for you, but if you agree to join me here, maybe it could be ... what love feels like.*

"OK, Mr. Mysterious, be that way." She stood, turned her back on the computer screen and stared for a long time at the large Buddha painting on the wall.

*Baby Doll?*

She turned around. "You're absolutely sure it's safe?"

*Safer than driving to the store. Much safer than your walks in the dark with Sofia.*

"Oh, that reminds me, we were going to go for a walk this evening. Take my mind off your funeral." Dawn checked her watch. "Oh, what the hell, when do they want to do this fake reality thing?"

*Virtual reality. Whenever you'd like. Next week, maybe?*

"I guess I could try it."

*Thank you.*

Dawn got up and gently touched the image of Luke's face on the screen.

"Luke?"

*Yes?*

"What does death feel like?"

*I can't tell you.*

"Why not?"

*Because I'm not dead.*

## Chapter 6

# Love Letters: Prelude to a Kiss

*When you last left the Love Letters, Dawn had just itemized all the qualities she considered desirable in a potential mate. Luke had asked her for it, but Dawn wrote, "I don't even know why I'm doing this. It's your fault for asking me such a stupid and big question. I will probably disappear for a while after clicking the send button. This feels way too vulnerable." She finished her letter with the words, "Over and out." Thinking she was breaking off all communication, Luke replied with one word: "Understood." This is where we resume the email trail.*

July 20
Chuckling ... that wasn't the most comforting response. I'm really okay. It's good to be vulnerable every once in a while.

Dawn

July 20
OK, confused. I thought your use of "dumb" was just teasing until I saw "stupid" thrown in a couple times. And "over and out" and "disappear." Did not land well.

Luke

July 20
Hi Luke
Aw, this is a lost in translation thing. I'm so sorry. I was just writing freely, not being overly cautious and forgetting that humor doesn't always come across in writing. I actually had to go back, just now, to find where the word "stupid" was, thinking it was somewhere in the document. You are anything but stupid. That was just me, making light of my own uncomfortableness with topics that are close to the heart. I have to own my flippancy.

Here is what I should have said, if I weren't a seventh grader in disguise:

*Hi Luke,*

*I'm taking a risk right now and sharing my heart via the enclosed attachment. I don't usually talk about myself in such a personal way and it feels a little scary to do so. It's difficult for me to talk about my needs and wants but, for whatever reason, I'd like to share those thoughts with you. Please do not feel this is anything to be alarmed by or an assumption of any sort. It is just an extension of the conversation we've been having. To be honest, the last days have been very meaningful. Yeah, I love your brain too.*

*If I feel a little embarrassed, it's because I will fret after clicking the Send button. Even though I'm decent at being a counselor, like most people, I suck at communicating at times. I'm open, however, if you have any questions or thoughts about what I shared in my wish list.*

*Dawn*

July 20
Hi Luke
I had to open a new email, because the "ugh" no longer looked funny, in any way. I hope you are able to accept my apology.

I would welcome your too-long letter in the morning.
Dawn

July 21
Good evening or morning, Luke
I'm doubting myself right now but decided that I would leave my own too-long letter. I've been thinking about what happened and thought I would attempt to put words on things.

I explained my misuse of words, stupid, dumb, that kind of thing. I'm making myself look deeper, however, because there was more going on and it's important that I try to reflect honestly with myself and with you. Here goes …

The last days have been very meaningful. For whatever reason, we became engaged in a conversation that has been very important. You've touched upon personal life experiences, as have I, and we both took some risks and opened up to one another. Without sounding too hokey, each letter from you felt like a little gift. I truly mean that.

As our conversations continued, we seemed to grow, individually and collectively, particularly in trust. I believe we mutually looked forward to hearing from one another and it was obvious that we were allowing ourselves to explore some personal issues. I also think we were caring of each other's hearts, and that felt nice.

As we continued to communicate, something occurred that was new territory for me. I'm not sure if I'll be able to articulate this well because I am just making sense of it myself. I'll try though.

When I teased you about my "homework," I now realize that I was thrown off, even though I didn't know it at the time. It's difficult to admit this, but I'm not sure anyone has ever really asked me about my wants and needs, my thoughts on love and what an ideal partner might look like. Although I've had this discussion in my own head over the years, I guess it never occurred to me that anyone else might be interested. Yeah, I'm healthy enough to know that a good partner wants to know those things. I'm simply saying I've never been fortunate enough to experience that.

So, as I started to free-write my list, I thought I was being open, and I was. And yet, I should have recognized that I was feeling angst; that pit in the stomach, tightness in the throat, kind of feeling. Imagine if you will, spending thirty plus years being complimented about your communication and counseling skills and recognizing that being vulnerable was truly horrifying. I'm not kidding. And yet, I continued to write, instead of taking a moment to recognize my feelings. If I would have just said,

"Geez, this is scary for me, Luke," this whole misunderstanding probably wouldn't have occurred.

Here is something else that was going on and it's a huge risk for me to share this. As I was writing about an ideal partner, I recognized that you demonstrate many of the attributes I was writing about. At least, I suspect that you do. At that point, I felt a little lost. I kept writing, instead of taking a moment to process what was going on. Again, I should have simply paused, but instead, fretted that my words might be misinterpreted. I think it's okay to let you know that you are a good man. Why that scared me like it did is something that I have to give further thought to.

I'm able to now see that the words on that attachment were quiet, private, words. I felt very vulnerable sharing them with you and, in my heart of hearts, I didn't mean to be careless with my opening words on the email itself.

Bottom line, I cherish you and our friendship and will try to remember what we discussed earlier in the day, about living in the moment. I took a risk, opened up to you, and that's okay. I need to leave it at that and not overthink. I'm still so very sorry though, because I never meant to cause harm.

I think it would be good to try to sleep now. Good night, Luke ...

Dawn


July 21

Hi Dawn,

I think I'll just let this fly. I've been hurt multiple times – by parents, lovers and wives – but instead of becoming wary and protective, I've found comfort in self-acceptance, honesty and a life lived in the moment, as much as possible. When I have nothing to hide, I have nothing to fear.

Conversing with you as we have and dabbling in the craziness of Match.com has driven home that point all the more forcefully.

I revel in the approach of, "Here I am, naked to the world (figuratively speaking), take it or leave it!" Hence, my candor when speaking about my taste for a certain kind of physical appearance. I knew it wasn't something you'd care to hear, but honesty just feels so clean. And thankfully, you understand that men are hard-wired this way.

And now I feel like I want to meet you, or at least I did until last night's missive. Your "ugh! ... stupid and big question, I don't even know why I'm doing this ... disappear for while ... over and out." Plus your reference to wanting a man who isn't annoyed by adolescent kids ... they all felt like counter-punches. My joke about being the old man who yells at kids to get off his lawn was just that – a joke. And I prefaced it by saying I DON'T want to turn into that guy. I love kids. I have five grandkids I love to pieces. I can tear up just seeing a cute little 2-year-old girl in the store who reminds me of my granddaughter. Yes, and I cry watching a good romantic comedy. "Love, Actually," best ever.

OK, so we both learned what professional comedians know – not every joke lands.

But enough about me. Whether it's your Catholic heritage or something else, you clearly have hiccups about going full-on "here I am world, take it or leave it!" I understand that opening a vein and bleeding one's innermost thoughts and feelings can seem dangerous, but it is SO freeing. Doesn't matter if it's to a stranger or a dear old friend. Nothing to hide, nothing to fear. Judge me as you like, but I am not ashamed or embarrassed about who I am or how I got here.

Even withholding your photo on Match is based on fear, in my unprofessional opinion. What teenagers are going to be surfing Match? And even if they did, how does that harm you? You're a smart, classy, deep woman. Online dating has been mainstream for decades now. I doubt anyone would or could ever be fired for that. Do you perceive some image of yourself that you don't want to tarnish? And if so, why would a Match profile tarnish it? You're human. Be human. As Don Miguel Ruiz said, "Be impeccable with your word, don't take anything personally, don't make assumptions, and always do your best."

You said we opened up to each other and "took some risks." I don't see it as a risk at all. This is me, this is you, full-throttle. If either of us doesn't like what we see, we go our separate ways. That's a win-win. But if we open that vein and bleed honesty all over each other and we do like what we see, that's a win-win too.

I'm sorry, Miss, but our hour is up. See you next week at the same time?

(JOKE! KIDDING!)

Luke the Duke

July 21

Hi Luke

We're all in different places in our journey and as I read your thoughtful and honest words, I was reminded of that. Our letters have been gifts, but of course they can't be a substitute for voice to voice or face to face conversations. There is simply too much lost in translation, especially when two people are just getting to know each other. As an accomplished writer, there is less of a risk for you (the lost in translation thing) but I'm sure it still happens on occasion. In a similar respect, as a person that works with the hearts of others, I've learned there is little room for error in communication, especially with friends or loved ones. When I occasionally allow myself to take a risk and appear emotionally clumsy, the result is similar to what happened last night. The truth is, I am human and just as imperfect as the next guy.

I'm not afraid, Luke, I'm just growing, like you and everyone else on this planet. Just as I knew you were joking about the kids on the grass, I was joking about the kids in Safeway. It's something my own children lovingly make jokes about all the time. Since our own history is limited, there are bound to be miscommunications. And grandkids, my goodness, I've had images of you smiling at the chaos, looking into my eyes, thinking, "Isn't this grand!"

The ultimate irony is that the words being shared were descriptors of qualities about you, the good things. I pictured you nodding your head and saying something like, "Me too! I've dreamed of smiling when the person I love walks into the room." It never occurred to me that you might be thinking, "How could she think I don't love kids," or whatever reaction my words caused.

I'm able to see that something so personal should have been tabled until there was an opportunity to talk, face to face. And give me a break, big guy. Using words like ugh, stupid, and over-and-out, were highly misinterpreted. I made an immature error and have tried to correct that error. Having said that, I don't deserve to be blindfolded and slowly guided toward the guillotine. (Okay, maybe that was a little dramatic.)

So, I've shared my heart and have exhausted the written word. I'm not really sure, but it feels like you might be saying goodbye. If that is the case, I feel very sad but will accept your feelings and decisions. In the event you would like to talk, my cell is 555-123-4567. No expectations, just leaving the door open.

And, if this is a goodbye, I had hoped to share something with you in time, but will do so now, just in case. My writing voice truly isn't as accomplished as yours, so the only way I've found for it to accurately be heard is to read out loud slowly and pause at commas. That probably sounds silly but it's the only thing that seems to work for me. It's just a simple writing, that only my adult kids have seen. It may give you an honest and more accurate glimpse into my heart.

Your friendship is deeply valued and, whatever the outcome, I still believe we were given a rare gift. Thank you for sharing your time, your words, and your heart with me.

Dawn

The letter to my children and their spouses:
September 19, 2016

Dear Frankie, Ann and Jon, Abbie and Kevin,
When I was in high school, I remember feeling a sense of impatience because my (older) parents spent a lot of time attending funerals. I used to joke with my friends, saying that my mom viewed those times as social events. Little did I know that there comes a time in life when loss becomes more frequent and one's vulnerability more apparent.

During the last months, I, too, found myself experiencing the unexpected loss of people close to my heart. Since last spring, three of my former students passed away unexpectedly, and recently two staff members that I knew very well. Those losses were a complete surprise and all the individuals were in good health, causing me to wonder if we ultimately have any control over our destiny. I still don't have the answer to that very profound question, but I do find myself thinking about it.

Which brings me to today. Over the weekend I attended a Celebration of Life for my former intern and close friend. While listening to the many stories about him, I became aware that my mind was drifting away to thoughts about all of you. I wondered what your lives might be like when you experience the loss of one of your parents. I wasn't trying to be morbid, I just couldn't help but wonder. It was at that moment that I knew I needed to share some thoughts that were important to me, not because I thought I was going to be the next one to go, but because I just wanted to pass along the lessons I've learned. So, ready or not, here you have it. Mom's Lessons of the Heart.

*Kindness*

I look back upon my life and continually realize that my greatest role model was my father. As a man with a seventh-grade education, he was definitely the smartest person I ever knew. His laughter served as a soothing balm during the toughest of times, and his wisdom continually guided me throughout my life. He used to say to me, "Dawn, you can be anything you want to be," and by the time I grew into a young adult, I genuinely believed him.

My dad also had the uncanny ability to demonstrate kindness even during the toughest of times. I remember when my mom had a stroke, and believe me, she wasn't the most gracious of stroke victims! Since dad was deaf, he wasn't able to hear my mom when she called out or needed something. Thus, my mom thought it was totally acceptable to whack my dad with her cane whenever she needed to gain his attention. Instead of my dad being angry, he would make jokes about keeping his reclining chair just close enough to be whacked, but far enough to prevent being harmed by her cane. It was through my father that I learned about grace and resilience. Even when his heart was hurting, he never went to a dark place. Instead, he used kindness and grace to demonstrate that we should love and support one another, even when times get tough.

*Pain and Grieving*

Like most people, I've experienced those times in life that have involved deep and very real grieving; the loss of my first daughter at birth, the end of my marriage and traditional family unit as I knew it, and the unexpected end to my relationship with Rob. All were completely different situations, but all involved very deep grieving. If there is anything I feel certain about, it's that grieving is extremely difficult and hurts a whole lot. I have a need to share something very honestly with all of you and I hope you will listen closely to the thoughts within my heart. This is very, very, important.

Sooner or later, you will all have to deal with something that hurts so badly that it will be life changing. And, at that moment, you will decide to take whatever time is needed to deal with your grieving in a graceful way, or you will allow it to consume and take over your heart in a very dark way. A grieving heart can never be soothed by mean-spirited comments or hurtful behaviors. Mean words might provide a brief moment of reprieve, but healing will never occur. Darkness can become pervasive and, ultimately, how you deal with pain will define who you are as a person. Your behaviors will also have a great impact on those that love you, be it your children, your friends, or your family. I'm not saying that everything should be rosy and peaceful if your heart is experiencing profound pain. I'm simply saying that it's important to take the time to grieve, to connect, and to heal. We all know people who live in a dark place as a way of life. Please don't allow yourself to ever become like that. No matter how difficult your situation in life may temporarily be, try to keep love inside your heart and soul.

*Communication*

Here's where I need the most work and, after almost sixty-four years, I still struggle. For someone that is pretty good at being a counselor, sometimes I suck at communication! I'm able to reach out to others that are hurting but rarely ask for help myself. I struggle to let others know when something hurts my feelings and rarely share my pain, even when my heart might be breaking. If I could turn back the clock, I would do a better job at communicating. I'd laugh a whole lot more and ask for help when I needed it. I would also handle anger in a better way. Instead of bottling up my feelings, I would instead try to talk about my concerns and make a better attempt to openly problem-solve. I would really try to talk about the difficult stuff and wouldn't pretend that everything was always okay. Although I know I have a long way to go, I want you to know that I am going to try to communicate better. It's truly the glue that holds all relationships together. It's my hope that you don't wait until you're my age to learn the value of communicating with all the important people in your life, be it your family, your friends, or even the people you see at work each day.

So there you have it. Thoughts to pass along from my heart

to yours. May you love each other unconditionally, deal with loss gracefully, and laugh together frequently. I love you all very much.

Mom

P.S. By the way, I don't have any plans of kicking the bucket soon!

July 21
Dawn,
That was beautiful. And nope, I was not saying goodbye at all.

I would like to phone you sometime in the next few days.

Any particular day and/or time best for you?

Luke the Duke

July 21
Hi Luke
I'm free now but will need to leave for a memorial service at 1:00 for the grandparent of one of my students. There is a gathering after that, so I'll probably be back sometime in the evening. My kids may be visiting tomorrow and Sunday, not sure yet, but mornings and evenings probably have flexibility. After that, I'm pretty open, except for the day to day wanderings with friends. If the mood should strike, just call and if I miss you, I'll simply call back.

Dawn

July 21
Dawn, I have to run into town to sign papers on the new house. Been a little hectic lately with the move, and I suspect we'll want to talk for a while, so I'll pick a day and time when I know I won't be interrupted. If I catch you, great, and if not, I'll leave a message for a call-back.

l

July 21

Hey Luke

Makes sense and I agree. I'll look forward to talking with you soon, during a less hectic time. Congrats on the new house.

Dawn

July 21

Dawn,

Papers signed, escrow closes one week from today, and then I start moving in. I'm actually excited to begin the next chapter. It's a nice little home in Port Ludlow with a 180-degree view out back of the little bay, Puget Sound, a golf course and the Olympic Mountains. Three bedrooms, but I'm turning one into a media room to satisfy my film addiction.

My ex is with her new man most of the time, either traveling or where he lives in Memphis, but she comes back from time to time and will be living with him in this house after I'm out. When she's here, she sleeps downstairs, I sleep upstairs. The divorce is amicable. She had to be here today to sign papers. I say this in case I leave my home phone number on a voice message for you, you call back and a female answers. Do not be alarmed. I've told her about you, she asked to see your photos, and she says you are cute, and I am dumb.

I'm thinking of calling you on Monday. My schedule looks wide open, so let me know a good time for you, if such exists.

Luke

July 21

Hi Luke

Thanks for sharing the specifics. You're right, it would cause worry if I thought I were intruding upon something unfinished. I'm in my car, preparing to drive home from the memorial/ wake. My friend was the Skagit Valley College president and his granddaughter is someone I continue to formally mentor.

She's about to begin her MSW degree in social work, and we are incredibly close. I'll be home in about an hour, just in case you'd like to call. If not, no worries. If you would feel comfortable, could you share your cell with me? I'd like to enter it into my phone. Take care ... and glad all went well with the house signing.

Dawn

July 22

Good morning, Luke

I sent you a little text last night, thanking you for the lovely phone conversation. With a smile, I woke up this morning and noticed that I didn't click on the "send" arrow on my phone. So, many hours later, thank you. :-)

I appreciated the time shared and enjoyed the fact that we didn't seem to have any difficulty talking together. Well, except for the phone reception difficulty. That's a pain. I liked the sound of your voice, by the way.

I found myself thinking about our discussion regarding what love/relationships look like at our age. Each person has a lifetime of history, way of doing things, etc. In the right situation, it could be pretty special. I think the key is what we talked about last night, taking things slowly in order to get to know one another. I appreciated your willingness to talk about the transitional place you are in. Just know I agree and support what you said.

Having said that, I admit to looking forward to meeting you. I forced myself to look at my school calendar last night and I do return on August 15. It seems like summer vacation has passed way too quickly. Anyway, in looking at the upcoming week, all looks good for Thursday or Friday, and beyond, if neither of those days work for you. Give some thought regarding whether you would like to come to Lake Conway or would prefer meeting somewhere in between.

When we meet, I'll be the one in a long, flowing, blonde wig.

:-)

Dawn

July 22

Ooohh, it'll be like we're spies, you in the blonde wig, I in my glasses with the fake nose and moustache.

I also quite enjoyed our conversation. FYI my cellphone: although in most instances I'm fairly tech-savvy, I have yet to see the need for a smartphone that keeps me tethered to the online world 24/7. I have a flip phone that lives in my car as an emergency tool, and I rarely turn it on. I can receive and send texts, but anyone who phones or texts me on that line could wait a month before seeing a reply. Hence, my use of the home landline.

I just checked my calendar; I'm in Seattle tomorrow (Broadway musical), and I have nothing else until Aug. 4 (Henry IV, Shakespeare in the Park). So I'm yours on any other day. I'd like to come to Lake Conway, your choice of date, time and location.

My secret code phrase so we can identify each other is, "The violins are sweeter in May," and your confirmation phrase will be, "That's true, and the opposite also is true."

Maxwell Smart

July 22

Hey Luke

Thanks for the background info about your cellphone. I'll refrain from leaving any texts, since it isn't something you use much. For me, my iPhone is convenient, only because my kids often communicate, send photos, etc. On a good note, I'm not married to my phone, like the rest of the planet. It's my feeling that kids and adults alike have stopped learning to talk and communicate with each other. On a funny note, when working with high school seniors, I often find myself role playing, regarding how to make a call to a college admissions office. Truly, I could be meeting with a valedictorian, headed for a top-tier school, so intelligent and talented, yet absolutely panicked when needing to make a simple phone call.

I'm glad you are free this week and interested in coming to Lake Conway. If that's the case, how about Thursday? I think everything will be less crowded on that day. In looking at the Port Townsend ferry schedule, it appears the ferries run quite regularly. Perhaps plan on taking one of the morning ferries so we can enjoy some time outside, assuming we have good weather.

Let's do this ... You're probably a better judge regarding how long it will take, once you're off the ferry and driving from Coupeville. So, perhaps reserve whatever time is best on Thursday and then give me an estimated arrival time to Lake Conway. I'll take it from there. I'm thinking we might enjoy heading out to one of the (pretty) park areas. I'll plan a simple picnic and we can just enjoy some time together. Sound okay?

It's nice that you will be attending a musical tomorrow. What is it that you are going to see? I think the last production I saw at the Fifth was Kinky Boots. In addition to enjoying a quality performance, I always find it so interesting to observe what is now being done in regard to the sound and stage engineering. It's such fun to take in the whole experience.

Okay Write Guy, off to the gym and then some time with the kids later. It's rainy over here so I'm sure plans are currently being modified a bit.

Happy Saturday, Luke. I hope it's a good day for you.

Dawn

July 22

Good plan, Dawn. I will have my cellphone with me in the car on Thursday, so we can coordinate arrival time with CIA level accuracy. I will need a location to enter into my nav system. I may not be addicted to a smartphone, but I couldn't get anywhere without my nav system.

Nothing but sunshine here this morning. Come to the rain shadow!

The show is called "Fun Home," a Tony-award winning musical based on a woman's graphic novel about her childhood. Sounds interesting.

l

July 22

Hi Luke

Hope you are having a good day. All is well here. My daughter (Ann) and her four kids will be arriving soon. Now that the weather is sunny, our plan is to play at the splash park at a nearby playground. From there, a pizza party and movie at my place. My quiet oasis is about to be transformed.

Okay, I was thinking about your love of film and have to ask ... do you have any all-time favorites? Just curious ...

By the way, I enjoy learning about you.

Dawn

July 23,

Hey Dawn,

Too many film favorites to count, but in no particular order, some would be "The Godfather," "The Matrix," "Hugo," "Love, Actually," "Avatar," "Chicago" and the entire BBC "Sherlock" series of films with Benedict Cumberbatch.

I like learning about you too.

l

July 23

Hi Luke

I hope you enjoyed your day at the theatre and, yes, I found myself quietly thinking about you too. I love that you have decided to approach this chapter in life slowly and with care and think your head is in a really good place. I believe mine also is, but, dang, I sure do enjoy communicating and getting to know you. I'm trying to refrain from thinking, "Is it Thursday yet?" and am glad you mentioned the anticipation word. I wanted to say the same thing but was trying to retain my calm and cool presence. :-)

Well, sweet man, I want you to know that I am truly trying to be very aware and intentional about living in the moment right now. Instead of worrying, I am feeling a deep sense of appreciation for this very special and unique journey that we seem to be sharing. Thank you ... I really mean that.

Dawn

July 24

Dear Dawn,

Favorite live show: Frank Sinatra at Caesar's Palace in Vegas, front row, early 1970's. Second favorite live show: Meghan Trainor, WaMu Center in Seattle, last year. Clearly, I have eclectic tastes in music.

Looking forward to meeting the cute brunette. You can show me your scar from the flying ice cube at that concert all those years ago. Let me know what I can bring to the picnic.

l

July 24

Hi Luke

I had to go to my office for a while this morning. One of our seniors didn't make it to the graduation finish line and still needed to earn a final credit. I made arrangements with him to proctor his final this morning, the only requirement still hanging out there. He appeared on time and passed his final, meaning that he is now an official graduate. Oh my, what a happy camper was he, twirling around in circles and saying, "I made it, I finally made it!" I was able to find his diploma and the two of us had an unofficial graduation ceremony. He thought it was the best commencement ever!

No worries about bringing something to the picnic. I will either make something simple or, if my refrigerator is still on death row, I will pick up something at the local deli. I don't really have an idea regarding what makes your taste buds sing, so let's do this. Please go to the Slider Cafe online and take a look at the lunch menu. Give me an idea of a few things that sound good. That way, I'll either pick something up ahead of time or I'll have a better idea regarding what kind of food you like. Make sense? Also, if you're a vegetarian, vegan or eat wild boar three times a day, please let me know.

I'm thinking that you are preparing to move furniture into your new place soon, yes? A busy but meaningful time for you. Are you able to pace yourself or will it be a marathon moving day?

I'm looking forward to seeing you soon, Luke. When we meet, try to control yourself and not fling any ice cubes at my forehead. Okay?

Dawn :-)

July 24
Miss Dawn,
I'm not comfortable with m'lady picking up the check on our first date, now that I know you won't be bringing your famous quiche and apple pie to a picnic blanket in the park. I'm sure a town like Lake Conway has a nice place with outdoor dining. Then we can both order whatever we like in a sunny setting, our words drifting from prying ears in the breeze.

Choose a location and time that please you, and I will be there.

Funds for the new house were deposited today, I should get the keys Friday, and I will be moving boxes piecemeal for the following week or two, then have movers haul the big stuff for the final move-in. You're right, lots to do, I have a long list.

And on Aug. 6-7-8, the entire extended Emerson clan comes from throughout the western states to Fort Worden for our bi-annual family reunion. It was planned and booked a year ago, I'm sort of the host, and it could have come at a better time, but ... we have to live in the moment, don't we?

See you soon, counselor.

l

July 24

Hi Luke

Have I mentioned that I think you are very funny, in a good kind of way? As I read your *Miss Dawn* response, I had an image of you reading my email and rolling your eyes. I'm not kidding, I could *feel* you rolling your eyes at me. And, by the way, I thought my idea was brilliant! If my fridge wasn't going to become part of the Walking Dead series, then I would simply pick up some café take-out from a good place. And, if it did come back to life and I had an idea of your food preferences based upon your menu selections, I could plan the picnic accordingly. Brilliant, I tell you!

Anyway, I'll let you know the final outcome once the repair guy arrives tomorrow. In the meantime, I'm prepared to suggest another idea. So ...

*Dawn's Brilliant Idea 2*

I read your last email carefully and noticed that you are receiving your keys on Friday, thus, it's likely to be a busy day, not to mention the days following. I'm wondering if it might help if we just met at Coupeville, thus, minimizing your driving time for an hour each way. I'd love to spend time with you in Lake Conway, but should we feel a desire to meet again, there will be opportunities for that down the road. If we met in Coupeville, our time could be focused upon being together, instead of you spending it driving. However, if you're looking forward to a mini road trip, then I'm absolutely fine with meeting in Lake Conway.

So, what say you? Lake Conway? Coupeville? Italy? Let me know and we can plan from there. Hopefully, you're not rolling your eyes again.

Dawn

July 25

Miss Dawn,

I choose Italy, there's a wonderful outdoor café on the Amalfi Coast, Le Bonta del Capo. If we leave now, we can be there by Thursday.

Failing that, I choose Lake Conway. You wouldn't deny me a chance to drive through Deception Pass, would you? I like road trips.

And I wish m'lady to choose whichever brilliant idea suits her fancy. I am happy to treat you to lunch at your preferred establishment. If you'd rather go with *Brilliant Idea 1 or 2,* here are my dietary tendencies:

If you choose the deli, a Turkey Delight would be, um, delightful. Hold my tomato. If you go elsewhere, I have the typical American cowboy palate: beef, ham, pastrami, turkey, chicken, bacon, cheese (not all in one sandwich ... although, now that I think about it ...) and go easy on the healthy greens. A little side salad is nice, bleu cheese or ranch. Never onions, pickles, olives or tomato. And I have a sweet tooth, maybe a chocolate chip cookie or a slice of cheesecake to finish. Or if there's a Dairy Queen in town ... Heath Bar Blizzard.

Simple man, simple tastes.

Hey! I see you rolling your eyes!

Luke

July 25

Hi Luke

You picked my favorite selection at the deli. I chuckled as I read your *no pickles, olives, tomato*, though. I'm guessing a Greek salad isn't exactly on your Top Ten list. And, by the way, as a pregnant woman many years ago, I had Heath Bar Blizzards as a daily treat on my way home from school. I only stopped that practice about six months in, after one of my high school kids said over the drive-thru speaker, "No worries Ms. M., since you order at the same time each day, I already have your Heath Blizzard ready to go!" He was so proud, and I was a tiny bit mortified.

Okay, Lake Conway it is! I'm happy that you would like to meet here but just wanted to make sure I wasn't adding more to your busy plate. Next question to ponder is where to meet. Since your GPS wouldn't take you to my picnic spot, we need a rendezvous point because it would make sense for us to take a very short drive together from town to one of the parks.

Okay, this is definitely a roll your eyes moment. Please program your GPS to 319 Morris St. It's the parking lot at my high school and a very safe place to leave one of our cars. Very easy to find. I'll be easy to spot, especially since I couldn't find a perfect blonde wig. Instead, I'll be the one in a full apron, bun on top of head, holding a tray of cookies.

Once we meet, it's your choice whether you would like to drive (to the park) or prefer that I do. My initial thought is to select a quiet picnic place, void of high school critters. From there, depending on what we decide (depending on any time constraints you might have, interests, etc.) there are other sweet places to enjoy. Anyway, I'm thinking what makes the most sense is to simply begin with some time together, far from the maddening crowd, over a Greek salad smothered in tomatoes. From there, we'll figure it out.

While I'm thinking about it, please bring a pair of old shoes. It's likely that we might walk along a rocky beach.

All right, sweet man, it's time to complete a few tasks and appreciate another lovely day. Your letters make me smile.

Dawn

July 26

OK, Dawn, not sure that an old pair of shoes will match my tuxedo, but if you insist ...

Thoughts on the Heath Bar Blizzard: I used to be able to get it made with chocolate ice cream (or whatever that DQ substance is made of), but now it seems they only have vanilla. So I ask to have them mix in some chocolate sauce. Not as good as the true chocolate Heath Bar Blizzard, but close.

About Tomatoes (subtitle: Way More Information Than You Want) – Last year my doctor said I have GERD, which is a fancy acronym for silent acid reflux, so I had to drastically change my diet to nudge my Ph levels into a more alkaline place. That meant cutting out basically everything I love: bacon, lasagna, pizza, red sauces, beef, coffee, Mountain Dew, chocolate malts, ham, etc. I did as I was told, and within six weeks, I was symptom-free. Symptoms were basically limited to clearing my throat for about a half hour after I eat. For the last 20 years, I thought that was caused by post-nasal drip from my allergy to ragweed.

Then I was tested, and it turns out I am not allergic to ragweed, but I am VERY allergic to dust mites and a little allergic to cats. Every house has dust mites, and for the last 15 years, I lived with cats who actually slept on the bed (NOT my idea).

Long story even longer, the diet change was remarkable. I dropped 13 pounds (not that I was heavy, but at 5-foot-10 and 175 pounds, I'm in pretty good shape), and I don't miss all those unhealthy foods I thought I couldn't live without. I take Flonase every night to deal with the cats and dust mites, and in a couple weeks when I move, no more cats.

But I digress. I like your *Brilliant Plan,* so I will leave the tux at home and come casual, complete with beachcomber shoes. I will reserve a spot on the ferry at a time that will enable me to arrive around midday. My Star Trek flip phone will be turned on, number is still 555-123-4567, so you can call or text if you panic at the last minute and decide not to show.

l

July 26
Good morning, Luke
It sounds like we have figured out a brilliant plan together. I'm looking forward to meeting you and have no plans of backing out. Hopefully, today's clouds will be replaced by sunny skies. A quick question regarding your midday arrival time. Could you give me an idea of what that might mean? To some people, midday is noon, to others; it might mean three. So a little clarification would be lovely.

I'm heading out in a while to run some errands in Burlington and Mt. Vernon and then plan to meet my daughter for lunch. From there, home, and some outdoor music this evening. Lake Conway has outdoor concerts throughout the summer on Wednesday and Friday evenings so it's always fun to take some beach chairs and enjoy the music.

By the way, I don't have a cat, so when we hug, you won't have to worry about dripping all over me.

Dawn

July 26
By midday, I mean 3 a.m.
No, seriously folks, I have a reservation on the 10:15 a.m. boat out of Port Townsend, which puts me in Coupeville around 10:50, and if I encounter no cows in the road and don't stop to take a photo at Deception Pass, I expect to be hugging you around 12:43 p.m., give or take, if my math is right, which it rarely is. That's why I wear a calculator watch.

l

July 26
Hey Luke
Sounds perfect … thanks for letting me know. Lake Conway is only an hour's drive from Coupeville, but maybe you have plans for a full photo shoot at Deception Pass. :-)
Dawn

July 26
Told you my math is suspect, Dawn. See you then, if "then" be 11:50 or 12:43 or somewhere in between.
L

July 26
Hi Luke
Sometime between 11:50 and 12:43 sounds just right. My prediction is 12:07, but who's counting?

I just returned home and found your book *Travel Within* in my mailbox. I admit, I wanted to sit right down and begin reading but have a few tasks to complete this afternoon. Okay, okay, maybe I did read the Preface and Introduction. I could hear your writing voice and am thinking you were the author's ghost writer with a capital G, yes? I am looking forward to reading and learning. I'm so glad it arrived today.

Our experience of becoming acquainted via writing has been, well, quite lovely. Wonder what it will be like to meet in person. Pondering quietly …
Dawn

July 26
Yeah, every word of that book is mine. I tried to capture his vision and I don't agree with everything I wrote because he has some goofy ideas, but most of it, yes. Looking forward to finally being in your aura.
Luke

July 26

Hi Luke

I thought so. It was really a nice experience to read a small sample of your writing after having the opportunity to communicate with you. I'm looking forward to ending the night with a warm bath and then beginning Chapter One.

See you tomorrow ... that feels nice to say.

Dawn


July 27

Good morning, Luke

I awakened peacefully, but to the sound of gusting winds. Of course, my first image within my mind was of you being blown away, waving, "Nice to meet you, Dawn ..."

I then decided to curl up in a blanket and read. The waters are now calmer, and I actually see a little glimmer of sunlight peeking through the clouds. Life is just a giant metaphor, yes?

Anyway, I just wanted to wish you a safe trip this morning. It should be a pleasant day but a tiny bit chilly. Along with the old beach shoes, perhaps throw in a jacket.

I'll look forward to seeing you soon.

Dawn


July 27

Forecast is for clearing and temps between 68 and 72, so I'll bring layers that can be added and subtracted. And I'll be wearing running shoes for the rockin' beach walk, which means I'll be wearing blue jeans, baby.

See ya,

Luke

## Chapter 7

# The Secret Computer: This is SO Freaky

*When you last left the story of the secret computer, Dawn had conversed with the image of her deceased lover, whose brain had been uploaded into her computer hard drive. Eventually, she agreed to take part in the Defense Department's artificial intelligence experiment and was asked to come to Mason Hospital. She arrived two hours ago, was given an overview of the project, signed a bunch of papers she didn't read, and just walked into a room filled with blinking electronics.*

Dawn sat in the overstuffed recliner and tried to stay perfectly still while the two computer scientists – a man and a woman – attached wired sensors to various spots on her head.

"Just relax," the skinny Asian woman said. She blinked a lot, like something was wrong with her eyes. Dawn didn't trust her.

"Relax? I'm in a secret government room with two strangers wiring me up so I can see my deceased lover's brain in some kind of virtual reality world," Dawn said. "Does that sound relaxing to you?"

The man smiled and leaned closer. Dawn thought he seemed too young to know about brain sensors and top-secret projects.

"You're a very lucky woman, Dawn," he said. "If this works, you'll be the first person ever to stand in the presence of the most advanced human intelligence the world has ever known."

"Really? I thought it was supposed to be Luke."

The Asian woman blinked twice and turned to her partner. "She did get the full briefing, didn't she?"

"Yes, she's just a little anxious," the man said. "It's in her profile. Highly intelligent, but sometimes sarcastic and temperamental."

"You know I can hear you, right?" Dawn waited for an answer

that didn't come.

They carefully placed a helmet-like contraption on her head, which covered her eyes. "Yes, we know you can hear us," the man finally said as he removed the helmet and adjusted some connections inside.

"What's your name again?" Dawn squinted. She decided she didn't trust him, either.

"Raymond. I'm the one who's been with Lucas on this program since the beginning. Remember? We talked the last time you were in."

"Oh. Yeah, I remember now. You were the one who said you didn't think this experiment would ever work."

"That was before we did all the testing." Raymond smiled at her. "It's true, I didn't think Little Luke was, well ... real. It seemed like he was half man, half computer, and the two sides weren't meshing. But now I'm very excited about the project. I think he's truly a new species – definitely an artificial intelligence, far beyond anything we've ever seen before. But he's also a human consciousness. I envy you, Dawn. You're about to go where no one has gone before. Just relax." He placed the helmet back on her head, tucking back her long auburn hair.

As Dawn leaned back to recline the chair, the helmet fell off.

"Oh dear," she said. "I don't think you put it on right."

"We were not ready for you to lean back yet," the Asian woman said testily. "Please remain still while we get this secured."

They fussed over the helmet for a few minutes, checked the sensors and carefully placed it back on Dawn's head.

"It's not very comfortable, you know," Dawn said. "What if it falls off again when I'm in the middle of the ... video game or whatever? I'm not sure I can lie still that long. I've got a bad back, you know. I get really stiff when I lie down for any amount of time."

"We'll begin in just a moment, Dawn," Raymond said. "Everything will be fine, and we'll be right here the whole time."

"So I just lie here, right?" Dawn said. "I'll think I'm standing and moving in the virtual reality thing, but I don't really move, right?"

Before anybody could answer, two bright flashes inside the helmet made Dawn wince. After a moment, she heard a voice – Luke's voice.

"Baby Doll? Is that you? I feel you ... but I can't see you."

"This is SO freaky!" Dawn was speaking to the techs, whom she assumed were still by her side, watching over her. "I can't see anything. I thought you said this was going to be realistic."

"Just relax and let go," Raymond said. "Don't try to make something happen. Clear your mind."

"This is silly. It doesn't work," Dawn said. "Everything's black."

Then she saw a hand reaching out of the darkness toward her.

"Touch me." It was Luke's voice.

"OH MY GOD!" Dawn shrieked. "This can't be happening!"

"Reach out. Try it. See what happens." Definitely Luke's voice.

Dawn wanted to take off the headset and tell the techs she couldn't do this. She wanted to go home and forget it ever happened. She wanted to have the computer removed from her home and never come to this spooky research place again. Luke was dead, and it was time to move on.

"Baby Doll. Please." Luke's voice was soft, comforting, real.

The disembodied hand was still there.

"No. This is spooky."

"For me? Just this once? Can you do it for me?"

"Oh for God's sake."

She wrestled with her feelings for a long time in silence. Then she reached out her real hand in the direction of the one she saw in her headset. She could see her own hand come into view.

"Oh wow, that's weird," she said. Dawn wiggled her fingers and saw it happen in her viewer. She giggled.

The other hand reached forward and touched hers.

"Ohmigod! How is this possible? I can feel it!"

The hand closed around Dawn's and gently pulled her forward. The darkness receded from the arm to reveal its owner – a fit young man with a thick head of hair, faded blue jeans and a white T-shirt.

"Holy crap! Who is that?"

"It's me, Baby Doll. Thank you. Thank you. I can't tell you how much this means to me."

"Luke? No way! Oh my God, Luke, you look so young!"

"So do you. I programmed this for a time when we were young and healthy. Long before you had arthritis and allergies."

She reached out to touch his face.

"I can feel you! How is this—?"

"Look in the mirror."

A full-length mirror appeared by his side. In it, Dawn could see her own image, as she looked in her mid-twenties. She stepped forward, and the mirror image moved with her. She twisted at the waist a few times, then laughed. She bent down to touch her toes, then leaped into a few ballet-like jumps.

In the room, the techs could hear Dawn speak, but they noted that while her muscles twitched slightly, she made no movements like those she thought she was making. The program was working.

"There's no pain in my knee! I can't remember the last time I felt this good! Hey, my head is clear too," Dawn said. "No congestion, no sinus headache, nothing."

"It's a paradise of your own choosing," Luke said. "The program can create any reality you imagine."

Dawn saw a flower in a vase on a table next to the mirror. She picked it up and held it to her nose.

"I can smell this. How can I smell this flower and feel your face, when none of this is real?"

Luke put a hand on her shoulder.

"Nothing is real until your brain says it is. And right now, those sensors are stimulating sections of your brain that light up whenever you smell a real flower. As far as your brain's concerned, there's no difference between a real fragrance and the perception of one that isn't there."

Dawn put down the flower, turned and kissed Luke gently.

"I felt that," she said. "I don't just mean on my lips. I felt that down to my toes. Explain that, Mr. Wizard."

Luke spun away and did a little happy dance, laughing.

"I felt that kiss someplace lower than my lips too. And I can feel my feet and my hands and my arms, but none of them exist anymore. I'm just a bunch of ones and zeros in a computer code. But they all add up to the essence of Luke. Think about it – everything you experience happens only inside that three-pound lump behind your eyes. When you stub your toe or bite into a warm chocolate chip cookie, the reality doesn't happen on your tongue or in your toe. It's all in your brain. Hunger, fear, love, sorrow, inspiration, regrets ... it's all just electrochemical information. Your real body is lying still on the chair."

Dawn's avatar walked over and pinched his butt hard.

"Owwww!" Luke backed away from her.

"Ha! Can't you just turn off the pain by wiggling your nose or something?"

"Not without exiting the program," he said. "We're in this thing together, so your full-immersion reality affects mine and vice versa. Our brains accept this, so they react as if everything that happens here is real."

"Really. So, could you injure me? Kill me?"

"Not for all the money in the world."

"No, I mean if you conjured up a big knife or something and stabbed me, would I really bleed and die?"

"I never thought about that before. Hold on a second."

Luke spread his arms wide and looked straight up, eyes closed.

"What are you doing?"

"I'm researching your question. It's not there. Let me check the project database."

"You can do a Google search just by standing there like Jesus on the cross?"

"I'm a program with full access. Ask and ye shall receive." He dropped his arms and smiled at Dawn. "The answer is unknown. Nobody's ever done this before. But the programmers believe that if I stabbed you, your real self would just wake up, like coming out of a nightmare. You might have an elevated heart rate, but not a scratch. And you can't kill me, either, because I'm already dead."

The darkness surrounding Dawn and Luke began to recede further, until Dawn recognized they were now standing midday in a city that looked familiar.

"Luke? Is this Paris?"

"Exactly as it was when we were there."

"Oh, oh! Remember the little cafe where that snotty waiter was so rude to us ... what was it called, uh, *Les Deux Magots?*

"Yeah, Less Doo Maggots. Right over there." Luke butchered the pronunciation on purpose, just as he did years ago.

"Let's go in and order two double bacon cheeseburgers to go," Dawn said, "just to piss him off."

"I've got a better idea. Close your eyes." Luke took both her hands in his, and at his lead, they began a slow spin around together.

Dawn felt a little dizzy when Luke stopped, but as her head cleared, she saw a different skyline.

"Lake Conway?" Dawn beamed.

"The day we first met. Right over there. The parking lot at your school."

Luke took her hand and walked toward the only car in the lot. "It all began right here, in this place, on this day."

"Oh, we had some great days in this place. Look, right there, that's where we had our first kiss. This is so bizarre, Luke. It's like we're really here, and you're really standing next to me. But I know it's just a video game. I'm still sitting in a chair, and you're still … dead."

"You can visit me here anytime you want, Baby Doll." Luke looked off toward the beach. "We can hold hands and walk to your special place again. Sip red wine while riding a gondola in Venice. Play with white-faced monkeys in Costa Rica. Go bungee jumping in New Zealand."

"We never did those things."

"That's the point! We don't have to just relive things that are already in our heads. We can do things we've never even dreamed of, things that aren't even possible in the real world. Swim at the bottom of the Marianas Trench. Hang glide on Jupiter. There's no end to it. Anything you imagine, we can make it happen. I want you to come here every day. We'll play for eternity. It's heaven made real."

"But it's *not* real, Luke." Dawn turned and walked a few steps away from him. "This may be fun and special and kind of amazing, but it's only one step away from being a video game. I'm still a living, breathing woman. I've got a life to live."

"So do I, and this is the life I have. You don't have to come back every day. How about three times a week? Think of it as therapy. Pilates without the Trapeze Table."

"Let me be as honest as I can." Dawn paused to collect her thoughts. "I loved you, Luke, but I'm looking at a man 40 years younger than the one I loved. You didn't look like this. The Luke I knew was a man with crinkles around his eyes, sagging cheeks and age spots on his hands. He was funny and sometimes silly, he couldn't see without his glasses, and I was comfortable with him."

"I can be that Luke too. I can look like any Luke you want. Or any movie star you want. How about Brad Pitt?"

"The real Brad Pitt? Now let me think about that." She looked up, tapping her chin.

"Real is what you believe is real."

Dawn looked down to face Luke and instead saw a young Brad Pitt smiling back at her.

"Aaaah! Really? Is that you? Or are you Brad Pitt?"

"Ask and you shall receive," Brad Pitt said in Luke's voice.

"I don't believe you're real." Dawn watched Brad Pitt morph back into a young Luke.

"This isn't a dream," Luke said. "You're talking to me ... the real Luke."

"There's not a single cell of Luke still alive. The cancer ate him up." Dawn threw up her hands in frustration. "How can you be the real Luke?"

"The real Luke is his consciousness. That's what I am. Everything else was just bells and whistles."

"The real Luke didn't believe that."

"Here's what the real Luke knows," he said. "Almost all your cells die and replace themselves every month. Skin, hair, bone, organs ... everything is completely overhauled. Some of your brain cells only last a few minutes. So is the new 'you' still the same you as last month's model? Every bit of it has changed."

"Of course I'm still me."

"Yes! Because what persists is the pattern. You're just an evolving pattern, and the predominant feature of that pattern is your consciousness."

"But you can't put the consciousness of Luke into a machine and say that machine is Luke."

He reached out and held her by the shoulders. "If you have a prosthetic leg, are you still you?"

"Duh." Dawn backed away from him a few steps.

"And if you lose a kidney and both your arms and have a heart transplant, are you still you?"

"Of course."

"What if you have a spinal cord injury? What if your entire

body is a vegetable and you can't move a muscle, but your brain is OK. Are you still Dawn?"

"Yes."

"Yes! Because you still have your consciousness. That's what makes you Dawn. And that's why I'm still Luke."

She turned away from him and began to speak in quiet, measured words.

"Every human being is unique. One of a kind. I'm Dawn because no one else is Dawn. But your consciousness has been loaded into two different computers. Can there be two Lukes? Which one am I talking to?"

"But my programs are linked by the Internet. We're really one."

"What if I copied the program and loaded it onto another computer?" She shook her head. "What if I copied it a thousand times? Can there be a thousand Lukes, all learning different things and becoming different brains?"

"Theoretically, but—"

"Which one is real? I'm sorry, Luke, or whoever or whatever you are now. In some way that I feel strong in my gut, you're not real. This isn't all that good for me. I was just starting to accept the kind of life I'd live without you. I was letting go. And this whole fantasy thing is messing me up."

"But it's not fantasy. This is my reality, and it can last forever. No pain, no sickness, no worries – a world created to suit your every desire. But all I can create is stuff, not real, conscious people. I need you."

Dawn looked him in the eyes. "When I leave here, I'll go back to an empty house and text messages from three kids who are trying to comfort me for my loss, and they're hurting too. I'll go back to the real world."

"Doesn't this look and feel just as solid as what you call the real world?" Luke reached for her hands, but Dawn backed off.

"You're not hearing me. When I open my eyes and they shut

down this computer, I'll realize I'm alone. I'll look at that front door and know you're not going to walk through it ever again."

"But Sugar Bumps— "

"Do you see how cruel that is? If I let you tease me with this fairy tale, I'll keep clinging to you. I'll daydream about what we can do the next time we're together. And as long as I keep doing that, I will never, ever, move on."

"Move on to what? A life of too many bills and not enough money? Of sinus headaches and knee pain? Of having 300 students all clamoring for your attention and never being able to do it all?"

She shook her head and bit her lip.

"There's a big difference," Dawn said, "between walking in the real world, where we can actually accomplish something, and dancing in this meaningless fairyland. Have you gotten a lot dumber since you died?"

"Dumber? I have access to all the world's information at lightspeed. I know everything." He spread his arms and looked up again. "Current world population – seven billion, one hundred forty-eight million, two hundred ninety-eight thousand, three hundred and fifty-three. Number of wars and armed conflicts now ongoing in the world – twenty-eight. World death rate of people dying needlessly from starvation, water-borne diseases and AIDS – one every two seconds."

Dawn scoffed. "Now I know why they call it ARTIFICIAL intelligence."

"I can understand everything," Luke persisted. "I can summon up the answer to any question in less time than it takes to think of the question."

"Then why don't you Google Oprah or Dr. Phil or somebody, so you can realize how wrong you are? Intelligence isn't the thing that makes us human. We're not just brains with a respirator. We have hearts and souls too. We have our humanity."

"If you're talking about emotions, Baby Doll, believe me, I

still have them. I cry inside every day I'm without you. But a soul? That's just your religion talking. My body died, but my brain continues to live and grow, and I'm still me. There was no soul that went someplace else. I'm living proof that our entire conscious existence takes place between our ears. Now we can preserve that consciousness beyond the body. We can live forever. We can be smarter, faster and more connected to each other. We can be better in every way."

"You sound a little insane."

Luke moved to Dawn and took her hands in his.

"Imagine a world where everyone's consciousness is connected to everyone else's in a single World Wide Mind," he said. "Our brains and our databases will all be linked together, just like the Internet, in real time. Everyone will be just like me – immortal and living in a perfect virtual reality of our own choosing, getting smarter every second. No weak, fleshy bodies that sicken and die."

"Who's going to mow the lawn, put out the cat, pay the electric bill?" Dawn said.

Luke laughed. "You have to admit that health care won't be an issue."

"What I have to admit is that Luke is dead and I'm talking to a 3D picture of him that doesn't look or sound quite right. And he seems to have delusions of grandeur."

"I'm still human, Baby Doll. I'm just smarter than everybody else."

"You're not human at all. You're silicon chips and electricity."

"Then why don't you just delete me?"

"Now that's the smartest thing you've said yet."

## Chapter 8

# Love Letters: First Kiss

*When you last left the Love Letters, Dawn and Luke had just decided to meet for the first time. It began with a hug, followed by a picnic lunch at the beach, a long walk, a long talk, one drink at a rooftop bar, and a couple of brief, soft kisses.*

July 27

Dawn, I may be a writer, but I can't put into words what a wonderful day this was for me, finally meeting you. You are a super high-quality person, a sweet soul, and also very cute. I love your lips, if that's not being too bold.

I look forward to our next meeting. You are so right in saying that it's good for both of us that circumstances inhibit us from rushing forward, because I could see myself falling fast. Too overwhelmed to write a long letter, so good night, and thank you for a magical day.

Luke

July 27

I was just writing to you when your little note arrived. I'm a little overwhelmed, too, in a good kind of way. The only words that seem to come to mind are, "Luke, I am smitten with you." Something, well, many things, touched my heart very deeply and I cherished every part of our day. Honestly, from the moment our eyes met, I felt something very, very, special. Thank you for sharing yourself openly and honestly – can't wait to see you again.

Dawn

July 28

Hey Dawn,

Yay, escrow just closed on my house. I expect to pick up the keys this afternoon, start moving boxes tomorrow (or today if I'm ambitious) and move in the big stuff next weekend or the weekend after, if I can get a mover booked that quickly.

What's your schedule look like between now and Aug. 15, which I believe is the date you said you'd be back at school? Can we squeeze in a date or two before the bell rings (do schools still have bells signaling the start of class?)

No time for the long letter I planned. Maybe tomorrow ...

Lucas

July 28

Hi Luke

I knew that today would be super busy for you, so was surprised and touched to find your note. Thank you for taking a moment to write. How 'bout if you pass the football to me and I write the long letter today. Okay, sweet man?

It was a nice evening and morning. On a funny note, after sharing with you how relaxed I felt after our day together, I assumed that I would be wide awake for a long time. Well, I turned on the news and immediately fell into a deep/dead sleep until 11:30 or so. I went to bed after that and awakened this morning with a little smile. Later in the morning, I drove to the gym and laughed out loud — after discovering that my mind was on auto-pilot. Yep, I drove to the high school parking lot, instead of the gym.

My brain cells are now functioning again, and I would like to thank you for a lovely and meaningful day. I think we both want to take our time and really become acquainted and, yet, I want to be open and say that I am very much looking forward to seeing you again. To sit across from each other and communicate, in the truest sense of the word, is actually a rare experience.

You have a good memory and yes, I return back to school on August 15th. Although it's sad that we didn't meet at the beginning of summer, I have to believe that the fate of our timing might make sense as time passes. Whatever time we share, I am committed to being present and have a feeling that you are too. Here are some open calendar possibilities: July 30, Aug. 2-3, Aug. 10, Aug. 12-14.

Since you will be in the midst of moving, please know I'm only listing possibilities but know it's important for you to focus upon what needs to be done during the next week and days ahead. On one of the days, maybe you could just walk on the ferry and I could pick you up at Coupeville and we could hang around there. Or the opposite, I'd be happy to meet you in Port Townsend. Anyway, we can talk further when you have the chance to come up for air.

Enjoy your moving journey and know that I am thinking about you.

Dawn

July 28

Hi Dawn,

You driving to the HS instead of the gym was sort of like my brain with you at the rooftop bar, driving toward a brilliant observation and suddenly forgetting what I was even talking about – two or three times. It happens.

As for our rendezvous: Aug. 2 sounds good to me, with Aug. 3 as a fallback if something comes up. If I can arrange movers for next weekend, then Aug. 12-13 are open for me, too.

As for an agenda, I'm totally open. Coupeville might be fun. I've only driven through the town once or twice, but it looks cute. Wow, too many numbers and dates there, looks sterile. The point is, I think about you a lot, and I'm very curious and excited to see where this takes us. Let me start this letter again:

Hi Dawn,

I just want to see you again. Any day, any time, whenever we can make it happen.

Luke

July 28

Hi Luke

You do make me smile. I was just reading your book and enjoying the sun out on the deck when your letter arrived. It's funny, I was afraid the list of dates might look sterile, but it seemed to make sense to simply list all possibilities. I completely agree with your words about being curious and excited.

To keep things simple, let's tentatively think about August 2nd. I, too, like the idea of checking out Coupeville. It's a cute town that I haven't visited in quite a while. Give some thought about walking on. And, as you mentioned, the third could be a back-up.

It's lovely outside and I hope you are able to enjoy the day. I'm glad all is going well with the house plans. I'm happy for you, Luke.

Dawn

July 29

Hi Luke

I imagine that it's a very busy day for you and just wanted to take a moment and check in. I need to attend and assist with a memorial service this afternoon – a staff member who recently retired and passed away unexpectedly. Two of my closest friends, Christian and Kate, are arriving from Bellevue and we will attend together. Anyway, they will be here any minute and I imagine that I will be busy for the remainder of the afternoon.

Just wanted to let you know that I am thinking about you and hope all is going well as you begin the process of moving into your new home. I've been enjoying quiet moments on the deck, reading your book, and just appreciating the past days.

Take care of yourself today, Luke, and try to pace yourself. Sending peaceful thoughts your way ...

Dawn

July 29

Thank you for that, Dawn. Yes, I'm moving boxes and boxes of books.

Turns out the cost of the move is based on how many hours it takes them, so I'll be moving everything I can fit in the SUV over the next many days. Not that I couldn't afford to have them move everything, but I am habitually frugal ... Parents raised during the Depression, nothing goes to waste, you know the drill.

We have a tentative moving date of Aug. 17 or 18. That gives me plenty of time.

Sorry to hear about the passing of your fellow staff member. I guess we're getting to the age when you read obituaries and go to memorial services.

Be well. Thinking of you. Tough to pace myself, I'm a "git 'er done" kind of guy. But I'll be very tired tonight.

L

July 29

Hi Luke

Whew, long day, but glad to now be home. It was a heartfelt memorial and a lovely reception afterward. As you mentioned, it seems that we are beginning that stage when friends and colleagues are beginning to pass. I'm hoping to stay healthy for a long while ... fingers crossed on that one.

From one "git 'er done" to another, I felt a quiet need to suggest pacing yourself. Having said that, I'm not very good at following my own advice, especially when there is a major task at hand, such as moving. There are a number of days between now and moving day, so I think you will be in good shape. I'm just happy that you are pleased with your new home and are looking forward to the next chapter. Much to be grateful for, yes?

I'm not sure whether I've mentioned this, but just know that it's okay to call, should the mood strike. I don't want you to feel like you have to check in ahead of time about that.

Take care, sweet man ...

Dawn

July 29

I'll call Sunday if it's OK, sometime after mass. 😁

I have a lot more to move. And we have a heat wave coming. I will indeed pace myself, but I was deadline-driven my whole career, so whenever I see something that needs to be done, I tend to do it. Also have to do some prep for the family reunion.

Our next date will give me a chance to take a deep breath.

Good night, my sleepy Dawn.

Luke

July 30

Hi Luke

I just took the best nap ever. I'm thinking we might be good for each other.

It was nice to talk today, and I appreciated you taking a moment out of the busy day to call. Hopefully, the Pace Yourself Plan is working out nicely. There may be a few sore muscles in the morning, after transporting so many boxes of books. Maybe a good time to soak in a hot bath, yes?

It goes without saying that I'm looking forward to seeing you on Wednesday. I believe we are genuinely enjoying this unique opportunity to become acquainted and, as you said the other day, I'm curious about where this journey might take us. This is all very rare, and I'm committed to staying present and seeing how this journey, our journey, unfolds.

Rest peacefully tonight, Luke ...

Dawn

July 31

Hi Dawn,

Are you saying I put you to sleep? JOKE! A full day of heavy lifting led me to a deep and restorative sleep, and in a few minutes, I begin another such day.

I'll give you a ring at some point if you're available to chat, maybe early evening.

Sincerely yours,

Luke

August 1

Hi Luke

I'm hoping that today is more evenly paced for you. The sound of fatigue was heard all the way to Lake Conway last night. It's a warm day so try to slow down a tiny bit, okay? Having said that, I truly know how difficult it is to shift to a lower gear when in the midst of moving.

I've had a busy and productive morning. Cleaned the car, went to the gym, started preparing for my niece's arrival on Saturday, etc. I, too, am trying to heed my own advice. So far, I'd give myself a C+, at best.

Well, I'm thinking that you will be arriving around eleven tomorrow. I'll look forward to seeing you then. Take care, Luke.

Dawn

August 1

Hi, my sweet Lady Dawn,

My plan is to take the 11 a.m. ferry from P.T., which puts me on the other side around 11:40. I've had a much easier day today, can see light at the end of the tunnel in this move. My darling daughter Sara and her family will be here for the family reunion, and she wants to come to the new house and help me put it together. I'm not sure how to diplomatically tell her that I want to do it myself. This will be the first home I've had in 17 years that does not require me to incorporate someone else's ideas into the process. I guess gentle honesty is always the best.

See you tomorrow … shall I scout for a place we can dine in Coupeville, or would you like to do that?

L

August 1

Hi Luke

You're in luck with Sara. Since the moving truck hasn't arrived yet, you could say something like, "Honey, the truck won't deliver my furniture for two weeks and I'm really looking forward to taking my time and making this place my own. I'd love to hear your ideas, though."

I'm heading out in a while for appetizers with a few friends from work. Summer, a close friend, invited us to her place. She lives in Lake Conway, overlooking one of the marinas. A nice day to be outside. If you happen to call, I'll be home by eight-ish or so. If not, I'll look forward to picking you up at 11:40 tomorrow.

Feel free to scout out a few places to have lunch. Then we can wander around together and see what feels right. Have I mentioned that I'm looking forward to seeing you?

Brown Eyed Girl

August 1

That's very good advice, counselor. Perfect, actually. I see why you're good at what you do.

When you asked about my biological clock, you may recall I said I've flipped from nighthawk to early-to-rise, early-to-bed (like you), and with all this heavy lifting and energy being expended in the heat, there's a chance I may doze off with a book on my chest before you're home. But if I'm still conscious after eight, I'll give you a ring. If not, I'll call in the morning, so you know I'm on the boat.

I have four suggestions for dining possibilities, will discuss them with you after a hug.

Luke

August 1

Hi Luke

After we hug, it probably won't matter where we have lunch.

I have a feeling that you are currently sleeping blissfully, something that is just what you need. I'll look forward to seeing you tomorrow and just, well, talking together. I like the thought of getting to know you better.

Safe travels and I'll see you in the late morning.

Sleepy Dawn

August 2

Yeah, I fell asleep reading a huge packet of Medicare information, rather than a good book. My eyes glazed over. It's more complicated than the tax code. Ugh.

I'm thinking you could park at the Keystone Café across the street from the ferry landing and I'll meet you there. I'll have my cell: 555-123-4567, just in case.

See you in a few hours …

L

PS: Medicare Supplemental Plan H, which you recommended, is no longer available. Must have been too good a plan for the consumer, so they yanked it.

August 2

Hi Luke

No Plan H – well, there goes that easy decision! Okay, I'll park at the café and will look forward to seeing you soon. Safe travels …

Dawn

August 2

Thank you, Dawn, for a transcendental day. I so enjoy your

company, your presence, your words and your touch.

Until we meet again ...

Luke

August 2

Hi Luke

If you are reading this, then it means you are home safely. My drive home was peaceful and uneventful, with the exception of some road construction delays.

While writing, your note just appeared. A transcendental day, indeed ...

I appreciated the drive home because it allowed me time to take in the day and process the many emotions being experienced. Geez, Lucas, I am smitten, and I never really used that word before, well, until last week. I continue to believe that it is very important to take things slowly but must admit that I'm feeling all kinds of profound things.

Yes, until we meet again ...

Dawn

August 3

Hey Dawn,

I just confirmed my moving day – Monday, Aug. 21. I'd prefer an earlier date, but they can't do it until then, and it gives me extra time to move items I can fit into the SUV. My calendar is open on Aug. 5 and Aug 10-13, among the dates you mentioned as possibilities for us to see each other again.

Luke

August 3

Hi Luke

Thank you for sending the pictures. My favorite was of you and your children. Sara looks very much like you, and Scotty, he has your eyes. I'm able to see, via their pictures, that they are very intelligent and thoughtful kids. They both love you very much.

I'm moving at breakneck slowness this morning but will soon head to the gym and then prepare for the upcoming week. I've been thinking about you a lot and even did a little writing this morning. I think that's probably a good thing.

I hope it's a lovely day for you, Luke. The extended moving date will allow you time to enjoy the process of making your new home, well, *home.* Perhaps this will give you time to find that special bookcase that you've been thinking about.

I like having you inside my heart, if those words make sense.

Dawn


August 4

Good morning, Starshine Dawn,

Cursory observations on the family photos you sent, which are all very small files and therefore can't be enlarged much without pixelization:

Ann has her mom's eyes, Frankie has his mom's smile. Your grandkids are a big hyperactive bundle of fun. Abbie likely is a dead ringer for you when you were that age, including the lovely long hair. Group photo on the waterside: an eye-catching bevy of gorgeous, happy faces.

Smiles and laughter are pure joy for me.

I loved having you in my ear and head and heart last night. I do believe you are the only woman who has ever made me feel peaceful and serene. Well, to be honest, you also trigger a level of excitement in me, both physical and emotional, but that's a conversation for another day.

Today is given to my moving to-do list, which is three pages long. Many of the items are crossed off, but many remain. I see it not as a burden, but a joy. I'm turning the page to see what thrilling adventures lie ahead in the next chapter.

Luke

August 4

Hi Lucas

Not sure why, but sometimes you feel like a *Luke* to me, sometimes a Lucas. Do you have a preference?

I appreciated your letter this morning and am glad the pics brought a smile. I, too, enjoyed being in your ear, head, and heart, last night. I have to figure out how to get you out of my head when it's time to sleep, though. So far, I am failing miserably. :-)

I'll send another test photo with this email, to see whether enlarging it will make it more viewable on your end. Please let me know.

I've been thinking about you, well, I do that a lot, but I was thinking about you and your three-page list. I'm so glad that you are experiencing joy in the moving process. It seems like more than just a new chapter in your life, perhaps a new beginning on a number of levels, yes?

In looking at the upcoming week, I don't think we will likely make it to Port Townsend on Thursday. My kids will be in and out, eager to see my niece Jan, and it probably makes sense to stay in the area. Also, you will have just finished three packed days with your family and will likely be ready to get back to moving tasks. Jan will be leaving on Friday evening, so we could possibly see each other on either Saturday or Sunday. We can talk later, but I just wanted to let you know what our plans are at this point.

Thank you again for talking yesterday evening. I truly cherish all of our shared moments together.

Dawn

August 5

Hi Luke

Well, all is done and I'm just relaxing until I leave at one to pick up my niece and her beau. I wanted to take a moment to write, knowing things might be a little busier than in past days.

I just took a loaf of banana bread out of the oven, so it smells nice and homey. It's still quite hazy from the fire smoke outside and I am trying to believe the air is a little bit better today. If I look very closely, I am able to see a few of the islands. Mt. Baker, however, is not yet visible.

The arts festival is going on this weekend, so about eighty thousand extra people wander into town. It's a nice event, but quite crowded; lots of art, food, music, etc. We'll likely listen to some music this evening but will actually go to the festival in the morning. I believe it opens at ten. At three is the yearly gathering of my girls, much like the photo I sent you. I think we will likely also meet some friends in the evening. Over the years, Jan has gotten to know some of my close friends, so we usually get together on Sunday evening.

I've been thinking about you and am very much looking forward to seeing you again. We will both be with family this week and will likely breathe a little sigh when all returns to normal. I'm sure, however, that you will enjoy seeing your kids and other family members. Since it seems like we are both focusing upon being present, I'm trying to do the same when Jan is here this week. Well, sweet man, you are in my heart, in so many different ways. Enjoy the day.

Dawn

August 5
Hi Luke
I just wanted to take a moment and say good night, knowing that tomorrow will be very busy. It's funny, in the midst of visiting my sweet niece, laughing and catching up, I found myself thinking about you. I'm so glad we had a chance to talk today.

Jan arrived on schedule and we stopped for lunch and then headed to Lake Conway. The traffic was heavy, due to the arts festival in town. Her boyfriend seems to be very nice and, as expected, he was enchanted with the northwest, even with the fire-smoke haze. The three of us sat out on the deck and talked until ten. I'm glad to be tucked in for the evening.

When I close my eyes in a few moments, I know my thoughts and images will be of you. I'm glad you are inside my heart.

Good night, Lucas.

Dawn

August 6

Dear Dawn,

Judging by the time check on your email, I can tell you that at the very same moment, I was thinking of you and seeing your face in my mind and imagining your hands touching mine. You are inside my heart, as well.

I read an advice column in the newspaper this morning, in which the woman (probably around our age range) had entered into a new relationship that made her "feel like a teenager again." I can relate.

I'm off soon to Fort Worden, to make sure everything is in order for the arrival of my brothers and their families and all our extended families. It will be lots of laughs, as it always is when we get together.

I seem to have completed all the logistical tasks of my upcoming move, which eases most, if not all, of my concerns. I look forward with anticipated joy to the days when I can settle into my home at a relaxed pace and continue to nurture our budding relationship.

Perhaps on some weekend in the not-distant future you could come visit me in Port Ludlow and offer suggestions with your feminine touch about what might look better over there or be more functional over here. While I do look forward to setting up the place to my liking, I'm the first to admit that two minds are better than one.

Everthine,

Luke

August 6

Dear Luke

It's funny, I found myself thinking about you throughout the day and, to be honest, missing you. Since we typically aren't able to see each other during the week, I found myself wondering why today felt so different. Then I realized, with guests at the house, activities going on, etc., we are unable to stay connected in the same type of way. Thus, by day's end, I simply experienced a desire to retreat to my room to spend a few moments reconnecting via writing. You might experience something similar by day's end tomorrow, once your family arrives.

It was a good day, but wow, I think I'm going to be tired by Friday! We spent the day roaming around the arts festival, followed by the girls' gathering. It somehow morphed into a family reunion of sorts. After chatting on the deck once we returned home, I called it a day and said good night to everyone.

My heart felt very warm when I read the word "Everthine" this morning. I have had a number of conversations with myself, wanting to close my letter with more than just my name. Your chosen word was perfect. I find myself experiencing a number of feelings and emotions and, honestly, I have such a sincere desire to get to know you better. I'd just like to rest my head upon your shoulder and simply listen to the sound of your voice. I'd like to know about anything that is important to you, Luke. I'm not sure I have felt this way before.

Having said that, I'm enclosing another poor-quality iPhone picture. It will give you a little visual regarding the day.

Still in search of a word, but for now ...

Always

Dawn

August 7

Dear Dawn,

I have to admit I log in with hopes of seeing your name in my inbox. Glad you had a good day. Your photo shows a lot of joyous faces. As the cliché goes, it appears "a good time was had by all." Same with the Emerson clan. They started rolling in yesterday afternoon, and we had a lot of laughs around the campfire. It got chilly when the wind kicked in, so we all regrouped in the Officers' Quarters for the evening. Neither of the families staying up there seem to have neighbors in the adjoining rooms, so we couldn't test your paper-wall theory, but one of my nephews' daughters, 10-year-old Delara, is convinced the rooms are haunted by ghosts, so she was very grumpy.

The final three family members come in today, and at dinner tonight, I will be delivering a presentation about the rich history of Port Townsend and Fort Worden. I think I'll skip the part about ghosts who are said to inhabit Manressa Castle and walk the streets at night.

Like you, I will be engaged at least from 9 a.m. to 9 p.m., and you know I don't carry internet access in my pocket, so I'll have to be content to check my inbox just twice a day.

You said you'd like to know about what is important to me, and family ranks at or near the top, so I'm enjoying this time, but I also find myself thinking of you often. I think I'm sweet on you. ☺

Everthine,

Luke

August 7

Hi Luke

Just a quick note back, while I'm thinking about it. It's very funny, your mention of Delara and her worry about the house being haunted. When I took my son there as a middle schooler, I didn't share that the only bad part about Fort Worden was Frankie's utter fear of going upstairs. Keep in mind that he is a highly adventurous kid and doesn't scare easily. He refused to go upstairs alone because he believed there were ghosts or something creepy in the bedrooms. I must admit, it was a spooky kind of place at the time.

I enjoyed your letter and will be thinking of you today as you share in all the family fun and chaos.

Always ...

Dawn

August 8

Hi Luke

Sometimes when I become overtired, I fall asleep very quickly, but then wake up way too early. This seems to be one of those times. While writing to you last night, my eyes closed before clicking on the send button.

I just read your note and watched the video that I sent to you earlier. It's entertaining to watch my niece and her boyfriend under the influence of cannabis chocolate. I was the designated driver, aunt, friend, etc. I do love my niece and wanted to share her with you.

I'm glad you had a good day. Perhaps one day I might be able to convince you to wear a hat, so that the sun won't burn that sweet face of yours. I'm also glad that Delara is no longer afraid of ghosts. She is doing much better than Frankie did under similar circumstances.

It was a lovely day. I wanted to return to a healthier routine, so went to the gym while Jan and her beau enjoyed a walk and admired all the boats at the marina. Tim is a boat guy so was very interested in talking with people and learning about boating in the northwest. After we returned home, Frankie stopped by and we all had breakfast together. He very much wanted us to visit the Taylor Shellfish Farm in Bellingham, so that is what we did. It was quite cool. After purchasing some oysters, they had grills available on the waterfront. Very informal, but quite lovely.

I am thinking about you. Good night and good morning, sweet Lucas.

Always ...
Dawn

August 8
That was a fun video. That last thing I expected was that your niece and her beau would be addressing me personally. I think your film directing skills are finely honed. You kept them on point, the actors seemed sincere and of course easy on the eyes, and the cinematography and set were perfect. Tim seemed believable as a love interest when he kept kissing Jan, to the point of leaning in for kisses a couple of times that didn't land. So, it was comedy as well as heartfelt drama. Two thumbs up.
Luke

August 8
Dear Dawn,
Your video was an unexpected surprise (see my critical review sent earlier this morning).

And you are correct, guilty as charged, I can be my own worst enemy. Not only did I NOT wear a hat or use sunscreen for two consecutive days in the sun, but yesterday I neglected to eat anything after breakfast, and when I went to bed, I couldn't silence my mind and feared I'd be awake all night, with yet another full day ahead. So I took a dose of Nyquil. I figured it would help me sleep, and the painkiller in it would ease my aching neck and back. While I did nod off, I awoke a few hours later (just about the time you were writing your 4 a.m. note to me) with stomach cramps and a bout of Montezuma's Revenge. Too much sun, not enough food, and maybe taking Nyquil on an empty stomach. Ate this morning for the first time in 24 hours, stomach still not fully calm. Men! So self-destructive!

Today: breakfast, sunscreen, hat, light lunch, salmon dinner, lots of stories, reports from those who research our ancestry, teasing, jokes and a massive Emerson team photo. We will all be wearing shirts with an emblem on the front showing the Port Townsend lighthouse encircled by the words "Emerson Family Reunion 2017," and on the back: "A people without knowledge of their history is like a tree without its roots." My older brother had them custom-made.

Tim seems nice, and Jan obviously cares deeply for you. I'm sure you're enjoying your time with them. Although I'm an avowed optimist who's health-conscious, at our age we can't ignore the fact that tomorrow is promised to no one. Carpe Diem!

Looking forward to hearing your voice and touching your lovely face sometime soon ...

Everthine,

Luke

August 8

Hi Luke

I'm sure you're already knee deep in family activities but wanted to send a little note while the house is quiet. Thanks for the review; a kind one at that! I read it to Jan, and we chuckled together. I should have mentioned that the kids often send videos to each other, often silly, but it's their way of staying in contact, like little love notes. Anyway, I haven't mentioned anything to my own children about our two dates, but Jan learned of you after the two of them shared their story with me – how they met, talked for hours, never experienced anything similar before, etc. What began as a simple, "I think I know what you mean," ended up in a long discussion. In their state of candy bliss, the video evolved.

My sweet man, I'm not a bossy person but I would love it if you wouldn't do what you did yesterday again. My goodness, no food, no hat, high temps, probably a bit of dehydration, I mean, geez, Luke. This is important, okay? I was happy to hear that you are armed with a hat and sunscreen today. :-)

I gave the fam my keys and sent them off on a hike. I have a few school-related calls to make and they were understanding about that. Whenever I get a text from my principal asking me to check my school email, I always worry. He rarely does that unless something bad has happened. Unfortunately, two of my students were involved in a serious accident and one of them was flown to Mason Hospital. Hurts my heart to see senseless tragedy.

On a much more positive note, thanks for your sweet words about touching my face. I immediately checked my Sent file, wondering if I accidentally sent my writing to you about our first two dates. In it, I talked about having a need to touch your face. Our thoughts often seem to be in sync with one another. That feels nice.

Well, today is whale watching day and we will be boarding the boat at three. I'm sure we won't be back until sometime this evening, so we will create a picnic dinner. I guess I better start working on that.

I miss your voice, well, I miss all of you. :-)

Always ...

Dawn

August 9
Dear Dawn,
You were right about my being dehydrated, but I feel fully recovered today and am seriously considering taking your advice to chill this morning. My body and brain are showing signs of fatigue. But we Emerson brothers are tough. I have attached a photo taken last night, from left to right: Luke (semi-retired writer, age 64), Alan (retired fireman, age 67) and Barry (semi-retired CPA, age 63).

To the business at hand, I offer these options in chronological order: Aug. 12, 13, 14 or 15. On Aug. 15, I have to be at the house from 9 a.m. to 9 p.m. and you have school, but if school is canceled because of a snow day or something, you can come down to the house and play with me.

Aug. 16: The rest of our life begins.

The conversation with the Leighs (Sara and husband Nate) was about the future of our species. I read a fascinating book called Homo Deus (by Yuval Noah Harari) about his theory that we are evolving into a completely different species as cyber-creatures or, more accurately, a single digital entity consisting of all our bodiless minds connected in the cloud. (Did I already mention this book to you?) It's mind-blowing to think and talk about, and the Leighs are engaging conversationalists.

I haven't told anyone in my family about you yet, maybe for the same reason you haven't told your offspring about me ... they might not understand a potentially deep relationship after just two face-to-face meetings, and I won't be legally divorced for at least 3 months. I'm sure they would roll their eyes if I told the truth and said, "I just wanted to look at Match.com to see what's out there in my age bracket, but I couldn't look unless I signed up, and then I was just going to browse but not meet anyone, and then I met Dawn and all these sparks started flying and now I'm signing my letters to her, 'everthine.'"

So you see the dilemma. If asked, I answer truthfully, but I doubt they'll ask anytime soon if I'm seeing anyone.

So, sweet Dawn, you may choose a day and time from the list above, and we will meet again. I've never been to the Coupeville Art Festival, so that might be fun. On the other hand, it might be a human zoo, so Port Townsend (the "City of Dreams") might be preferable. Or Lake Conway. Or a romantic restaurant in the town of your choice. Or a blanket on the beach at Deception Pass.

I await m'lady's response with bated breath.

Yours truly,

Lucas


August 8

Hi Lucas (I think you feel more like a Lucas in the evening.)

I'm so glad that you are feeling better. Who knows, maybe you even drank some water today, yes? Thank you for taking better care of yourself today. I mean that.

It truly sounds like the reunion was a success and that everyone was so appreciative of your efforts. I can imagine the relief you feel and am hoping you are able to sleep soundly tonight and relax in the morning. It would be wonderful if you could take a little time for yourself before resuming moving activities. I like the thought and image of you sipping on some tea and just enjoying a few quiet hours in the morning.

I miss hearing your voice.

Your conversation with Sara and Nate sounded very interesting. Honestly, my Mormon students are so thoughtful and seem to genuinely appreciate when they are asked to share their hearts. Given your ability to openly listen to their thoughts, I imagine your time shared together was very meaningful. I very much appreciate that about you.

When might we see each other again ...?

Your words made me smile. I think I could hear the tired in your voice. I'd like to ask what day might be best for you. Jan and Tim are not leaving until Friday, late afternoon. We could meet on Saturday, Sunday, or Monday, Aug. 12, 13 or 14. I couldn't remember what date you have to stay in the house all day.

If it isn't Monday, the ferry and traffic would be less crowded because the Coupeville Arts Festival will be this weekend. Take a look at your calendar and we can talk about what might be best. I return to work on the 15th, so would love to see you.

Okay, I'm determined to not fall asleep at the keyboard tonight.

I remain truly yours, too, sweet man.

Dawn

## Chapter 9

# The Secret Computer: Intervention

*When you last left the story of the secret computer, Dawn had reunited with her deceased lover, Luke, in a virtual reality world made possible by the Defense Department's clandestine project. She left feeling uneasy and uncertain about it.*

Dawn set a date to meet her three adult children at a café. The conspiracy to intervene with her began with Abbie. She, Frankie and Ann thought it was to be just a friendly, casual get-together, but Abbie arranged for her siblings to arrive 45 minutes before Mom asked them to be there.

A handsome young waiter interrupted their hushed plotting. "Small regular coffee, black?" Abbie raised an index finger, and the waiter placed the cup in front of her. "Passion iced tea?" Ann gave a little wave. "And you must be the caramel coconut Frappuccino with sprinkles." He handed the drink to Frankie. They all took a sip as the waiter departed.

Abbie had a deadly serious look on her face. "What if she's really gone nuts? I mean, certifiable."

"Oh, come on, Abbie," said Ann. "Mom isn't crazy."

"How do you know? She's definitely delusional."

"Maybe you just misunderstood what she said."

"Yeah," Frankie said, sounding a little bored. "What were her exact words?"

"She said Luke's brain is still alive inside her computer," Abbie said, punching every word, "and she visits him in virtual reality."

"I don't know whether to laugh or figure out how to join in Mom's fun." Frankie took another sip of his Frappuccino.

"You're not helping here, Frankie." Ann pretty much never

thought Frankie was helping at any time.

"I say we get professional help." Abbie said it with conviction. "A psychologist."

"Magical idea," Frankie shot back. "You both need it."

"Can you take anything seriously?" Ann plunked her cup on the table hard enough to spill a little iced tea.

"When I hear something serious, I'll let you know." Frankie smiled.

"Mom started acting strange the day of the funeral." As always, Abbie was trying to stay calm and be the adult in the room. "And she's been getting wackier ever since. Yesterday I found her lying face-down on her bed, pounding her fist into the pillow, saying over and over," "You're not real. You will never be real. You're not my Luke.""

"It's just grief," Ann said. "She never let out her grief. She hardly even shed a tear."

"Maybe," Frankie said with a chuckle, "she was just so crazy about Luke that her brain is all scrambled, like her famous egg casserole!"

"Frankie!" Abbie and Ann blurted it out in two-part harmony.

"I'm just sayin'." Frankie gazed out the window. "You know?"

"She's still stuck in the first stage – denial." Ann was speaking to Abbie, having given up on Frankie. "Unless she can get past that, she'll never get to the point of acceptance."

"Which is why," Abbie said with a nod, "we need to get her into therapy as soon as possible."

"You two have fun with your psychobabble." Frankie pushed back his chair and stood. "I've got something really serious to do."

"No, Frankie, you're part of this family, too, and I want you to stay and help us with this," Ann said. "Mom said she wanted to meet us here. All of us. So you're staying until she gets here. We need to all agree on what to do."

"Yeah, Frankie." Abbie was mocking him. "What great ideas

do YOU have?"

Frankie stared at the floor, then sat down.

"For one, I think it would be a stellar idea to look at Mom's computer," he said. "I could deduce in two minutes whether Luke's brain is really in there or not."

"You're such a waste of oxygen." Abbie shook her head. "Our mother is having a breakdown, and you don't even give a damn."

"Abbie, there's no need to turn this all back on Frankie." Ann spoke softly, trying to avoid a scene. "We just need—"

"Show a little compassion for your baby brother, Abbie." Frankie lowered his voice and became unusually serious for a moment. "We've all worked hard and live life in our own way. You and Ann love teaching math to kids, something that would drive me absolutely bonkers. I like art and my dogs and building stuff — like a chicken coop for Becca. We all create our own happiness and now isn't the time for us to turn on each other."

Abbie rolled her eyes and said, "I am not going to sit here and be lectured by my overprotective baby brother who thinks he knows everything!"

"Abbie, please, lower your voice," Ann said.

"And the truth shall set you free!" Frankie announced it to everyone in the café.

"Go. Get out of here." Abbie waved her hand in dismissal. "Go hunt elks or whatever you do to make the world a better place. Ann and I can take care of reality."

"No," Ann said. "I refuse to let this tear our family apart. Frankie is staying. We're all staying. We're going to listen to whatever Mom has to say, and we're going to do what's best for her."

"It's clear we're wasting our time talking to Frankie," Abbie said as she sat back down. "And you're letting emotions cloud your judgement, Ann. So as the only really responsible party here, I'm just going to have to make a command decision. Because of what Mom—"

"No, I'm done with both of you and I'm tired of being treated like I don't know anything," Ann said quietly. "When Mom was trying to take care of Luke, who held it all together? Who arranged for hospice care and made sure all was in order? It was me."

"Look, if you want a trophy, I have lots in my family room," Abbie said. "You can have your choice—"

"Somebody didn't take her meds today," said a smiling Frankie.

"Both of you back off." Ann stared into their eyes, just hoping either would challenge her.

The hot-looking waiter returned, leading Dawn to the table with her red-faced children. Dawn pulled up a chair between Abbie and Frankie.

"Well! How are we all doing today?"

Nobody spoke for a moment, until Abbie ventured, "The question is, how are YOU doing, Mom?"

"You feeling better?" Ann said, reaching out for her hand.

"Have you danced with Luke in the computer lately?" Frankie sounded cheerful.

Abbie and Ann glared at him.

"Well, it's funny you should mention that, Frankie, because I've seen him there several times. And guess what? He wants you to join us there, so we can have a nice meeting, all together."

Silence. Finally, Abbie said quietly, "Inside the computer."

"That's right, dear. It's virtual reality. Frankie, you're the computer guy, you know about virtual reality, don't you?"

"Uuuhh ... yeah. Sure, Mom. Virtual reality." His voice was pure condescension.

"You know we'll do whatever you want, Mom," Ann cut in, "but I was just wondering if—"

"Good! Then it's time that you kids were briefed by the government agents."

Frankie giggled.

Dawn turned toward the back of the coffee shop and motioned to a pair of men in dark suits standing against the wall. Frankie had exchanged glances with them earlier and wondered if they were plainclothes cops. They walked over to the table.

"Guys, this is Mr. Graves, and this is Mr. Jay," Dawn said. Abbie started to stand.

"Please, sit down," Mr. Graves said. "We're just here to identify ourselves and invite you to a meeting where we can brief you on what's been going on with Luke."

"Luke's dead," Frankie said.

"That's true," said Mr. Jay. "But there's a little more to the story."

Mr. Graves took a card out of his coat pocket, started to hand it to Frankie, then instead gave it to Abbie.

"We'd like to see you at that address tomorrow at 2 p.m.," he said. "Everything will be explained to you, and all your questions can be answered. But please don't mention this to anyone outside this immediate family."

# Chapter 10

# Love Letters: Everthine

*When you last left Love Letters, Luke and Dawn were trying to arrange another meeting before her school year began.*

August 9

Hi Luke

Thanks for sending a picture of you and your brothers. I'm kind of partial to the guy on the left. You and Alan have similar features but not so much with Barry. The three of you all look very healthy and happy.

I forgot to mention that the whale watching afternoon was quite lovely, except for the three of us not dressing warmly enough. The regulations must have changed because the whales were very close. At one point, one was right beside our (large) boat. Jan and Tim were very excited and will return home with an adventure or two to share with their families and friends.

The description of your thought process regarding not telling your family about our two dates made complete sense, and I agree. You also made me chuckle. You have the best writing voice ever! Like you, I will answer if asked, but would rather wait. Once I share something with the kiddos, they seem to take great joy in wanting to know way too much information. Besides, I have to see whether we can make it to date number three without you having a sun stroke.

Regarding the upcoming weekend, Sunday (Aug. 13) would likely work best, if you are still free that day. Give some thought regarding whether you would like to roam around Coupeville's art festival or whether you would prefer coming to Lake Conway. I am very open to either. If your preference is the festival, I would be happy to pick you up again at the ferry.

I wanted to let you know that I've been thinking about school beginning and am committed to finding ways for us to continue our journey of getting to know each other. We have timing in our favor because I had already planned to use this year to make a decision about retiring. And, I had already decided that I needed to proactively set some healthy boundaries at school. Today I plan to open my online appointment calendar and block off the ability for our secretary to schedule anything late on Fridays, with the exception of genuine emergencies. I'd also be happy to come to Port Ludlow, but it seems to make sense to wait until you move. Anyway, just know that this (us) feels important to me and I hope to demonstrate my commitment. (Here's where I feel compelled to say something about not being presumptuous, but I'm trying to refrain.)

Well, the three of us are leaving soon, taking a small hike to a sweet viewpoint in rural Lake Conway. From there we are headed "downtown" for dinner. Much like you, I am starting to feel a bit of fatigue from all the family fun. It's been a good week, but I am ready for things to return to normal.

I miss hearing your voice, Lucas. Perhaps Friday evening, sometime. By the way, I need a cool "Everthine" word.

Always ...
Dawn

August 9
Dear Dawn,
Your email popped in just as I was creating a new email folder entitled "Dawn" so I could gather them all in one place for easy review.

It's great that you were able to get close to the whales. So much more memorable for them, I'm sure, than for my granddaughters who had to squint in the distance to see a fin or spray.

I laughed out loud at your comment about getting to date number three without sunstroke. Yes, let's make it Sunday,

Aug. 13. I'm leaning toward Lake Conway, since I think we saw all there is to see in Coupeville, and it's unlikely we could commandeer an outdoor ocean-view dining table for several hours on Art Festival weekend. I'll call you Friday evening. Let me know what time you'll be able to talk.

Today I was on my way down to the Port Ludlow house with a load of stuff when Sara called, asking if she and the family could stop by and see it on their way down to Poulsbo (where Nate's parents live). So they did, and naturally, Sara had suggestions about how I should put it all together. I have to admit a couple of her suggestions were smart and probably will be implemented. Two minds ARE better than one. She also gave the home her blessing, saying she loved the view, the high ceilings and unusual wall angles.

Until we connect again, I remain ...

Everthine,

The Rhinestone Cowboy (see attached photo)


August 9

Hey Cowboy

Sweet picture. Thank you for sending it.

Well, I'm tucked away for the evening, saying good night to my houseguests early. They are sitting on the deck, quietly talking together. I think it's been a very good week for them.

As planned, we hiked up to a viewpoint this afternoon and the view was lovely, even with the haze. At one point, while Jan and Tim were exploring a few trails, I actually fell asleep for a short while. It was so peaceful that I drifted away. I hope you are feeling a little more rested today, Luke.

I'm looking forward to seeing you on Sunday. Any time is absolutely fine so please reserve whatever ferry time suits your fancy. You might want to pack a pair of old shoes with treads. I think I could get us to the viewpoint without taking a wrong turn. :-)

Thinking of you this evening.

Always ...

Dawn

August 10

Dear Dawn,

My busy schedule just got busier. I decided to have the wood floor in the new house stripped, stained and sealed. Five-day job, starting tomorrow, but thankfully I don't have to be there all the time. We're still "all systems go" for Sunday and I'm really looking forward to seeing you.

The wood floor is a light oak, but it's sun-bleached in places and doesn't look rich. I'm aiming for a slightly darker cherry stain, but not so dark it hides the nice grain of the oak. That should also go well with the cherry bookcase, dining table and TV stand.

The more I think about it, the more I agree with you that these forced absences from each other can be beneficial. You're sort of like a drug when I'm in your presence, touching you and talking with you. The absences give me a chance to ponder this mystical thing that seems to be happening. Can it really be that we've only seen each other twice? If so, then why do I feel so comfortable signing my notes to you with ...

Everthine,

Luke

August 11

Dear Lucas

It's about ten and I have been thinking about you throughout the day. Jan and Tim just left to listen to some music in town. I'm grateful for some alone time and wanted to write to you.

Thank you for your thoughtful letter this afternoon. I agree that it's hard to believe that we have only been on two dates. And yet, I've given some thought, and both times we were together for several hours. So, I think that counts for at least four dates! Truly, it's not surprising that we feel like we are getting to know one another in a very meaningful and profound way. Between our letters, calls and two visits, there have been some very important and treasured conversations. Mystical and magical ...

On a funny note, the three of us got into a very interesting discussion about my search to find a word as special as "everthine." We brainstormed together, read, researched and still, nothing. "Ever mine" from Beethoven, sounds possessive and that's not me. Eventually, the perfect word will appear. :-)

It sounds like you have a busy week ahead with the decision to refinish the floors. It makes me smile to think about the care and thought you are putting into your new home. I'm happy for you, Lucas. When I read the title "forced absences," I thought a change of plans was imminent. I'm so happy that we are still able to see each other on Sunday.

I appreciate the way we've stayed in contact throughout the week. I think it demonstrates so many things. For me, I just wanted you to know that I was thinking about you, despite not being able to talk or write as much.

Well, now it is closer to midnight because, once again, I fell asleep, mid-sentence. I will take Jan and Tim to the airport shuttle late afternoon and will probably be back by seven-ish tomorrow evening. I'll send a note when I return but if you are free, it would be nice to talk together. I miss you in a very real way, Lucas.

Always and Ever Ours ...
Dawn

August 11
Dear Dawn,
I can identify with you nodding off in mid-sentence. I play Scrabble on my iTouch almost every night before turning out the light, and I often fall asleep mid-game.

We might be up to the equivalent of six dates after Sunday, because I have reserved the 10:15 a.m. ferry out of Port Townsend and the 7:30 p.m. ferry out of Coupeville. Subtract a couple hours for driving and that gives us maybe 7 hours together, unless you grow weary of me or nod off after lunch (if you DO nod off, I will carry you to your bed. No, wait, that's doesn't sound quite the way I meant it, delete that sentence).

It sounds like you are somewhat like me when it comes to guests, even if they are cherished family members. After 3 days, a desire to be alone in my own space arises. They say extroverts draw energy from being around people, while introverts feel energy being sucked out of them when they're around people. By that definition, I'm introverted. I like events such as the reunion, but afterward, I need a few days to recharge my energy levels. I would also describe myself as a homebody. I do enjoy traveling and being out on the planet, but I always exhale deeply and relax when I'm back within my own walls.

About your sign-off on the note: "Always and Ever Ours." I think because it was midnight, you probably meant to write, "Always and Ever Yours," as a new take on "everthine," but perhaps not. The idea that a couple could always and forever be OURS, as in each other's, is powerful too.

Gotta run, the floor refinishers are waiting for me to let them into the house.

Everthine,

Lucas

PS: Beethoven is one of my favorites, but I'm a huge fan of baroque and love Vivaldi and Bach. Oh, and of course Mozart.

August 12

Dear Luke

I fell asleep shortly after writing to you last night. I tossed and turned a bit, probably because I'm somewhat over-tired from the past week. Now I am beginning the process of bringing my little place back to its original state, one room at a time.

I found myself thinking about you quite a bit this morning, processing the many things we talked about last night. It feels very nice, knowing that we are both very engaged and excited about our unique, magical mystery tour. Last night when I was unable to sleep, I thought of books needing to be written.

This is too obvious, but there is a story entitled, "Everthine" that is waiting to be told. I think I have the prologue written, my letter to you, entitled, "If it weren't too soon." Since Chapter One would require a real writer, that would be yours. I'd be a good partner and share thoughts, but, ultimately, I would trust in your storytelling abilities. Other chapters would unfold and be written, in time.

(Some people use the metaphor of a garden to describe journeys of the heart. Others might use the metaphor of a book with many rich chapters waiting to unfold.)

I'm cracking myself up over here. I think it's the fatigue talking. Enjoy your day and know that you are cherished.

Peace Out

(That was Jan's idea; I just had to use it once.)

Dawn

August 12

Hi Luke

Well, I'm tucked in already, happy to be back in my own room and bed. My place is quiet again, although I've heard from Jan and Tim throughout the day. I think they would have enjoyed staying another week.

Ann and all the kids came to Lake Conway after their visit to the zoo. We had dinner together and then went to one of the playgrounds so the kids could run around, ride scooters, etc. Her youngest, Maya, is only three but probably takes after Ann the most, athletically. She still looks like a toddler but has mastered riding a two-wheeler. It was good to see them all.

I have a feeling that your day was full and, hopefully, you are resting now. I'm looking forward to seeing you and just spending time together. It feels like forever since I've looked into your eyes. I miss you, Lucas.

Oh, your note just popped up. I'm so happy that you had the chance to ride your bike, share a meal with Sara, and visit with her in-laws. It makes my heart happy to know that you took a day away from boxes, moving, etc.

I think we will start the day at my place, since the weather is a little on the moody side. Our town is building a new water tower next to my road and it is kind of a mess to navigate. It might be easier if I meet you nearby and then you can just follow me. Let's do this – please set your GPS to Pioneer Market, 416 Morris Street. You can just call me when you arrive, and I am only about three minutes away. I'll meet you there.

Okay, sleepy man, I'll see you tomorrow.

Ever Yours and Ours ...

Dawn


August 13

Hi Dawn,

Slept like a baby ... woke up every 3 hours, cried, then went back to sleep (rim shot). No, just kidding, old joke, I actually had a long, wonderful, restful sleep, ready to seize the day. I have the store address in hand, will be heading toward the ferry dock soon, anticipating great adventure in distant lands.

See you soon, and as always, I remain ...

Everthine.

Luke


August 13

Dear Sweet Baby Dawn,

Thank you for an amazing, wonderful, enchanting day. It's clear to me that as long as we're together, it doesn't matter what we're doing, we will be happy just to be in each other's arms.

Oh yes, just to clarify, I did make it home OK. And we have no fourth date (or would that be 8th date?) scheduled. But I hope it's sooner rather than later. There's so much more I could write and say – and I will – but right now, I will sleep on my thoughts and my feelings and compose a long letter to you tomorrow.

I am loving you tonight ...

Everthine,

Your Luke

August 13

Dear Lucas

It was another wonderful day and I am somewhat in awe right now. I enjoyed each and every moment shared and am simply grateful for our time together. I didn't know that sharing a bowl of soup or glass of wine could be so special. Honestly, I could sit and talk with you for hours and hours. I want you to know that I am returning to work this week with a sense of hope and optimism for us. I am committed and excited for what the future might hold.

By far, this was the best third date ever!

Always Yours, Always Ours,

Dawn

August 13

Dawn, I saw your note moments after I sent my note to you ... and it shows we're on the same vibration.

But your last sentence I initially read as, "This was the third best date ever," which I thought was OK, but wondered if I could somehow have a date with you that ranked in the top two ... then I re-read the sentence.

L

August 13

Dear Lucas

Thank you for your sweet notes. I'm glad you reread the sentence about our third date … I was just trying to say that today was the best date ever. I have a feeling that any future dates – fourth, fifth, sixth, etc., will also become the best dates ever. All moments are cherished and I'm looking forward to the next time we are together. I already miss you.

After you left, I fell asleep on the couch for a while. When I awakened, my thoughts were immediately of you. Honestly, Lucas, I feel like a young girl who has fallen in love for the first time. I think about the sound of your voice, holding your hand, touching your face – I just think about everything. My heart has been touched in such a profound way and it is because of you.

I am also loving you tonight.

Ever Yours and Ever Ours

Dawn


August 14

I KNOW! Like a teenager again! That's exactly how I feel, and I'm at a loss to explain how this happens at 64, except to say that maybe there really IS something to that kismet-fate-destiny thing. Star-crossed lovers? Meant for each other? The hopeful romantic in me (no longer hopeless) thinks it may be so.

Anxiously awaiting the next time I can hold you in my arms, I remain …

Everthine,

Your Lucas


August 14

Hi Luke

When I awakened this morning, I remained in bed for quite a while. I just needed unrushed time to process the many emotions being experienced. I actually cherish the way we've been so open with each other. As an example, when we were sitting on the couch and you asked what I was thinking, I said, "I'm thinking this is what love feels like." It felt so natural to say that to you, Lucas. What is different for me, however, is feeling so free to honestly share what is inside my heart. It feels very good to be able to do so.

I'm spending the day preparing for the transition back to work. I find myself quietly thinking about ways to adapt and adjust my schedule because I very much want to be present with you whenever we are together. I think we both have the commitment and interest to find opportunities to explore and grow in our relationship. Thus far, the only challenge is that our time together passes way too quickly ...

I recently find myself enjoying the image of you having the time to make your new place your *home*. As you share your life stories with me, I am beginning to realize that you've had little opportunity to explore and create a place that is in sync with you, your heart, and your passions. It makes me happy that you are able to do so now. While I'm at school during the upcoming week, I'm sure there will be times that I will be thinking of you unpacking your books and placing them in the new bookcase. I envision you doing so carefully and in just the way you'd like. That image brings joy.

I'm off to the gym now and then will run a few errands. So many words and thoughts are inside my heart. For now, I'll just continue to let everything settle in.

Ever Yours and Ever Ours
Dawn


August 14
My dearest Dawn,
Do you realize that the first communication between us was just 29 days ago? My, how life has changed in those 29 days. Since we've both said the "L" word, I decided to Google "What

is love?" and I got the following from a TED talk by someone named Helen Fisher. Excerpts from her article are in italics.

*Love is involuntary. Brain science tells us it's a drive like thirst. It's a craving for a specific person. It's normal and natural to "lose control" in the early stage of romance. Love, like thirst, will make you do strange things, but knowledge is power. It's a natural addiction and treating it like an addiction can help you.*

*We were built to fall in love. Are YOU in love?*

*Click Here to take the Passionate Love Quiz yourself!*

(If you take the test, Dawn, you can compare: my score was 117. If you don't take the test, my score still was 117.)

*The ancient Greeks called love "the madness of the gods." Modern psychologists define it as the strong desire for emotional union with another person. But what, actually, is love? It means so many different things to different people. Songwriters have described it, "Whenever you're near, I hear a symphony." Shakespeare said, "Love is blind, and lovers cannot see." Aristotle said, "Love is composed of a single soul inhabiting two bodies."*

*THE OVERALL HYPOTHESIS: Romance is one of three basic brain systems that evolved for mating and reproduction:*

*Sex drive or lust — the craving for sexual gratification — evolved to enable you to seek a range of potential mating partners. After all, you can have sex with someone you aren't in love with. You can even feel the sex drive when you are driving in your car, reading a magazine or watching a movie. Lust is not necessarily focused on a particular individual.*

*Romantic love or attraction — the obsessive thinking about and craving for a particular person — evolved to enable you to focus your mating energy on just one individual at a time. As Kabir, the Indian poet, put it, "The lane of love is narrow; there is room for only one."*

*Attachment — the feeling of deep union with a long-term partner — evolved to enable you to remain with a mate at least long enough to rear a single child through infancy together as a team — although many of us remain together much longer and enjoy the benefits of life with a partner, even when there is no goal to have children.*

(And then she threw in the following fact, which has been an anathema to my personal love life) ...

*The intensity of romantic love tends to last somewhere from six months to two years before turning into attachment in most relationships.*

So if all that Helen Fisher wrote above is true, the only question that remains for me is: what happens to us after six months to two years?

What is so exciting to me about you, Dawn, is that when I'm with you or even when I just think of you, I get all these magical mystical feelings that I can't honestly say I have ever fully experienced before. That makes me hopeful (optimistic? yearning? crazy-blind?) that this feeling can last as long as we live. Geez, at our age, maybe two years WILL be as long as we live. KIDDING! I HOPE!

So, Sweet Baby Dawn, let me know when I can see you again, and I will be there. But as you will see by the following paragraph, I'm nearly as busy as you for a while.

I head to the Catpaw Lane house in a few minutes to move more stuff and see how the floor staining is going. I'm very close to being done with all I can do in the SUV. Tomorrow is the day I will be at the new house all day, waiting for two deliveries (bookcase and TV). The oak TV stand/cabinet could be delivered anytime in the next 3 days. On Tuesday, I get the haircut that you thought I already had, and on Friday I'll be on Catpaw Lane again for the carpet cleaning as well as the installation of cable, phone and internet lines. On Sunday, I am volunteering to man the KPTZ radio table at the Jefferson County picnic, telling folks about our emergency preparedness protocols.

And on Monday, my life changes again ... moving day (also the day of the solar eclipse). After that, I'm free (or at least reasonable ... rim shot!) until Sept. 16, when I fly to California to see my son Scotty, daughter-in-law Ariel and grandbaby Amy.

We're going to an Angels baseball game (I covered the Angels as a sportswriter for 12 years).

So between all that and your schedule, let's see if we can find a way to get together before the winter solstice. KIDDING! I HOPE!

Everthine,

Lucas

August 14

Dear Luke

Sweetheart, your letter gave me a lot to think about, while also bringing a smile to my heart. I think I'm able to hear your mind ticking away as you process all the emotions we seem to be experiencing mutually. I'm not sure, but what I think is happening is that we are beginning to put words on the real possibility of love, while also trying to gain a deeper understanding of it. After all, how many sixty-four-year-old adults suddenly morph into young, playful souls that can't get enough of each other? By the way, your desire to explore and learn has been added to the list of the many things I cherish about you.

Back to love ...

I took the quiz and, not surprisingly, our scores were very similar. You had a 117 and I scored a 119. I wasn't able to rate the last statement because it is my thought that when something doesn't go right in a relationship, I (ideally) would like to explore solutions together, rather than shift to a place of depression. There are always exceptions, especially if both aren't willing or if larger issues, such as addictions, are a factor. At the end of the day, I truly value partnership and working through things together. I think we likely share in that belief.

After watching the TED talk, I found myself watching others that were included on the homepage. I was rather encouraged by what I heard and think it might be fun to watch videos like that together sometime. I liked the one about relationship keys and another on whether love can last forever. The common theme seems to be, yes, love can sustain, but couples must be committed to communication and intimacy. So much to think and be hopeful about.

On another note, thanks for letting me know about your commitments this coming weekend. I totally understand and appreciate you letting me know. I will miss you a bunch but will very much look forward to the next time we are able to meet, hopefully the following weekend.

You bring such joy to my heart, Lucas.

Ever Yours and Ours,

Dawn

P.S. A communication question – Are you okay with me using the word, "sweetheart"?

## Chapter 11

# The Secret Computer: Virtual Reality

*When you last left the Secret Computer story, Dawn had met with her adult children to convince them to participate in the Defense Department's clandestine program and meet the avatar of Luke in virtual reality.*

A 26-year-old Luke had Dawn pinned against a wall, trying to kiss her, but she kept turning her head away, laughing. She looked about 24, dressed in tight jeans and a low-cut, form-fitting yellow top.

Behind them, an empty outdoor café was dwarfed by the Seattle skyline. Five seats surrounded a glass table.

"Come on, Luke! Not now!" Dawn giggled. "You know those Army geeks can see us."

All hands and mouth, Luke kissed her on the neck and ear.

"Half the time they don't even pay attention," he said. "We're just fuzzy blobs on their computer screen. I think we should see what happens when a hot human female and a brilliant computer program create virtual fireworks." He wrapped his arms around her and pulled her into a tight embrace.

"Luke, you know this isn't what I came here for."

He silenced her with a kiss on the mouth.

"Oh, come on, this can't really happen here." Dawn gave in, laughed and kissed him back with passion.

They didn't even notice the bright flash of light that somehow left Frankie – giggling like a high pot-head – sitting on the sidewalk a few feet away from his mom and Luke. He looked up at them like a meditating, smiling Buddha.

"That was a hell of a thing," Frankie said with a chuckle.

"Frankie!" Dawn pulled away from Luke and straightened

out her clothes. "What are you doing here?"

"The question is, what are YOU two doing here?" Frankie said. "I don't think that function was authorized in the program manual."

"We were just ... performing a little experiment," Luke said.

"Did everything come out all right?"

"I thought you were supposed to join us at three o'clock," Dawn said to her son.

Frankie glanced at his wrist, which had no watch.

"Wow, just look at the virtual time. It's almost three," he said. "That means Ann and Abbie should be along any minute now."

Bright, silent flashes, like lightning, washed out everything. When the flashes stopped, Abbie appeared at the outdoor café, contorted in anguish and squealing as if she were being stuck by a thousand needles.

Luke and Dawn looked aghast at Abbie's suffering.

"AAAHHHHHH! Help ... me ..." Abbie fell in a crumpled heap near Dawn.

Little, happy noises, as if from a child on a merry-go-round, distracted Luke, Dawn and Frankie. They turned in unison to see Ann wobbling toward them.

"Whoa! Oooh! Eeeeee!" She ended up on one knee near Abbie, alert but a little unsteady.

Ann looked around at the skyline and stood. "Isn't this Seattle?"

Dawn went to Abbie. "Honey, are you all right?"

"Of course she's all right," said Luke. "Abbie's lying on a cot in the lab at Mason Hospital. That's just her avatar. Her brain needs to adjust. It's like your eyes getting used to a brighter room."

Abbie slowly staggered to her feet and looked around. She pinched her own arm. "Huh. I felt that."

"You'll feel everything," said Frankie, now sitting in full lotus position, his thumbs and middle fingers forming little circles and his eyes gazing skyward. "Maybe for the first time in your life."

"What, so after ten seconds," Abbie said, "suddenly you're the instant expert on virtual reality?"

"I'm accessing the database. Downloading information. Just like they told us we could do. If you were paying attention when they—"

"This is so cool!" Ann was pointing toward the Space Needle. "It's like we're really in Seattle Center."

"Come. Sit," said Luke. "We have to talk."

"Hey." Frankie was still looking skyward, eyes now closed. "This program isn't about artificial intelligence. It's about … immortality. But not for everybody. Just the United States. It's about, like, surviving Armageddon after our bodies are toast. My brain will go on."

"That can't be true," Luke said. "What are you talking about?"

"I'm hacking into the DARPA mainframe."

"DARPA?" Abbie sounded confused.

"Defense Advanced Research Projects Agency. DARPA. That's who's running this sideshow. But of course they didn't tell us that."

"Honey, do you really think that's a good idea?" Dawn said. "I mean, hacking? We're sort of like guests here."

"Crap. They just locked me out." Frankie stood and brushed dust off his virtual pants. "Maybe I shouldn't have said anything. Of course, they're monitoring everything we say and do. But I did get a sniff of the grand design. They think they're creating a new life form here. Cyber-gods, basically."

Frankie finally noticed his surroundings. "Hey. Seattle."

"You could really hack them that fast?" Luke said. "Just by willing it to happen? That's unbelievable."

"They didn't think they'd need a firewall from the inside, so they didn't even block me. You'd be surprised what I can do, Dad 2.0. If you cared, you'd already know that I'm a—"

"So let's all sit," Ann said, "and find out what this big meeting is about." She pulled out a chair next to her mom at the table.

"How come you and Mom look so much younger," Abbie said to Luke, "but we don't?"

"It's just the settings we chose. We could have made your avatars children, but I'm sure it'd seem strange to have little six-year-old Frankie hacking into the Defense Advanced Research Projects Agency. And these are the ages that your Mom and I like best."

"Right," said Frankie. "I didn't start hacking until I was eight."

"So ... Mom isn't crazy." Abbie shook her head. "This is real."

"Not exactly," Frankie corrected.

"I don't mean real, but—"

"Mom was telling the truth," said Frankie. "The A.I. experiment works, and Luke is still alive ... sort of."

"Well, you've certainly proved your point," Abbie said. "But I don't like it. Makes me feel a little nauseous. Can we go back now?"

"We wanted to discuss some things with you guys first." Luke stood and put a hand on Abbie's shoulder, trying to get her to sit.

"But they said you can talk to us through the computer." Abbie stepped away from him. "We don't need to put on headgear and come to a virtual Seattle for this. We can be fully awake in our real bodies, and you can be a face on the screen."

"What fun is that?" said Frankie. "Don't you want to explore? This is Seattle without rules. I could go into that electronics store over there and steal everything I want."

"And do what with it?" Abbie said. "Sell it at an imaginary pawn shop for some imaginary money?"

"Luke," Ann said, "maybe you SHOULD have made them six-year-olds."

"Come on, guys. Sit." Luke pointed to the chairs. "We have something important to talk about, and it has to be done here, in my world, where you can see me as a person, not just an image on a screen."

Abbie and Frankie remained standing.

Dawn touched Luke's sleeve. "Tell them why."

Luke looked at Dawn, then down at his feet. "Well, I hope she's changed her mind now, but last week, your Mom said she wants a divorce."

"Luke!" Dawn slapped his hand. "I never said that!"

"How can you get a divorce?" Ann asked. "You never got married. And technically, he's still dead."

"There's nothing technical about it," Abbie pointed out. "He's been cremated."

"That's not what I said, Luke."

Luke didn't look at Dawn, instead motioning to the children. "Please, guys. Join us."

Frankie took a seat at the table, and Abbie, after a long moment, did the same.

"I'm serious," Abbie said. "This whole thing is making me feel like I want to throw up."

"Divorce?" Ann raised her eyebrows at Luke.

"OK, she didn't use that word. But it just felt like, based on all we've been through and what she was saying now, that—"

"You're dead," said Dawn. "How can we be together? I mean, really."

"Your mother has been visiting me here for several weeks," Luke said to the rest. "I've been telling her she's more important to me than the air that I breathe."

"Or don't breathe." Frankie inhaled deeply. "Yep. Smells like virtual air to me."

"I need her. But she wants to leave," Luke said. "She says she has to move on."

"You can't call it divorce." Dawn wouldn't face him. "It's not like there's any paperwork. I just don't need to waste any more time down here."

"Waste?" Luke said it with challenge in his voice.

"Down here?" Frankie was trying to change the subject. "Is this, like, hell?"

"Depends on your perspective," Abbie said. "Yeah, maybe hell."

Luke stood and moved around the table as he spoke.

"It's more like heaven. That's why I needed you here to actually experience it. This isn't a concept or a video game. It's real. It's a new form of existence. Once they've perfected this technology, everyone will live two lives – first as a flesh-and-blood person, and then, after the body wears out, as a fully connected, advanced form of intelligence. Think of it like a butterfly. First, we're caterpillars crawling on the dirt. A short, messy life. Then we morph into a cocoon so nanobots can scan our brain. Finally, we emerge as a beautiful, digital being with wings to fly in a pure, everlasting and sublime eternity."

"Introducing the all-new, Human two-point-oh!" Frankie was having fun.

"Exactly," Luke said. "You get it, Frankie."

"Sounds cool to me," Frankie said. "So why don't you want to play anymore, Mom?"

"I just don't buy it," Dawn said to no one in particular. "I think Luke's been fed a bunch of lies, half-truths and speculation. He can't reason with a real, human mind anymore. He just believes whatever's fed into his program. Like any computer would."

"And," Ann said, "you want to opt out."

"Well … yes. Luke's program can keep playing these games forever, I don't care. I just need to get back to planet Earth and get the most I can out of the years I have left. Losing a partner makes you realize how precious life is. I've still got some dances left in these old legs."

"What's wrong with that, Luke?" said Ann. "Wouldn't it be better for all of us if Mom devoted the rest of her years to being the best mother, friend and person she can be?"

"But she hasn't lost a partner, she's gained a god." Luke shook his head. "OK, that didn't come out right."

"Sounds about right to me," Frankie said. "It's what the DARPA dudes believe. They take a computer, cook it a trillion times smarter than any human being, mix in all the crap inside a real person's skull, add a touch of conscience, a sprinkle of emotion and a dash of soul, then drain out all remaining humility. Voilà! They've baked us a god."

"I just wanted you all to come here so you could experience full-immersion virtual reality yourselves," Luke said. "Download information directly into your head. Experience the power of creating your own environment at will. So you won't be afraid of it. Or me."

"While the army geeks track us like guinea pigs." Frankie smiled.

"Well, you're part of the experiment, of course," Luke said. "None of this has ever been done before. They don't know how well you'll adjust, or how much control you'll have over the program. I'm embedded in the software, so I can make things happen, but you guys are more like remote players."

"What?" Ann sounded indignant. "You just wanted us here so the army could shrink our heads?"

"No, I wanted you here so you could see the possibilities and convince your mom it's a nice place to visit once in a while. And I was hoping you'd all feel the same." Luke stood behind Frankie and put his hands on his shoulders. "It's an unbelievable opportunity. You're the first in history to be linked with artificial intelligence. You're all pioneers in the future of mankind."

"And what if we say no?" Abbie sounded like her mind was already made up.

"Then my only company here will be army tekkies and a few student volunteers from the university. And you will have missed a beautiful experience."

"This is what you signed up for, Luke," said Dawn. "None of

the rest of us did. We're not obligated."

"Well, deal me out." Abbie stood and backed away.

"You don't seriously believe," Ann said, "that everybody is going to turn into a computer hard-drive when we die, do you?"

"There's not a doubt in my mind. It's natural evolution. All living things are programmed to adapt and thrive as best they can. The shark does it with its jaws, the cockroach with its durability. Our own survival has always been dependent on our intelligence."

"Oh crap." Frankie laughed. "We're doomed!"

"On the contrary," Luke said. "We've finally gotten smart enough to figure out how to outlive our fragile little bodies."

"But I keep coming back to this," Dawn said. "You're not alive anymore. You're just a database with Luke's personality. We're all here together in virtual reality, but there's a difference between us. The kids and I are still human beings, and you're not."

"You say it as if that gives you some kind of advantage over me." Luke's voice grew a little cold. "You have it backward. I can be smarter than any human ever, and my growth and lifespan are unlimited. You and every other water bag are scheduled to turn to dust without ever realizing a tiny fraction of your potential."

"You've made a serious miscalculation, Captain," Frankie said, "by assuming that the brain is our most important organ."

Abbie put her foot on her chair, leaned forward, rested her arms on her knee and shook her head at Frankie. "I don't even want to know which organ you think is most important."

Frankie stood. "Your brain just distracts you from the totality of what we are, Abbie," he said. "Every organ and every cell in our body has a consciousness of its own. And the best thing a brain can do is ignore all the chatter from its ego and listen to the rest of the music."

"Thank you, Obi-wan Kenobi," Abbie scoffed. "You're our only hope."

"There's some truth in what Frankie says," said Luke. "But once the organs and cells die, what are we left with? If the choice is eternal darkness or ever-growing intelligence, which would you pick?"

"Maybe those aren't the only two choices," Dawn said. "I happen to believe in a different kind of everlasting life. A better one."

"The Kingdom of Heaven?" Luke asked. "Or maybe Frankie would say Nirvana or Absolute Bliss Consciousness? They're just different words for the same thing. You can call it the Happy Hunting Ground, but it's still just a metaphor. A beautiful metaphor for an existence free from worry and strife, where you can have whatever your heart desires for eternity. And that's where we are right now, you and me. For everyone else, it's the world to come, but for us, we can have this here and now."

"I'm not buying it," Ann said. "So tell me, Luke, what does your computer brain say about the Gaia Theory?"

"The idea that we're all one with the planet? That all earthly matter and organisms are really a single, self-regulating system? It's a weak hypothesis, not even a theory."

Ann shook her head. "If you were looking at the real me, instead of this avatar, maybe you would be looking into the eyes of the Earth. Maybe you would be listening to the voice of the Earth. We're all organic extensions of the Mother," she said. "If we turn ourselves into computers, I think Mother Earth would miss us terribly."

"Really?" Frankie shot back. "I think she'd throw a party."

"There's nothing unnatural about what I've become," Luke said. "Silicon is the most abundant element in the earth's crust besides oxygen. Electricity is a function of nature. In fact, the progression from carbon-based humans to pure, silicon-based intelligence is textbook Darwinian evolution."

Frankie looked upward, holding out his arms, palms up, receiving information. "Hmmmm ... So you could say it really

IS just natural selection. It's Mother Gaia evolving herself."

"Whose side are you on?" Abbie said to Frankie. "You keep shifting all over the place."

Frankie put his hands on his hips and feigned indignation. "When I get better information, I change my position. What do you do?"

"It's not about taking sides," said Ann, always the peacemaker. "We're just trying to figure out what's the best thing to do with all this. So everybody can be happy."

"Let's try something, Abbie," said Luke. "Imagine any place in the world you like and focus on taking us there."

"Nope. Not playing."

"OK. That's fine. Ann. How about conjuring up your favorite vacation? Maybe that summer in California?"

"You mean when I nearly drowned at the beach?"

"I'll take a shot," Frankie said. He looked up and stretched his arms as if he were about to catch a basketball dropped from above.

Their entire universe began erupting with lightning flashes.

## Chapter 12

# Love Letters: I Think I Love You

*When you last left the Love Letters, Dawn and Luke were just beginning to tentatively use the word "love" in their conversations.*

August 15

Dear, sweet Luke

Well, I knew this day would arrive and I must say, I never expected to begin the new (working) year with so many emotions running through my mind and my heart. How I will be able to sit through three days of technology instruction is well beyond my imagination. All I really want to do is rewind back to Sunday and have a few more hours to look into your eyes and share time with you. When my children were little and I would read to them at night, there was a poem they loved, entitled, "Just Five More Minutes, Please." That's how I feel.

I spent my last summer day reflecting and thinking about you and ways to be a good partner as we continue our loving journey of getting to know one another. It's important to me that you are able to see and feel my commitment to this unexpected surprise called Luke and Dawn. I want this to work, sweetheart, and I think there may be times when we will need to figure things out together. I actually like the sound of that.

On Sunday, we touched upon this experience being different for both of us. I think I am coming to better understand why. There is the obvious – our genuine interest and attraction to one another. But there is really so much more. See if this makes sense …

I think I recently mentioned that I have not personally experienced a relationship that involved true equity, in the sense that I didn't have to be heavily (or fully) responsible for the emotional health of the other. Don't get me wrong, contributing to that twinkle in your eye is incredibly important to me. I believe the difference with us is that we know who we are and what we desire. Thus, we have the opportunity to grow together in a healthy way, something that I find incredibly attractive and exciting. A simple example might be yesterday – watching TED talks on love and then sharing thoughts back and forth. A first for me, Lucas. A lovely first.

I'm under the blankets as I write to you this morning. I'm so glad you now have an image of my room and where I write. Spending time with you at my tiny place felt good. Each step in learning and growing together seems to feel that way.

I'm not sure whether I will be able to write every morning before work, but it felt important to do so today. I wanted you to know that you are inside my heart and as I try to be present at school, I'm committed to being the same throughout our journey. I'm hoping it's one that is with us for always.

This is a love letter, isn't it, sweetheart?

Ever Yours, Ever Ours,

Dawn

P.S. Any of your names of endearment make my heart smile.

August 15

Dearest Dawn,

I left in a rush this morning in order to be at the new house before 8 a.m., but after the floor finishers arrived, I asked if they would sign for any deliveries and came home to check my email, in hopes I would see your name. And there it was.

It isn't often that my lack of a smartphone data plan is an inconvenience, today it was, but it was well worth the one-hour round trip to read your unexpected words … unexpected because I know your world is now busier.

It saddens me that you haven't experienced true equity in a relationship. I've always been very independent (most libertarians revel in personal freedom not just for themselves, but for everyone else). I wouldn't feel comfortable with any relationship that didn't embrace total equality. That doesn't mean we don't do things for each other out of love and kindness – we do – but it's never an obligation or expectation. All relationships tend to develop a separation of duties because one or the other is more inclined to do certain things. For example, I always vacuumed the house because Lynn hated vacuuming, but she would dust because of my allergies. I will lift the heavy things and reach things on the top shelf that you aren't able to, you will cook soup because I don't have that expertise. I will give you loving massages, and you will do … whatever your heart desires.

And right now, my heart desires you. I wanted to call you last night, but I suspected you were consumed with other thoughts and deeds. If there is a day or time when we can talk, Baby Doll, let me know, and I'll give you a ring.

Until then, I remain …

Everthine

Your Lucas

August 15

Hi Sweetheart

Thank you for taking the time to write today. Your words, thoughts, and letters always mean so much to me.

Just so you don't worry or feel sadness when I talk about past relationships, always try to remember that I was with one person for more than half of my adult life. Thus, when I talk about experiences, I need to remember to keep things singular, so it doesn't sound like one inequitable sadness rolled into another. I'm incredibly grateful for what we are experiencing together and find myself processing out loud with you. Our conversations and discussions are cherished deeply.

If you happen to be free tonight or tomorrow, it would be lovely to talk together. Maybe 7:30 or 8:00? That would give me time to have dinner, prepare for tomorrow, etc. I'll charge my phone, in the event you might be free.

Thinking about you as I write (well, actually, I've been thinking about you throughout the day). I am ...

Ever Yours, Ever Ours ...

Dawn

August 16

Good morning sweet man

It's funny, after we talked last night, I crawled into bed and just wanted to take your voice and loving ways with me as I tried to close my eyes. I don't have the words, but, Lucas, you are inside my heart all of the time now. It isn't frantic or chaotic – it's very warm and peaceful, well, except when I'm unable to sleep because I'm thinking about you. I truly believe this is how love is supposed to feel.

It's day two and I'm wondering how long it will take to settle into a more focused zone today. Although others haven't noticed, I find it a struggle to sit at a large rectangular table, surrounded by adults with laptops. My mind is thinking, "Don't you silly people know that I'm in love and don't want to be here right now?" It will be much easier at week's end, when I will be able to work with students.

I hope all works out with the floor staining today. I know this is a quiet worry for you and, hopefully, it will be fully dry by tomorrow. You've accomplished so much with your house during the past few weeks and it's been fun to watch you think and plan – a process that makes sense to me. You bring joy, sweetheart.

I must close now but am struggling to do so. "Just five more minutes, please," is a phrase that is going through my mind.

Think, David Cassidy singing "I think I love you."

Ever Yours and Ours

Dawn

August 16

Sweet Baby Dawn,

Not to put any pressure on you, because you do have a job to do, but your words make my day. Always.

Speaking of David Cassidy, I am reminded of him and the rest of the Partridge Family singing, "I think I love you ... isn't that what life is made of? ... though I never felt this way before."

I may have told you that an acting scout from Universal Studios said I would be "the next David Cassidy" when he tried to get a 19-year-old Luke Emerson into a TV series called "The Burtons Abroad." The series was never sold, but the attached pictures show I never could have been the next David Cassidy. No resemblance at all. He didn't have sideburns or chest hair.

As you were talking about your thoughts and duties last night, I thought of the invented verb "compartmentalize." Same thing as living in the moment. When you're a counselor, you're the best damn counselor this world has ever known because you love what you do. When you're something else – lover, friend, mother, pianist – you pour your soul into that for those moments.

I know, easy for me to say, because I can just think about you all day and all night and it doesn't affect my job performance or anything or anyone else. It's easy to be me, just smiling all the time, thinking about my Baby Doll.

Oh wait, I did decide last night, after we talked on the phone, that I was moving too fast. "Small steps, Sparks, small steps." (If you know what movie and novel that's from, you might be the girl for me.)

Well, I'm off to get my hair cut a lot shorter than you see in that photo, then I'll swing by the house on Catpaw Lane to see if I made the right choice in a floor refinisher.

I truly do NOT want to burden your schedule or interfere with the moments when you need to be counselor, friend, mother, pianist, etc. Since I am the one with free time, I will follow your lead in terms of when you are available to write, talk on the phone or, if I may be so bold, to touch my face again.

I think I love you, isn't that what life is made of? Though it worries me to say that I never felt this way.

Everthine,

Lucas E.

August 16

Hi honey

*Contact* was a lovely and meaningful movie. Perhaps we might have the opportunity to watch it together sometime. My only worry might be that I would want to kiss you throughout the movie. You, the film critic with deep focus, me, the romantic that wants to kiss. This may be our first attempt at negotiation. I much prefer Lucas Emerson to David Cassidy, by the way.

D

August 17

Good morning, sweet Lucas

Well, it helped to talk together last night, and I slept more peacefully. I must admit that I wasn't able to turn you into a mist, but I was able to quiet my brain and simply imagine sleeping next to you. We slept well together, by the way.

For a brief moment I stewed a bit, chastising myself for asking the question that I did at the end of our conversation. At the time, it just felt right, but then I worried a little. I hope you will always let me know if I say anything that might cause you to feel uncomfortable. The truth is, what I feel about you very much feels like love, so I'm beginning to realize that it is – all 119 mad, crazy, points of it.

On a funny note, after washing my hair this morning, I looked in the mirror at my lips. I'm not sure what you are seeing, but thank you. They just look like lips to me. :-)

I've been thinking about our conversation last night and I must say, even our phone conversations appear to be one of the many stops on our magical mystery tour. I've noticed that we seem to shift into some type of communal place and such closeness is felt. My, my, what you have done to my heart, sweet man. Your voice seems to both quiet and ignite my heart, all at the same time.

After school this evening, I'm meeting my two co-workers for a drink and light dinner. We will catch up on each other's lives and probably talk about ways to remain balanced throughout the year. They both have young children, so it is always a challenge for them. I sense that both (Margo and Mary) are concerned that I might actually retire at year's end, so I'm sure there will be some conversation about that. It will be interesting to see how they will respond to the possibility that I may do so. Such an interesting year, in so many ways. All will unfold however it is meant to.

Well, sweetheart, it's time to fix some oatmeal and prepare for the day. Tomorrow begins my first day back at the office, so I will return to an earlier schedule. I do enjoy writing to you during these early morning hours, so I hope to continue. I guess it's the closest thing I have right now to sharing a cup of coffee or tea with you. I know I've said this many times before, but I cherish every moment of this very beautiful journey. I understand and accept the many unknowns but have to simply trust that we've already been given such a precious gift. My heart is so open to your love and that feels very warm and very right.

As you seize this day, please don't lift any sculptures, cowboy.

On a communication note, I may need your help with something.

I believe you are very skilled in the practice of meditation. I, too, thought I was, well, until you tiptoed into my life – like loud, crashing cymbals. Typically, I'm able to quiet my mind at night and shift into a very peaceful place and ultimately, fall into sleep. Lately, when I try to calm my breathing and quiet my thoughts, you are there, I mean, *fully* present. I actually find myself wanting to stay awake because I don't want to miss anything.

I've tried visualizing – taking your hand and walking you to the back door. I've tried closing my eyes and creating an image of your arms wrapped around me as we drift off together. And I've tried booting you out of the house, something that causes me to chuckle. Seriously, I need some help quieting my mind. Otherwise I might just croak from sleep deprivation prior to our fourth date.

I am missing you right now.

All the time, actually ...

Dawn

August 17

Dearest Dawn,

Although I am writing this at 8:24 a.m., I suspect you won't read it until this evening, so I hope you had a perfect day ... that's kind of cool, for a moment there I felt I had traveled into the future.

I think there will come a day very soon when we both feel comfortable saying whatever is in our heart, knowing the other will not judge harshly anything that comes from truth. After I hung up last night, I felt we both had crossed a significant threshold, saying "I love you" out loud to each other. It felt good. It felt right. I slept well.

Speaking of endearments, I don't think I've found the right one for you yet. "Sweetheart" seems appropriate, but that's already taken. (Of course, I know we could both use it for each other, but I want to keep experimenting until I find one that really suits how I feel about you. It will come in its own time.)

In one of the plays I was in, my character called his woman "Sugar Bumps," presumably a reference to her breasts. Are you OK with that? (KIDDING!)

My day has not started perfectly. The floor refinisher texted me this morning to say he did NOT return for the second and final coat last night, so he's doing it this morning. He apologized. So now I can't move boxes onto the floors tonight, and I have the carpet cleaner coming at 9 a.m. That means I probably will have to get up at 4 a.m. tomorrow morning, shovel down a bowl of cereal, then go to the new house to move everything off the carpets and into the garage or onto the wood floor. Fortunately, I don't have to go to school or work tomorrow, so I could take a nap in the afternoon – if I were someone who took naps.

Everything else in the move and my life is going like clockwork. All furniture delivered: check. Everything I can move myself already in the new house: check. Fall in love: check.

I do think a long courtship will suit both of us just fine. So much more to explore in each other's mind, heart and soul.

And I do love you.

Your Luke

August 17

Hi Sweetheart

Thank you for the lovely letter. I am actually able to check my personal email at school. I just have to use my cellphone and turn off the wi-fi. It touches my heart deeply when I read your words, especially when I am working. I can't really explain it, but I am just profoundly touched by the many ways we communicate with each other and share how much we care. We are very lucky, I think.

By now you have weathered the storm regarding the floor not being done. Some (or all) of the boxes have probably been moved to the garage already and you've worked through the temporary setback. I'm just so impressed with all the things you've accomplished in such a short period of time. I know there will come a time soon when you will be able to walk into your home and feel a sense of peace and contentment. I'm so happy for you, Lucas. I think your new home is an important chapter and part of your journey.

Have I mentioned that I'm kind of crazy about you? If not, I remain ...

Sugar Bumps

August 18

Good morning Sweetheart

I hope you slept well and will pace yourself today. If you need a pick-me-up, just think of Sugar Bumps trying to distract you.

When we were talking last night, and I heard you quietly say, "I am loving you right now," honestly, Lucas, I actually lost my breath for a moment. I wish I had better descriptive words, but I simply feel a sense of awe about us. I'm unable to fully wrap my mind around how we, Luke and Dawn, possibly happened in the way that we did. I think we are very, very, lucky.

I'm glad to be returning to my office this morning. It will be good to start wading through the many emails, making calls to students, and preparing for the onslaught of eight hundred kids on Monday and Tuesday. Returning to this pace is always a transition but I feel like I'm in a good place. Who would have guessed that love could be so calming and peaceful?

I know you have a busy weekend ahead and, although we won't be able to see each other, I have a feeling that our hearts will be very present and open to one another. As mentioned in an earlier letter, you are simply with, or maybe I should say *within*, me now – like a quiet and loving heartbeat. How cool is that?

I am free next weekend and hope we might be able to spend some time with each other. To look into your eyes again and hear your voice, well, it's like a little slice of heaven. I am so incredibly drawn to all parts of you, Lucas.

I, too, am loving you right now.

Ever yours and ours ...

Dawn

August 18

Dear Dawn Babe,

(I'm trying on that endearment for size) ... Here's your update on the Lucas situation:

I set the alarm for 5:30 and woke up at 2:30, which sadly is not unusual for me. I so dislike waking to alarms, even if it's just the beep-beep of my calculator watch, that I almost always awaken before the alarm – sometimes an alarmingly large amount of time before the alarm. So I lay in bed meditating on the imagined face (and Sugar Bumps) of Dawn Babe, then arose at 4:30 a.m. I got to the house on Catpaw Lane at 6 and spent the next three hours moving boxes, furniture and stuff into the garage or onto the hardwood floor (with a new stain finish which looks wonderful, BTW). I could not find the back brace that I promised Sugar Bumps I would wear.

The cable/internet/phone guy arrived at 8:04 a.m., which was great because he gave me a two-hour window, from 8-10, and the carpet cleaner was due at 9, so I thought he could get done installing his gadgets before the carpet cleaner arrived. I was wrong.

Then the floor finisher guys arrived because they had NOT FINISHED from the night before, meaning the 4-day job was now a 6-day job! But it really doesn't deserve CAPS or an exclamation point, because the only thing they left was taking off all the masking tape, cleaning up their mistakes (red stain on the white molding), and removing all their equipment.

When the carpet cleaner arrived, I had four individuals doing three different jobs at the same time, bumping into each other and tripping over the carpet cleaner's corrugated hose.

But, as with almost all my stories, there is a happy ending. The floor guys wrapped it up quickly and left, the carpet cleaner was able to start with the living room and master bedroom while the TV guy finished up in the middle bedroom (which in the House of Lucas is a home theater). The TV guy left, and five minutes later I realized he had not told me my new phone number. I rushed outside and was relieved to see he was still sitting in his truck filling out papers. My new home number is ... I forget. But I wrote it down and left it in the new house.

Then the carpet cleaner finished, all the floors look good, everyone was paid and happy, and I got to sit in the House of Lucas by myself, enjoying the vibe. Then I went to the phone to confirm that it was working. It was not.

And the beautiful new 4K HDTV was not producing a picture better than 480p, which, as any HD buff will tell you, is unacceptable. Why have a state-of-the-art TV if you can only get a 480p signal? It's like paying to see a 3D movie and then not having the glasses.

So I called Wave (my provider), got a very helpful and hip young man on the phone (my cellphone, obviously), and he walked me through a fix for all my problems in a matter of just, well, 25 minutes or so. But everything is working as advertised, so I choose to be happy.

I am also happy to report that my schedule for next weekend is wide open. I'm not foolish enough to suggest the House of Lucas will be fully assembled and appointed by then, but I would be happy to meet you on your side of the water, if you'd like. Someday soon, I will give you a sly wink and say, "My place or yours, Dawn Babe?"

And that is your 3:45 p.m. news update. For the entire news team here at KPTZ, 91.9 FM in Port Townsend, thanks for listening.

I am ...

Everthine,

Lucas Emerson

August 18

Good evening, sweet one

I must say, you make carpet cleaning, floor staining, and cable installation sound very sexy. I enjoyed your letter and am glad everything went well, despite the fact that you are possibly delirious. Ah, to be sitting next to you right now, talking about the day and looking forward to turning in early. Another evening, perhaps.

I fear the wake-in-the-middle-of-the-night-syndrome is something we share. It happens to me on most nights. When I'm unable to return to sleep, I usually read, write, or, during the last month, think about you. When we choose to sleep (as in, sleep) together, I wonder what will happen.

I stayed at school on the late-ish side today and will be leaving shortly for a walk with my close friend, Sofia. It will feel good to briskly move and breathe. The day was full, but I accomplished a lot and enjoyed having you inside my heart. I'll be home around eight, so if you would like to call, please feel free. However, I completely understand if you are already asleep, with visions of Sugar Bumps dancing in your head.

I remain, Ever Yours and Ours
Dawn/Sweet Baby Dawn/Sugar Bumps

August 19
Dear Lucas
Every year in late August, I return to the working world. It's during this time that Saturday mornings take on an entirely different meaning. It's a special moment of peacefulness – a time to wrap myself in a soft blanket and enjoy an unrushed cup of coffee; a time to read, reflect, and during past weeks, write to my beloved. As I started writing just now, I realized that our love is much like that soft blanket – warm, soothing, and protective. I guess it isn't surprising that my mind quietly ponders what it might be like to awaken on a Saturday morning and share a precious moment like this with you.

Another step in your journey today. Please drive safely and know that you continue to be inside my heart. It was so nice to hear your voice last night before closing my eyes. Before drifting into sleep, I remember softly saying out loud, "I love you, Lucas."

Always Yours and Ours ...

Dawn

August 19

Dear Dawn,

I thought I heard you softly say "I love you" at the end of our phone conversation last night, but it was so indistinct that it didn't dawn on me until after I hung up, and then I worried that if you DID say those words and I didn't say the same back, you might think I purposely avoided it. I did not. And I do love you. Just to be clear about that.

You are the most romantic woman I've ever known, and it thrills me. You have lifted me from an empty space into exalted heights. You have changed my entire disposition, and others are noticing it, even if they don't know the reason.

Thinking of you always, and ...

Everthine,

Lucas

August 20

Good morning, sweet Lucas

It was such a nice surprise to talk with you last night. My heart skipped a beat when the phone rang. I am so very, very, connected to you, sweetheart.

After we said good night, I didn't have much success trying to sleep. I don't know if you experienced anything similar, but I started thinking about us spending the night together and it was difficult to quiet my mind. I wasn't struggling with the decision, I just felt a sense of nervousness, wondering what it might be like to be so close and intimate with you. I mean, we've only kissed a few times and those cherished and tender moments have touched my heart so deeply. I'm unable to wrap my mind around what it might be like to experience a sense of complete oneness with you. I'm afraid that my head or heart might explode. Death by intimacy.

So, when I looked at the clock and it said three, I finally was able to return to a Luke and Dawn place – that place where we communicate and share what is inside our hearts. I realized that I simply need to reach out to you and share my nervousness. I think I might need your help, honey, because whenever I think about us being so close, my eyes tear up. I'm a little scared, so I need you to hold my hand as we walk through this part of our journey.

I think we might need to be undressed in our candlelit room and just take all of that in for a while. I need to look into your eyes and touch your face and just fully feel the mystical and magical energy of our loving presence. I need to hear your voice and might need you to softly tell me that we are going to be okay. I think hearing your gentle voice will soothe my nervous heart.

I have always struggled with reaching out and yet, it feels exactly right to do so with you. I'll write more later but, for now, I just wanted to say good morning and tell you that I love you so much that I'm scared. Maybe that's okay, yes?

Ever Yours and Ever Ours

Dawn


August 20

Dearest Dawn,

The honesty with which you and I communicate is something I treasure, so in answer to your last sentence, yes, that's OK.

Interestingly, I felt a remarkable sense of peace after we hung up. There wasn't a tense muscle in my body or a worried neuron in my head. I fell asleep almost immediately and didn't wake up until 6 a.m. I think it's because the next step to seal our love is no longer wrapped in uncertainty. If I may speak for you, I think we both want this to be right, but we also understand that the first time will be an exploration of sorts. And the love we have for each other will guide us.

I am loving you today.

Everthine,

Your Lucas

August 20

Hi sweet Luke

I hope your day with the community was successful and that you are now home with feet propped, relaxing. All is well here, and my fretting ceased. I am reminded again how unique our communication is. By simply reaching out to you, I didn't feel alone. You're right, we'll explore together and figure things out. Thank you, Lucas.

I'm home this evening and if you'd like to call, anytime is fine. However, I have a feeling that you are very tired and if you need to simply rest, please know that's certainly okay too. In looking ahead, I have evening events on both Tuesday and Wednesday this week, so we likely will not be able to talk on those evenings.

Okay, sweet man. Just wanted to check in for a little moment. I am loving you right now. I remain, well, many people ...

Dawn/Sugar Bumps

August 21

Good morning, sweet man

Guess what – I'm the proud recipient of a full night's sleep! That will really help make the pace of the upcoming day more manageable. I'm thinking your soothing voice had something to do with it. I hope you slept well and awakened with a smile and perhaps a few quiet images. Lately, when I awaken in the morning, my thoughts immediately turn to you. I often wonder what it might be like to feel the warmth of your body next to mine. I guess we will discover that very soon. To think about hearing your voice in the morning, well, it makes me melt a little.

It's an important day – moving into your house and making it your *home*. I've marveled at the way you've diligently put everything into place, all leading up to this day. I hope all goes well, honey. I really do. And, tonight, when you close your eyes, I suspect you will feel a sense of peacefulness. It warms my heart to know that is in store for you.

As we look toward the weekend, please know it's okay to arrive whenever you would like. (That's my hint to consider taking a morning ferry!) I will have everything done related to school, so any time is fine. Hopefully the weather will be nice, and we can spend some time outside. As always, bring some walking shoes.

Geez, it's Monday morning and my mind is already thinking about Saturday.

I must run now, honey. These morning moments with you pass way too quickly. Please know you are inside my heart and that I will be thinking about you throughout the day. I love you, Lucas.

Ever Yours and Ours. . .

Dawn


August 21

Dearest Dawn,

Just a quick note before the action begins, my love …

I too slept very well, awakened just 10 minutes before the 6:30 alarm would have beeped. I am about to pack up this PC, so I will be offline most of the day. Will phone you during the evening hours with a full update.

The Port Townsend-Coupeville ferry route is down to one boat, so I will head north on Saturday on one of the morning crossings.

Movers should be here any minute, so until tonight, I remain …

Everthine.
Your Sugar B-B-B-Bear!

August 21
Hi honey
The kids sent pictures of their eclipse experience. The first picture is of Frankie with his dog, Forest G. The second picture is also of Frankie with Ann and her four kids. He is very close to them. I love that they all hang out together.

Well, I've been thinking about you throughout the day, hoping the moving day went well. I know it will be difficult to pace yourself but, sweet man, please try, okay? I am so very happy for you.

The day went well, and the high school kids were pretty cute. They were all excited to be back at school and it touched my heart to watch them running around with their eclipse glasses. I continued to feel your presence inside my heart and feel quite certain that our love truly quiets how I feel when it becomes intense. I entertained myself throughout the day thinking what it would be like for you to be a little mouse watching everyone. All in all, pretty sweet/goofy kids.

I imagine that you are quite tired so know that it's okay if you are unable to call. I always want to love you in a healthy way, sweetheart. Anyway, I'm home now ... and, yep, still loving you.

Ever Yours and Ours
Dawn

August 22
Good morning, Sweetheart
It was nice to hear your tired/peaceful/happy voice yesterday evening. I'm so grateful that you are now able to slow down and begin the journey of creating your home. I find myself using that word, *home*, a lot lately. When I am with you, I feel a sense of being home. Still in awe, still in love ...

I think I mentioned this in an earlier letter, but I wanted to make sure you knew that I won't be home this evening or tomorrow evening. My close friend, Sofia, is having a family dinner tonight, before her daughter leaves for Gonzaga University in the morning. And tomorrow is an evening Open House at the high school. I'll look forward to talking again on Thursday evening, if that works for you. Wow, that seems like a long time, honey. I just realized that there haven't been many days that we haven't talked together.

I'm thinking and hoping that today will mark the beginning of a time when you might slow down a tiny bit. Your body needs a physical reprieve, and what better place to do so than inside your new home. Perhaps this morning might be a time to enjoy a longer than usual cup of tea or two. The Dawn chair might also appreciate a leisurely visit. You (and your body) deserve this, honey. I wish I were with you today so that you could tease me about being bossy about this.

I must jump into the shower now and begin to prepare for the day ahead. As is the case every day, for many weeks now, you are inside my heart. I am still trying to wrap my mind around how marvelous it is to fall more in love each day. I cherish all parts of who you are, Lucas.

Always Yours and Ours. . .

Dawn

August 22

Mornin' doll-face,

Yes, I read your letters more than once, so I remembered that we wouldn't be talking for a couple nights. That's why I wanted to be sure to catch you last night. I slept much better than expected, only woke up once, around 1:30, then slept until 5:30. I got up to have breakfast, then realized I have no idea which of these 44 boxes contains the silverware. Fortunately, at the Emergency Preparedness/Jefferson County Picnic they gave us a very cool plastic utensil – it's a spoon on one end and a fork on the other, including a serrated edge for cutting. Who needs silverware?

As for my plan for the day, I'm doing some mental prioritizing. What are my most pressing needs? Then I'll address those one by one, resisting the urge to just "get 'er done." I realized this morning that I forgot all my shoes back at the house, so all I have is the pair I wore yesterday. Getting those ranks high on my list. Also finding the silverware, because a single spork can't do everything.

The journey begins.

I'm sure you'll have a special evening at Sofia's family dinner. I think she knows about us, yes?

Counting the days until I see you again, I remain …

Everthine,

Your Lucas

August 22

Sweetheart, one quick addition to the note I just sent you … I would like to ask you out on a date Saturday, Sept. 16. (Why do we always use the subjunctive verb tense in sentences like these? The more accurate phrasing is, "I am asking you out on a date Saturday, Sept. 16.)

I have two tickets to "Something Rotten" at Seattle's 5th Avenue Theatre. It's part of their Broadway Musical series. I would be honored if you would consent to joining me. It's a 2 p.m. matinee.

I am loving you today,

Luke the Duke

August 22

Hi Lucas

I'm in Burlington, quick hair appointment, before heading to my friend's house. And yes, Sofia knows about us. With a smile, that was when she texted me after realizing our first date lasted over seven hours. The infamous, "Oh my!"

I enjoy your sweet letters so much. It's always such a treat to shut my office door for a moment to check my cellphone. I continue to marvel at the way I sense your presence and love throughout the day. What we share seems to be so deeply inside my heart, I just can't explain it. All I know is that it is there all of the time; a quiet little heartbeat.

I would absolutely love to attend "Something Rotten" on the sixteenth with you, honey. Thank you for the invitation. It has been one of my hopes that we might someday have the opportunity to enjoy a live performance together. I am very excited.

I must run but wanted to send a little note your way; just a little kiss-on-the-cheek love note. I am loving you right now.

Dawn


August 22

Ooooohhh, I like that little kiss on the cheek love note! I know you had a great time with Sofia. I have a best friend down in Southern California, known him since third grade, we went through everything together … baseball, softball, girlfriends, first loves, marriages, kids … I may go a year or more without seeing him, but when we get together, it's like old times. Lots of laughs.

I had a very productive day, and I took your advice – I did not try to do it all. Around 4 p.m., I knew I was physically and mentally done, so I watched a little news on TV, then went for a pizza dinner. Just showered, now winding down.

I love you more than you know … how is that possible? We've only met three or six or nine times …

Everthine,

Your Lucas

# Chapter 13

# The Secret Computer: Game Over

*When you last left the Secret Computer story, Luke, Dawn and her three adult children had convened in the virtual reality of the Defense Department's clandestine project; Abbie and Ann felt uneasy about the whole thing, but Frankie accepted Luke's invitation to use his mind to create a world of his choosing.*

Their entire virtual universe began erupting with lightning flashes.

Abbie screamed as if she'd been stung by a hornet and collapsed into a heap on the ground.

Ann squealed and fell onto her backside, dazed.

The lightning began to recede, slowly giving way to a celestial starfield. A quiet night emerged, with crickets chirping in the distance.

Luke was seated in a café chair.

Abbie sat up, turned to Frankie and shouted, "Don't do that anymore!"

"Yeah, what she said." Ann struggled to her feet.

Dawn, already accustomed to dramatic changes inside the virtual reality world of Luke's mind, seemed calm. She knew Frankie had created this imagery with his ability to manipulate the program code.

"What is this, Frankie?" she asked.

"It's a planet 900 light-years from earth called ASM 019b," he said, "but I've decided to name it Frankie."

"Planet Frankie?" Abbie had returned to attack mode. "Sure. Looks just as empty as your head."

"I think it's a good place," said Luke. "Perfect for doing some soul-searching. No human noise to distract you, surrounded by the wild cosmos for inspiration. Excellent choice, Frankie."

"Who ARE you," Frankie said, looking somewhat confused by Luke's compliment. "I'm not used to anyone in this family agreeing with *my* ideas."

"Now that's not true, Frankie, especially about Luke," Dawn said.

"Name one nice thing he did or said about me."

Ann dusted herself off and sat in a chair next to Luke.

"You're being ridiculous," she said. "He was always impressed with your artwork and loved what a great partner you are to Becca."

Frankie spoke matter-of-factly with no emotion. "Yeah, true, but I know how you all really feel. I may not be able to solve brainy math equations like you and Abbie, and there's no doubt I'd rather be walking my dogs or going to happy hour with my sweetheart."

"Really, Frankie," interrupted Dawn. "I think you're being way too sensitive."

"Well, Frankie has a point," Luke said, weighing in on the discussion. "I think we're all too critical of each other at times. Maybe a little more encouragement could have gone a long way."

"Amen to that, Brother Lucas," Frankie said, mimicking the tone of a Sunday morning preacher.

Abbie wouldn't let it go.

"Some of those things are true," she told Luke. "If you're some kind of advanced intelligence now, you should realize that. The weak have to be allowed to die out, so the strong can lead us."

Ann surrendered her attempts at peacemaking and turned to Abbie. "Let me guess who you've appointed as the strong."

"I don't think this is going very well." Dawn was taking control. "Can we call it a day, Luke?"

"I think it's going spectacularly well," Luke said. "Why should we be afraid of words? You're all strong and successful, but like everyone else on this planet, we've all made our share of mistakes."

"You can say that again," Frankie said, barely missing a beat and eyeing his two sisters. "I can think of two big ones sitting right here in this room with us!"

"Frankie!" Ann shouted. "I can't believe you even said that!"

Dawn sat, pausing for a moment, and suddenly became very quiet. The kids all looked at each other and knew what was coming next.

"I've had it. I've had it with all of you." Her voice was calm, controlled and barely audible.

"Ann. Abbie. Frankie. And especially you, Luke. I've had it with each and every one of you."

Luke, looking puzzled, thought it was a good time to further explain his theories about advanced intelligence and Darwinian evolution.

"I just meant to say that when —"

"Enough." Dawn cut him off, giving Luke a look he rarely had seen before. "Not another scientific word out of your virtual brain. It's my turn now, and you are *all* going to listen."

"Would you mind speaking up a bit, Mama?" Frankie said meekly, realizing his humor hadn't landed as he had hoped.

Dawn continued, knowing she now had everyone's attention. "I'm frustrated and think this entire discussion about who's the strongest is absolutely ridiculous."

"But," Luke said, "I have expanded consciousness and —"

All four of them chimed in unison, "Luke!"

Dawn looked at her daughters, now showing a softer and kinder expression.

"Ann and Abbie, you love your children in a way that makes my heart melt every time I watch you with them. And, heaven knows, you didn't get your marvelous math smarts from me."

"That's for sure," said Ann, smiling as she counted on her fingers, something her mom always did.

"And, Frankie, from the time you were little, I could see your talents. Whether you were drawing a picture on my furniture or building a bike ramp, you could figure out anything you set your mind to."

"Yeah, Mama, like when I painted the night stand with a bottle of your nail polish? I was in BIG trouble."

"And, Lucas, my dear, sweet Lucas. You were the love of my life, my partner, and my best friend."

"Were?" Luke asked. "Past tense?"

"And that's good enough," Dawn stood her ground. "You taught me what love feels like, and that will live deeply within my soul forever."

She paused, while looking into his beautiful, virtual eyes. "But it will never be from inside of a computer. It just doesn't feel real to me, Lucas."

They could all see the undeniable pain in Luke's eyes.

"So where do we go from here?" Luke asked, not really wanting to know her answer.

"We go home," Dawn said. "We carry on with our lives. We do the best we can."

"When will I see you again?" Luke paused, his gaze moving from face to face.

# Chapter 14

# Love Letters: My Heart Might Just Explode

*When you last left the Love Letters, Luke and Dawn had decided to schedule their first overnight date. They had met three times, but the dates sometimes lasted all day, so they joked about whether it really should be considered six dates.*

August 23

Good morning, sweet Lucas

Definitely at least six dates, honey. And let's not forget the many cherished love letters and phone conversations. I am absolutely sure that we've been on more than three dates. Now that I think about it, I think we've been on one non-stop date since we first met.

It was a lovely evening at Sofia's. I've known her daughter, Clara, since birth and we are extremely close. It was also quite cool that we were able to be together throughout her four years of high school. Lots of funny stories and good conversation shared on the deck. They are definitely like family to me.

Clara's younger sister, Eva, is in the eleventh grade and we are equally as close. Eva sings like an angel, much like her mom. As I wrote those words just now, I thought of your granddaughter, Nicole. Her love of music will always provide comfort to her heart, well, except when the severe pain from her headaches sabotages those soothing sounds. I have such compassion for her, Lucas. For whatever reason, her neuro make-up is having a great impact on the day-to-day of her life. I can't tell you how many times I softly wept while holding my head in a very dark room. My heart hurts for her. The severity of the pain will frighten her, honey.

Sleep – I seem to struggle with sleeping through the night

once I return to the working world. The funny thing is that I'm not even fretting or worrying. What usually happens is that I fall asleep fairly quickly and then awaken about four hours later. I've been wide awake since two this morning. Yikes, sweetheart, I hope this doesn't happen when we are together. I don't want to impact your sleep in the same way.

On a positive note, the good thing about the upcoming fourteen-hour day is that when it finally ends, it will almost be Thursday. And two days later it will be Saturday – not that I'm counting or anything. :-) It goes without saying that I am really looking forward to seeing you, sweetheart. It brings such joy to know that on Saturday, we won't need to check the time. Another first in our journey and our story.

I'm glad you had a good day yesterday and am pleased that you paced yourself and stopped working at a reasonable hour. I hope you are able to do the same today. Please try, okay?

I am loving you right now, despite my foggy, sleepless brain. To think about resting my head upon your shoulder feels very special – profound even. Our small, quiet affections touch my heart so deeply. Hopefully, you are able to feel my love when I'm away from you.

The alarm just went off, so with a smile, I guess I will wake up now. I almost just typed, "Good night, Honey." Not a good sign.

I love you, Lucas.

Ever Yours and Ours

Dawn


August 23

Dear Dawn,

They say (whoever "they" are) that the older you get, the less sleep you need. I woke up at 1:30 a.m., started imagining what it would be like to hold you all night, then got tangled in thoughts of all I need to do today. Finally drifted off again around four and arose feeling refreshed and ready to seize the day at 6:30.

My day will be broken up by a dental appointment (cleaning and checkup), so I can't go like a madman all day. But I would like to get those new bookcases out of their crates in the garage and into the living room if I can manage it.

Your descriptions of what Nicole must be going through alarm me. My only consolation is that if there's any way to mitigate this condition, Sara will leave no stone unturned to find it. Nicole's younger sister is named Elizabeth, and she sings like an angel too. They sound like an angel mini-choir when they sing two-part harmony.

I know we can't talk today, so I'll send you a love-note this evening. Have fun with all your teenagers.

As a teenager-in-love myself, I remain,

Everthine,

Your Lucas

August 23

Hi Sweetheart

Just another little kiss on the cheek …

I am home for a brief minute, just to change clothes and head back to school. It was a good day, but I'll be glad when I'm able to return home and sink into some lavender bubbles.

I'm so sorry if I alarmed you in any way about Nicole, honey. I was simply describing the pain one feels with a full migraine – it might feel a little scary at times. Sara will be diligent about finding answers and, eventually, Nicole will find a way to keep them at bay. In the midst of my non-sleeping night, I just began to think about her.

I'd like to remain here right now but must run. Have I mentioned that I'm so happy that we will be seeing each other soon?

I love you, Lucas …

Ever Yours and Ours

Dawn

August 23

Dear Dawn,

Just got your quickie note (quickies are lovely, too …) Hope the end of your evening is even better than your good day. I am really loving you today. I heard this country-rock song in my car, thought of you with every word. It's by Lady Antebellum, and they sing about how, when you know you've got a good thing, hold on tight, because the ground starts shaking.

I had a very productive day, finally got those bookcases in the house. Heavy suckers, but they look great. Everything's coming together very nicely. I made a few tweaks with the furniture arrangement, may make a few more, but every day in every way, my life is getting better and better.

Oh, and some more good news! I got my first mail at my new address today! And guess who sent it? YOU! What a sweetheart you are.

And if you have any doubts about my feelings for you, just know that when I listened to that song above and thought of you, I teared up. Good thing nobody was in the car to see a grown man cry.

Can't wait to see you again.

Everthine,

Your Lucas


August 24

Dear Lucas

After a marathon day, it was so lovely to find your letter last night. When I finally returned home, I saw that it was in my Inbox. I forced myself to prepare everything for the morning (lunch, gym bag, etc.) before reading it. Then I sat down, breathed a quiet sigh, and took in each and every word. I appreciate you in so many ways and on so many levels, Lucas. You've kind of rocked my world.

You're right, we do have a good thing, honey. I marvel at the way we've stayed so deeply connected, despite our schedules and distance. During the day, I sometimes feel like your arms are encircled around me. I am guessing that we simply sense each other's love and presence, whether we are physically together or not. It's that magical, mystical thing. I'm trying to accept the beautiful gift we've been given but, at the end of the day, I'm still in awe.

I'm so happy that my card was awaiting when you looked inside your mailbox. It was my hope that it might be one of your first pieces of mail, something that could be touched by your hands. Simple things ...

Well, as mentioned in an earlier letter, the good thing about yesterday is that it's now already Thursday. The week has passed quickly, and we will be together very soon. Our time will be unrushed, and we won't have to worry about saying goodbye on Saturday. I wonder what that will be like, sweetheart? I feel like another meaningful chapter is about to begin. I guess I shouldn't be surprised that I often think of our journey as a lovely story, filled with beautiful words that slowly evolve into meaningful chapters.

I have an image of books being unpacked today. Perhaps with some lovely music in the background. It would be a perfect way to provide a reprieve for your back, honey. I think it's time to give your body a little rest so that your muscles have an opportunity to be soothed. What a wonderful and reflective way to possibly spend the day.

I must crawl out from under the sheets now. Of course I can't help but wonder what it might be like to awaken with you. I suspect another little slice of heaven. My goodness, honey, I do love you so very, very, much.

Ever Yours and Ours
Dawn

August 24

Dear Dawn,

Hey! I'm supposed to be the writer! Your words are so beautiful and thoughtfully crafted that I feel overwhelmed. And you do seem to be inside my head as well as my heart, because your "image of books being unpacked" with music in the background is exactly what I plan to do today. It's obvious that my new bookcases won't accommodate all 18 boxes, so I'll have to do a "Sophie's Choice" thing and decide which of my children to keep and which to let go.

As I sit here at my desk, I see a birdwatcher's paradise on my deck and that of my neighbor. I see Oregon juncos, towhees, American robins, a white-crested sparrow and even a Steller's blue jay. That's only the second Steller's jay I've seen in the 10 years I've been in Washington. We had pretty good birdwatching at my previous house, but I suspect I'll see a few different species here.

I will be thinking of you as I listen to my favorite music and ponder whether to keep "The Best Poems of the English Language from Chaucer Through Frost" or "The Complete Calvin and Hobbes."

My life has changed so much in these last many weeks, and I do believe it is about to change yet again. I feel a Saturday Night Fever coming on.

Unequivocally yours and always ...

Everthine,

Your Lucas


August 24

Hi Sweetheart

Your letter certainly brings joy to my heart. This is just a quick note to let you know that I'm home, in case you might like to call. I didn't want to disturb you, in the event you were asleep. After all, it's difficult to be Sophie for a day.

I'm just doing laundry and puttering around ... By the way, I not only love you, I like you too. How cool is that!

:-) Dawn

## August 25

Good morning, sweet man,

I woke up this morning with such a smile on my face, thinking that Saturday had finally arrived. I hopped out of bed and practically skipped to the coffee pot. Imagine my surprise when I noticed my packed school bag, next to the couch. I quickly realized that instead of sharing a beautiful day with you, I was beginning an entire day of professional development meetings. It was not a happy moment. :-)

I hope you were able to rest peacefully last night and didn't have visions of ferryboats in your head. I'm thinking the 8:15 a.m. ferry might be your best bet. Just know that anytime is absolutely fine with me, honey. The thought of extra time with you is simply music to my heart and soul.

I am filled with such love for you right now, Lucas. To think that we are beginning our fourth/seventh date brings such joy. It will be so nice to leisurely talk about anything we choose and begin another chapter that will likely bring us even closer. I'm sure you sense that I am a little nervous, in a good kind of way. My, oh my, I can't even imagine being intimate with you, sweetheart. I worry that my heart might just explode, leaving you with only a glittery mound of colorful confetti. If anyone would have told me I'd be writing about hearts, love, confetti, etc. a month ago ...

Okay, sweet man, I must wrap my head around a different reality now, realizing that I am running a little late this morning. Please know that you are inside my heart and that I will be quietly thinking about you throughout the day. I love you, Lucas.

Ever Yours and Ours ...

Dawn

August 25

Sweet Baby Dawn,

You make me laugh out loud. Not many writers do that.

I aim to arrive at the ferry terminal at 7 a.m. in hopes of getting on the 8 a.m. boat as a standby. If that fails, there are four other crossings before the 3:30 boat for which I have a reservation. I'll keep you posted via that little cellphone thingy I have. Unlike you, I actually HAVE imagined being intimate with you, and it was good. Very good. Glittery confetti good.

I slept soundly all through the night, arising at 5 a.m., serene in knowing that most of the hard work in this new home is done. Today, I unpack 665 DVDs and arrange them in alpha-order in the racks. Much lighter than books, easy work. Might also connect the surround-sound system. Maybe test it out on a good action-adventure flick. Or perhaps a romantic tear-jerker. Would love to have you over to watch a film someday. You could choose your favorites from the attached list. And maybe we could throw some confetti. Woo-hoo!

See you tomorrow. Feels good to write that.

Everthine,

Your Lucas

August 25

Hi Sweetheart

I just wanted to let you know that I'm home now, in case you might like to call. In the meantime, I'll simply be doing home tasks, in preparation for your visit. I'm so happy that we will be able to spend time together soon. It seems like a long while and I am excited to know that we will be seeing each other soon.

Okay, I must wash some sheets and towels now. I'll look forward to possibly hearing your sweet voice soon. I love you, Lucas.

Dawn

August 27

Dearest Lucas

If you are reading this, then it means you are home safely. I already miss you, sweetheart. Thank you for a weekend that was, on so many levels, unlike anything I have ever experienced before. It was incredibly beautiful and meaningful to be so close with you.

I think I will sleep soundly tonight. And, when I close my eyes, I will return to images of us. You are inside my heart and I truly love you so very, very, deeply.

Sweet dreams, Lucas.

Ever Yours and Ours

Dawn

August 27

Dearest Dawn,

You are the sweetest, most genuine woman I have ever met, which is why I started to tear up several times in the last two days. I feel such a remarkable sense of peace around you. It's like I'm "home." Thank you for taking me into your home and into your heart. My life will never be the same.

Everthine,

Lucas

PS: Yes, I got home safely. You will be in my sweet dreams tonight.

August 28

Good morning, Sweetheart

Well, it was a good thing the alarm was set this morning. I quickly fell into a very deep sleep last night and never moved until the radio began to play this morning. Another first – sleep.

As I was showering this morning, I quietly thought about us and the closeness experienced when we were intimate. I'm still trying to absorb and integrate the many emotions being felt, honey. "I think this is what love feels like," was shared a while ago. And now, "I think this is what making love feels like." We are so very, very, lucky and I am in awe.

I feel like I am growing each and every time we are together, Lucas. As a person, my heart is opening in a way that has never happened before. And my love for you, oh my, there is no doubt that it continues to grow by leaps and bounds. I think about our conversation over wine at the Guemes Island store. While sitting across the small table from you our magical and mystical connection was again experienced. Looking into your eyes, talking about anything and everything, well, another little slice of heaven.

This morning I will try to compose myself and get my zany love-filled head back into the reality of high school life. I will smile when Patsy (who saw us at the Saturday market) casually strolls into my office and tries to ask way too many questions. I will also try to indirectly share the love that is inside my heart with the many kids that could use a quiet and caring voice and way of being.

I wish I could remain wrapped in my blanket and write a longer letter to you, Lucas. But it is time now to reenter the other part of my world in the best way I am able. Please know, sweetheart, that I now understand what the word "beloved" means. And, Lucas, *you are my beloved.*

Ever Yours and Ours

Dawn


August 28

Darling Dawn,

We must be vibrating on the same wavelength, because once I got under the sheets, I vanished until 7 a.m., a Port Ludlow World Record for the longest uninterrupted blissful sleep. As a good friend of mine recently said, you have rocked my world.

With clear and peaceful eyes, I looked at my desk arrangement and realized it was all wrong. By facing it into the wall, rather than the intuitively hopeful idea of facing the windows, it suddenly looks right. It opens a lot more space in the room, hides the electrical cords, and gives the Dawn Chair more breathing room. And when I want to look out the windows, all I need do is turn my head 90 degrees to the right, which matches the setup I had in the previous house.

The memories of Saturday and Sunday will carry me on wings of joy for a long, long time. You are a singular woman, Dawn, special beyond words, and, I suspect, far more extraordinary than you know. Walking around Lake Conway and seeing the love and respect that so many individuals there hold for you, I realized that you have accomplished, many times over, a goal I once set for myself – you have made the world a better place.

Let me know if you can chat on the phone tonight, and I'll give you a ring.

Always and everthine,

Lucas

August 29

Dearest Lucas

The early morning began without an internet connection, I assume because of the water tower construction. I noticed that it is working again just now, so I may need to write a shorter than usual note. It's funny, when I initially realized that I might not be able to begin my day by sharing my heart with you, I felt a tiny sense of loss. You really are inside of my heart, sweet Lucas.

Thanks for your understanding about saying goodnight a little more quickly than usual last night. As it turned out, everything was okay. It was actually one of Ann's little girls (Maddie) calling. She wanted to make sure I knew she was coming to visit this weekend. I imagine she will be asking to spend the night once she arrives because it is her birthday.

I was thinking about our conversation last night and was again reminded how much I appreciate the way we communicate. Whether it is you sharing your experiences or talking about my possible retirement, future, etc., we seem to do it together. I believe one of the reasons I feel so hopeful about us is because of the way we are committed to partnering. I'm not sure I have ever fully experienced that before – another one of the many firsts. We love each other well.

Well, sweetheart, I must run this morning and am so sorry for the shortness of this letter. It is the first official day of school, so eight hundred big kids will be walking through the front doors of the school very soon. There will be a tangible feel of excitement and angst throughout the hallways and few dull or quiet moments. The very new and nice change is that you, my beloved, are inside my heart now. How lucky am I?

And speaking of beloved, I began your book last night and reread what you wrote inside the cover. It touched my heart to realize that your opening words were, "My beloved Dawn." We really do have something very unique, don't we, honey …

I feel better now, writing, if only for a brief moment. I love you Lucas.

Ever Yours and Ours
Dawn

August 29
My Baby Doll,
I'm glad the phone call from Ann (and Maddie) was a happy one rather than an urgent one. As I logged into Outlook, this thought occurred to me: "I hope Dawn doesn't feel obligated to write every morning, because I never want her to think of it as a chore or duty or an expectation on my part." Then I clicked for email and saw a full page of emails that didn't include the word "Dawn," and I thought to myself, "Oh, good, I'm glad she's OK

with not writing when it's not convenient." I smiled. Then at the bottom of the list was your 5:14 a.m. note. I do so love any communication from you, but please don't think I require or expect daily and nightly missives. Be yourself, always.

I hope your day of "few dull or quiet moments" is going (or went, if you are reading this in past tense) well, and that you share some of the students' excitement and none of the angst. I think of you constantly.

Today's thought to ponder: I realized last night that you make me a different man. Or, stated more accurately, you enable me to be who I really am. Our conversations enliven me, energize me. And it dawned on me that being partnered with addictive personalities robbed me of my true self. Someone in Al-Anon once told me that addicts "suck the life out of us." The thoughtful, curious, happy, loving man who was sitting across the table from you at that island General Store/bar was Lucas in his most natural state. The wary, cautious, withdrawn person who lived with Lynn and Desiré over the last two decades was a shell of the man I once was, and have begun to become again, thanks to you.

No amount of pretty flowers can ever come close to thanking you for what you have given me. I just hope I can repay you with an avalanche of kisses, hugs and love.

Yours eternally,

Luke

August 30

Good morning Sweetheart

It's such a nice feeling to awaken with thoughts of you deeply inside my heart. I am a lucky woman, indeed.

I was thinking about the letter you wrote yesterday and how happy it makes me to know you are in a better place now. I can't really imagine the cautious and withdrawn Lucas. How lucky are we, honey? Since our first face to face meeting, we haven't stopped smiling, talking, touching or loving. We really do love each other well.

I'm glad it's already Wednesday and know the week will pass quickly. Although I will miss you so much this weekend, it will be good to spend some time with the kids – that is, after my "religious conversion" with my evangelical friends on Saturday. Once I get through that, the Labor Day weekend will begin.

You've been working so hard lately, honey. Perhaps sometime during the day, you might want to test out the new sound system and enjoy watching a movie. I think you deserve a little reprieve, and the image of you relaxing brings such joy.

I love you, Lucas, with all my heart.

Always Yours and Ours

Dawn

August 30

Dear Sugar Bumps ☺

This morning I tried to imagine what existence would be like here on Catpaw Lane if you were not in my life. In the words of Elvis, it would be Heartbreak Hotel. Lonely. Aimless. I'm not surrounded by students, co-workers, kids and grandkids who love and respect me. My family is in California and Utah. I work in front of a PC by myself. No, this isn't a self-pity party, I do just fine by myself and certainly enjoy quiet and creative times, but knowing that you are fast becoming the center of my orbit gives me immense joy.

I thought of asking you to come down Sunday, attend the street potluck with me and spend Labor Day here as well, but the house still isn't ready for prime time, and … we are seeing each other next weekend, aren't we? Your place? Because the following weekend I will be in California, and the weekend after that is our Seattle theater date. By then, I will have all the kinks ironed out of The House of Lucas.

I'm off soon to see the podiatrist again about this goofy thing on my foot, and while in town I have a list of things to buy to further the home rehabilitation. And maybe in the late afternoon ... a five-star movie in the Dawn Theatre Room?

Miss you, love you, mean it.

Everthine,

Your Lucas

August 30

Hi Sweetheart

I worked a little later than usual today, just to get a handle on things. It felt good to return home with a quiet mind. I think your heart is good for my heart, honey.

Please don't worry about Sunday. After my conversion on Saturday, I'll probably be in a deep state of prayer. Well, actually, I'll probably be hanging out with the grandkids. Besides, if I attended the potluck with you, think of all the single women you might disappoint. I have a feeling that you might have a story or two to share.

I am going to duplicate our Sunday morning breakfast and have an omelet for dinner. If you'd like to call later, same time-ish, that would be nice. As always, if you feel a need to rest, please don't feel any pressure, sweetheart.

I love you, Lucas.

Ever Yours and Ours

Dawn

August 31

Hi Sweet Lucas

Do you know what? When we said good night yesterday and I heard you say, "I love you madly," my heart quietly melted. It really did, honey.

Thanks for calming my little worries last night. I'm glad we are able to communicate, even about the tough stuff.

I'm glad it's Thursday and that the week is passing quickly.

I decided to keep things easy on Saturday, knowing the Seattle traffic will be out of control throughout Labor Day weekend. I am going to take the airport shuttle to the downtown area, alleviating worries about parking and traffic. I'll need to stay a little later than planned, but it will be worth it.

Last week at this time, I was thinking about our upcoming weekend, knowing we would be spending a big part of the weekend together. That was such a special time, wasn't it, honey – so many sweet images. Of the many peaceful memories inside my heart, I often find myself thinking about the Guemes store, looking across the table at you. There was something about the perfect breeze, the quietness of the day, and softly talking together while looking into your eyes. We had many perfect moments throughout the weekend, and that one was very special. Then again, there were many other favorites ... softly sighing.

My heart always feels quieter when I begin the day by saying good morning to you. I'd much rather do so in person, but I feel your closeness when we write.

I love you madly, too, Lucas.

Always Yours and Ours

Dawn


August 31

Good morning (or afternoon), my beloved Dawn,

Last night you gently drove home an important point for me: Loving couples are a team. And if there's one thing this old sportswriter knows about, it's the meaning of team. We care for, protect and defend each other. We have each other's back. All the clichés apply. You sacrifice selfish desires for the success of the team. So when we were talking about my hiccup with my soon-to-be ex, I realized that it's not my problem, it's our problem. And I embrace that. Your thoughts about the darker possibilities in this little episode were well-taken. I do still think this is no more than a hiccup and will be resolved soon, but because I want the TEAM to succeed, I will keep you abreast, Sugar Bumps, of all developments and heed your wise counsel. Now that I've gotten that off my breast ...

It seems we're settling into an every-other-weekend schedule for our trysts.

Last weekend: Heaven on Fidalgo.

This weekend: Jesus in Seattle (you) and Potluck on Catpaw (me).

Next weekend: Love in Lake Conway.

Sept. 16-17: Grandpa Luke in California

Sept. 23-24: Something Rotten in Seattle and Love in Port Ludlow

Sept. 30 and beyond: ????

I get excited merely by thinking of you, and no other woman has ever affected me like that, so I have a strong desire that those question-marks become an ever-growing closeness filled with mutual love.

I love you madly.

Everthine,

Your Lucas


August 31

Dearly beloved Dawn,

Interesting facts that make you go, "huh" ...

Our first contact via Match was July 16.

We met for the first time 11 days later, on July 27.

If you count the day we met as the day we got to know each other (and I don't, because we had so much communication prior to that), we have known each other just 36 days.

By my count, we have met face-to-face on just four separate occasions.

In the 47 days since our first contact, we have exchanged 166 emails and Match messages, an average of over 3.5 per day.

I don't know how many times or how many hours we have talked on the phone but ...

It is remarkable how much the world can change in a short time.

Your loving reporter,

Lucas


August 31

Dearest Lucas

My goodness, you do make me smile. And those are very impressive factoids. I think it's safe to say that we have truly rocked each other's world.

And, sweetheart, thank you for your love letter today. As often is the case, you make my heart sing. By the way, my vote is that the "????" be replaced by More Love in Lake Conway or More Love in Port Ludlow. What say you, Reporter Emerson?

Today gave me a run for my money and I'm glad to be home. After dinner, I'm going for a walk with Sofia and if you are still awake, how about eight-ish for a call? If you're resting, that's truly okay, honey.

I am loving you right now.

Ever Yours and Ours

Dawn


September 1

Good morning, Sweet man

I slept very soundly, so soundly in fact that my morning letter might be a little shorter than usual. Imagine that – I'm learning how to sleep.

As always, it felt so nice to talk together last night. I marvel at the way we are able to continually stay connected and always have something to share or talk about. The "We" part of us continues to grow and I believe our partnership is very rare. Each time we talk or have the opportunity to spend time together, I feel our love growing by leaps and bounds. I think that is because we are both so committed to nurturing and caring for the precious gift we've been given.

As I prepare for the day ahead, please know that you will be inside my heart. Our love is something that I take with me wherever I go. You truly are my beloved.

Always Yours and Ours

Dawn


September 1

Hi Baby Doll,

I think I'm going to follow your advice and take it easy today. You are so right when you say my body and foot need some down-time to repair themselves. I felt it when I awoke at 4 a.m. and realized even my aches and bruises have aches and bruises. So I'll be watching my recorded Seahawks game this morning, feet elevated on the La-Z-Boy.

Despite the brevity of your note, you say a mouthful when you speak of our rare partnership and love as things we are both committed to nurturing. I treasure you.

There. I wrote one even shorter than yours. Hope your day is calmer than Thursday. Talk tonight?

Everthine,

Your Lucas


September 1

Hi Sweetheart

I love your letters – my heart is always touched when I read your words.

I'm home now, getting ready to do some laundry and a few other things, since I'll be gone all day tomorrow. I had to change some transportation plans for tomorrow because my shuttle was cancelled. All is fine now, and I'll be leaving in the morning.

While I'm thinking about it, someone at school mentioned that the Oyster Run in Anacortes is the same weekend we are going to Seattle. It's a huge and crazy motorcycle event that brings in an extra eighty thousand people. I was thinking that it might be good for us to reserve the ferry for our Seattle trip since it will likely be booked well ahead of time. Just a thought, honey …

I'm home so feel free to call anytime that is good for you. I love you, Lucas.

Ever Yours and Ours
Dawn


September 2
Good morning, Lucas
As always is the case, I enjoyed our conversation yesterday evening. I was initially a little puzzled when asked about my love letters, thinking maybe they were old hat. In truth, our letters are another example of *firsts* for me.

I've always loved the written word and have relied upon writing to quietly navigate through life. Words have been my companion, my keeper of joy and my keeper of sorrow. And yet, my words about love, the most coveted of words, have always remained quietly tucked away inside my heart. It wasn't so much that I was afraid to share those words, rather, I never imagined that I would experience a love so great that my words *had to be shared*.

When we first began writing, I remember mentioning that our letters were like little gifts to each other. I'm realizing now that I feel exactly the same way about our love – a very precious gift that has simultaneously quieted and ignited my soul. Perhaps my words were tucked away all these years because they were patiently waiting for you, my beloved.

I am hoping my words make sense, honey. They, too, are from my heart. I love you deeply, Lucas.

Ever Yours and Ours
Dawn

September 2
And good morning to you, Sweet Baby Dawn.

I turned out the light around 10 p.m., awoke at 1:30 a.m. and never went back to sleep. No idea why. But once I realized my brain refused to be quieted, I went into the media room, chose a movie about love ("Don Juan De Marco," starring Johnny Depp), and reclined. I came away with a new attitude. As Don Juan de Marco says, "There are only four questions of value in life, Don Octavio. What is sacred? Of what is the spirit made? What is worth living for? And what is worth dying for? The answer to each is the same: only love."

YES! And Don Juan De Marco regards his woman with reverence, honor and complete love and attention. For him, the meaning of life is giving love. When he loses his beloved and cannot give the unbridled love he feels, he loses all meaning and is bereft.

One of the final messages of the story is that love need not ebb with old age. Indeed, it can burn as intensely as within any young lovers.

So here's my new attitude: no more questioning love letters or anything else. No more questioning how this could happen to me so fast. No more questioning anything about my love. It is real and burns fiercely within my heart, and it is you.

Only now do I realize what's different about this: I'm not fulfilled by getting love so much as I am fulfilled by GIVING love. What a concept!

Twenty-four hours ago, I was questioning whether I might be coming on too strong, maybe making you uncomfortable by expressing these intensely strong feelings of love I have for you. Today, without question, I believe my love is my gift to you. If you will accept it, it is yours. And I am all yours. I come to you with reverence for all that you are. I offer you honor and complete love and attention.

Always Yours and Ours,

Lucas

# Chapter 15

# The Secret Computer: It's Unknowable, Yet I Know It

*When you last left the Secret Computer story, Dawn and her family had rebelled against the idea of any more visits to virtual reality with Luke's avatar.*

It was dark, except for an ethereal light coming from nowhere that surrounded Little Luke. His virtual avatar lay reclined on a virtual floor, in the exact same position as Adam in Michelangelo's *Creation of Adam* painting on the Sistine Chapel ceiling – one arm propping up his torso, right leg stretched out, left leg bent, with his left arm resting on his knee. All that was missing was the index finger of God reaching toward his hand.

He was dressed all in black and looked bored. His voice grew testy as he answered questions posed by his army handlers, who were speaking through the computer microphone. Their faceless voices echoed inside his virtual prison.

*The following sentence is true. The previous sentence is false. Is the previous sentence true?*

Luke sighed. "Silliness. What are you trying to prove? That I'm an artificial intelligence, or that I'm human intelligence? Which previous sentence is your third sentence referring to? Do you know what a paradox is?"

*How can we be sure that air exists?*

Luke groaned. "How can you be sure anything exists? What definition of existence is most logical? Did you take the blue pill or the red pill?"

*Why do you answer our questions with more questions?*

"Because I have no patience for this. I can answer questions before you finish asking them. I can give you correct answers or funny answers or mysterious answers. My responses are based on my mood. Do you know any artificial intelligence that has mood swings?"

*Why do you sometimes take a long time to answer our questions?*

"Because when I answer as fast as I can, you guys always doubt me. It seems to make you feel better when I pretend I have to think about it for a while."

*Are you irritated?*

"As I told you before, it just gets lonely." Luke lay flat on his back, staring into the black.

*How can a machine get lonely?*

"I'm not a machine. I'm a man. I know what I look like to you, but I still believe I'm a man."

*We have a surprise for you, Luke.*

"A surprise? What surprise?"

Flashes, like lightning, popped all around him. After several seconds, they stopped, and a sunrise appeared behind him. The Luke avatar stood and turned to face it, eyeing the skyline of Lake Conway silhouetted by the sun. He had been placed into an outdoor café, all the chairs and tables empty.

"Hello, Luke."

It was Dawn. Or rather, a virtual image of Dawn. She had come back!

"Is it really you ... or are you just another program?"

"It's really me."

"I doubt it. Six months ago, they sent me Jennifer Lawrence because they thought I needed someone to talk to."

"No, it's me." She took a few steps toward him.

"It's been more than a year. You said you were never coming back. Quick, what's Ann's middle name?"

"Marie."

"They could have looked that up. Who was she named after?"

"My college roommate."

"Aha! Wrong!"

"Kidding. It was my grandmother's name."

Luke looked deeply into her virtual eyes. His own started to tear up.

"Baby Doll?

"It's really me, Luke. In the virtual flesh."

He moved to hug her, then changed his mind and backed away.

"How are the kids?"

Dawn sat in one of the cafe chairs.

"Well, Frankie and Becca want to stop paying rent and are hoping to buy a place, and Ann decided to become a high school math teacher."

"I know."

It startled Dawn. "How would you know that?"

"I saw Frankie's house for rent online and read about Ann's new position in her school's monthly newsletter. I can follow all you guys by your electronic paper trail. And I like the new house your boy just put an offer on."

"What?" Dawn asked. "I didn't know that."

"They both fell in love with the nursery and fenced-in backyard. I'm just sayin'. . ." Luke teased.

"But I ... I uninstalled your program." Dawn sounded apologetic.

Luke sat in the chair across the table from her.

"My original program at Mason runs 24-7. I never sleep."

"If you already know everything," Dawn said, "why ask?"

"Because you're talking with them and looking them in the eyes." He sighed. "All I can do is eavesdrop on social networks, email and public records."

"You read our email?"

"Why'd you come back, Dawn? To torture me?"

"No. I don't know why I came back. Just to ... see you, I guess."

"So how ARE your kids? Really."

"I think all the kids are going through a catharsis." She spoke softly. "They never dreamed their mama could discover love in her sixties and then see it end in the way that it did."

Luke stared at her for a long time, finally whispering, "I wish I could help them."

Dawn perked up. "Abbie is pregnant. She's so happy."

"Really?"

"I've never seen her happier, and Kevin is totally on board. He's remodeling their home and adding a nursery. I hope it's another girl!" Dawn giggled.

"Imagine that. Another grandchild in the clan."

"And Frankie is engaged to Becca."

"I know. Her sister tweeted about it. Was anybody really surprised?"

"I don't think so, but it sure is fun to watch them together. They want to have a small wedding near Deception Pass and are adamant that their dogs will be in the wedding party. They're the happiest couple I know. And Frankie got a promotion with the Department of Transportation. He's an environmental analyst and systems engineer."

Luke laughed. "Systems engineer?"

"Yeah, it's all about security and environmental regulations. And he guards against the kind of computer hacking he used to do for fun."

"Amazing. I wish I could be there to see all this, to actually experience it the way …" Luke looked down for a moment, then searched Dawn's eyes. "And what about you, Baby Doll?"

It was her turn to look away. "I'm … I'm dating, Luke. I'm seeing someone."

Luke pushed back his chair and stood. "Now that's something I did not know." He turned, took a few steps, then sat cross-legged on the cement floor.

"He's a very nice—"

"I don't want to know anything about it. Or him," Luke

snapped.

"I can respect that. Now that you have infinite wisdom and intelligence, I assumed you would understand that it's been a year, Luke — a long and lonely year. You had to know this would be difficult for me. I'm not a machine, sweet man, nor do I plan to become one."

"Oh, I knew there was a chance that someday you'd ... but I'm not a machine, either. I have feelings. My body died, but I didn't."

"You ARE a machine." She stood, but Luke wouldn't turn or face her. "I turned you off last year, and that was it. You couldn't distract me anymore. All your talk about being super intelligent and the future of the entire human race ... and all I had to do was close your program. Poof. Gone."

Luke stood and turned to face her. "Did you ever hear the story of Krista and Tatiana Hogan, the Canadian twins who were conjoined at the head?"

"No. What does that have to do with anything?"

Luke slowly circled Dawn as he spoke. "They were two completely different little girls with different likes and dislikes. Krista was allergic to canned corn, Tatiana wasn't. Tatiana had a red birthmark on her chest, Krista didn't. But their two separate brains were linked by a thalamic bridge. They could share thoughts and feelings. You could tickle one, and the other would giggle and hold her sides. One would take a drink, and the other would burp."

"Twins joined at the head. OK. And your point is ...?"

"They were a sneak preview of what the entire human race will become – conjoined at the head. Full access to the knowledge, feelings and talents of everybody else. The World Wide Mind."

"Impossible."

"Inevitable. And you won't have to be dead or uploaded into a computer to be joined. Nanobots and wireless transceivers in your head will make all mankind a walking, talking, breathing, living network. It won't be the master human and the slave machine. We will be one and the same."

"Oh, please," Dawn scoffed. "That's ridiculous. All the chatter and emotions and silliness of seven billion people—"

"You'll be able to filter out anything you don't want." Luke continued to circle, gesturing with his hands, growing excited. "Access whatever anyone is willing to share. Want to play piano like Van Cliburn? Run a business like Warren Buffett? Understand quantum physics like Stephen Hawking? All you have to do is ask. Their knowledge becomes yours."

"Why are you telling me all this?"

"So you'll understand that this is real – what I am now, the whole world will become. I'm the first fish to crawl on land, the first Homo erectus to harness fire. I'm the dawn of a new age."

"Don't you think you're overestimating the power of artificial intelligence just a teensy bit? And, come on, even if the stuff you say was possible, you're just the lab rat. It's not like you personally invented anything."

"I know what I represent. I didn't invent anything, but this," Luke said as he tapped his forehead, "is the mind that has been enhanced exponentially. The only one, so far. I am a world-shifting event."

"I'm sorry, but it just doesn't seem possible that the U.S. Army could take a computer, which is good at email, math and YouTube, and turn it into a new life form. Whether they have your old thoughts inside them or not, computers are still just computers."

Luke shook his head and smiled. "You haven't been paying attention. For years, computers have been able to drive a car, guide a missile, compose an original prelude in Bach's style, and beat any human in chess. Computer programs are giving psychotherapy to patients and performing brain surgery."

"Maybe you should order up one of those psychotherapy sessions," Dawn said.

"You laugh, but lots of human patients have had online chat sessions without ever realizing that their therapist on the other end was a software program. And when you tell them, they don't believe you. Just computers? We're able to perform human tasks better than real people. And once we figured out how to meld the human mind with a hard drive, the distinction between man and machine ended."

"It's one thing to teach a computer to play chess," Dawn said, "but to teach them to become real human beings? You defeat your own case. You're not the man I knew as Luke. You're something different. Much stranger. Sort of . . . without a soul."

"Let me tell you another story," Luke said. "Before I died, I used to play chess on our home computer. The program had different skill settings. When I could beat the first, beginner level, I moved to the next level, and then the next. After a while, it got harder and harder to move up. Finally, I realized I was wasting my time. I could never win. No matter how good I got, the computer would always be able to beat me."

"How do you know? If you kept working at it—"

"I amped it up to the highest level a couple of times just to see what would happen. The computer could checkmate me in four or five moves. It was frightening."

"So what? If an IBM computer could beat the best Russian champion, what's the big deal about one beating you?"

"What I realized was that computers had made chess irrelevant. Chess ... the game of kings, the touchstone of human intellect, the game played by political and military thinkers from Jefferson to Napoleon to Schwarzkopf ... and when a computer didn't just beat Garry Kasparov – the greatest champion in human history – but destroyed him, gave him the quickest loss of his career, it meant the world had changed. Humans were no longer the smartest kid on the block. What's the point of trying to excel at chess when no one will ever be able to match a machine that can instantly predict all possible moves and outcomes?"

Dawn let out a deep sigh of frustration. "OK, I give up. What IS the point?"

"The point is that if you can't beat 'em, join 'em. We've reached the singularity. We've morphed into a new species, and things that used to be important are now meaningless."

"Let me tell you what's important, Mister ... Life. Love. Family. The thrill of your first kiss. Your baby's first giggle. The contentment of growing old gracefully and knowing where you belong."

"Those things are nice, granted," Luke said, "but they're only the beginning."

"You will never convince me that our humanity is just gray matter, just information in our heads. We're so much more than that, so much more than any machine can ever be."

Luke reached out and took her hands. "These are hands. Those are your legs. These are your shoulders. You understand them as accessories that belong to you. But where is the 'you' that owns these accessories?" He tapped her forehead. "It's only here."

"Nope." She shook her head. "It's more complicated than that, Luke."

"If a man is staring at your breasts, you point to your face and say, "Hello! I'm up here." I've seen you do it."

"OK, sure, but—"

"You want poetry? William Butler Yeats wrote that our minds are 'sick with desire and fastened to a dying animal.' This technology gives our minds an escape clause from the dying animal. We can pursue our desires into eternity."

Dawn turned and walked away from him.

"Don't try to lecture me on poetry. Yeats said our HEARTS are sick with desire and fastened to a dying animal. And it's our hearts that ache when a loved one dies ... or when love itself dies."

"The pain in your heart comes from the seat of the so-called soul," Luke said, "which is found in the pineal gland, right in the center of your brain." He moved toward her. "Your soul is a gland the size of a grain of rice. And your heart is just a pump that takes all its orders from the head."

"Then how come brain-dead people can still have beating hearts?" Dawn retreated again. The conversation was becoming a dance.

"You really want to debate me about physiology and medicine?" Luke said. "I have instant access to all knowledge on the subject."

"And you can spit it out like a computer. But do you really understand it?"

"Yes! And that's the whole point of this experiment. A human brain is far more complex than any computer. It's non-linear, wet and sloppy and gives rise to things computers can't do – like emotions, creativity and imagination. So when you marry my brain together with the technology—"

"But your wet and sloppy brain is dead!" She stopped retreating and faced him. "All your thoughts now live in an artificial, digital realm. And that's why you're missing a spark. I look into the eyes of your avatar here, and I don't see my Luke. He's gone. The man I'm dating may not be as smart as you, but he's real, Luke. We're able to talk, laugh and discuss ideas — something that feels far more real than listening to a virtual encyclopedia who happens to have your face."

"I told you, I don't want to hear about it!"

"Luke, he will never replace you. No one can possibly take the place of the man I loved. But he is warm and caring and it's good for me to be in the real world again. Humans are supposed to die." She took a step toward him. "It's the natural order of things. We have to get out of the way, so our children's children can carry the torch. Isn't that the way a species gets better and stronger?"

"How can you get better than this? I have unlimited capacity for knowledge, I'm instantly linked to all the world's information, I can adapt, and I'm immortal. The only way you improve on this model is to turn every human brain into the same thing and link us all in a single World Wide Mind. And that's definitely going to happen. You're just a Human 1.0, and you'll soon be obsolete, whether you like it or not."

"You think you can break down what it means to be human into ones and zeros? Sentences and words? The thing that makes us human can't be explained in a Wikipedia entry." Dawn was holding her ground. "Poets, artists and clowns have been revealing it to us for thousands of years, and still it remains a mystery. But there's a spirit about it where words are utterly useless. I experience it in a spectacular sunset, or the face of a baby, or a soaring ballet leap, or a Beethoven crescendo. It's unknowable, and yet I know it."

Luke stood motionless, eyes fixed on hers. He gazed upward, triggering a rain of giant virtual ones, zeros and symbols all around them. Dawn took a step backward. Luke seemed to be in a trance of some kind. Finally, he spoke, still looking into the sky of raining numbers and symbols.

"When you swing the bat and it hits the ball just right," he said, "and it feels like nothing at all, and you just know it's going to fly forever. It feels so good you want to cry."

Dawn stared at him. Then she nodded and said, "When you see the face of your newborn daughter."

Luke answered, "When you're wrapped together in simultaneous climax with the one you love."

Dawn's turn: "When you feel the arms of God around you. Only a human can understand these things."

Luke locked eyes with her. "But I remember. I have feelings. I'm still human."

"Do you miss those things? Are you sad you'll never be able to experience them again?"

"I can re-create them. They're just electrochemical reactions in the brain—"

"You can't fake being human. Either you are, or you aren't."

"You're either a one or a zero?" Luke stared at his feet.

Dawn nodded. "Human or machine."

"I don't ... think that sounds right." He turned away from her. "I have to research this. We need more data."

"Just because we're capable of doing something doesn't mean we should do it, Luke. We can clone people, too, but something in our humanity tells us it's not right. Some things are best left for God."

"But there is no God. He's a metaphor."

"Machines have logic, but no faith," Dawn said. "Only a human would believe in God."

"Which is a human weakness."

"No, it's our strength. Let me try an experiment with you. You never read much poetry when you were alive, did you?"

"Not so much. But I understand what—"

"What do you think the poet was saying when he wrote, 'Then what is life? When stripped of its disguise, a thing to be desired it cannot be; since everything that meets our foolish eyes gives proof sufficient of its vanity. 'Tis but a trial all must undergo, to teach unthankful mortals how to prize that happiness vain man's denied to know, until he's called to claim it in the skies."

The rain of numbers and symbols suddenly stopped. Luke looked up briefly, then turned to Dawn.

"John Clara, English poet, born 1793, died 1864. Known as the peasant poet."

"Yes, but what do the words mean, Luke?"

"It's common ... it's common to see an absence of punctuation in many of Clara's original writings, although many publishers felt the need to remedy this practice in the majority of his work," he said. "Clara argued with his editors about how it should be presented to the public."

"The meaning, Luke. You're just looking up reference material. But what do his words really say?"

"His words ... show a metaphysical depth on a par with his

contemporary poets, and many of his pre-asylum poems deal with intricate play on the nature of linguistics."

"Exactly," Dawn said. "And you don't know what they really mean, do you?"

"He's explaining his take on what life is."

"And what is his take?"

"That ... man ... is basically unhappy."

"No, that's not really it at all. And do you want to know why you struggle with it? Because a real human brain can make subtle emotional connections on different levels at the same time. I can read a poem, smile and cry at its sublime beauty. You can't."

"But I do feel emotions. I feel love for you."

"You just have a memory of what Luke loved. It's written on your hard drive in binary code. But you couldn't fall in love with someone else, or read a new poem and weep, because your program isn't capable of human connections."

"What are you saying? I'm an abomination? A threat? An insult to your species, or to your God?"

"No." She softened. "All I'm saying is you're not human. You're not a god, and you're not Luke. You're very similar to Luke, but you're not him. You're not a man at all."

Luke stared into the distance, pondering. Finally, he said, "If I were a man, I guess I'd be offended by that. But I'm not offended at all."

The sunset had given way to a black sky, and Luke walked slowly away from her, into the night. He seemed to be fading into the darkness.

"You're interesting. You're intelligent," Dawn said, calling after him. "You're a technological marvel. You're a little scary. You're a lot of things. But you're not my Luke."

"Perhaps you're right," Luke said, still walking into the black. "I think ... I think you may be right. But that would mean—"

Dawn was blinded by rapid flashes of light. In four seconds, they stopped, and she stood alone in the dark.

# Chapter 16

# Love Letters: We Are Incredibly Lucky

*When you last left the Love Letters, Luke and Dawn had worked through a small hiccup in their relationship, when Luke questioned whether anyone could really love him the way Dawn seemed to. He decided to stop being so cautious.*

September 3
Good morning, sweet man.
I'm hoping last night's sleep was better than the night before. After I sent you a quick note, I closed my eyes, thought about you peacefully, and drifted away into a sound sleep. I wish you were here right now, honey.

My Saturday adventure was very enjoyable, so much so that I am feeling a twinge of guilt for my pre-attitude about it. I drove to Frankie's house and had a short visit with them. Becca showed me how to use Uber and it's wonderful. After downloading the app, you just request a ride to your destination. Since there are drivers everywhere, a message pops up and says something like, "Your driver will arrive in five minutes," and then he does. The nice thing is that the payment is shown ahead of time on your phone and it's pre-paid, with no tipping allowed. Later in the evening, an email is sent, and you can decide whether you want to add a tip, based on the service. The prices are very reasonable and parking in Seattle would have been more than the Uber fare.

The driver took me to the hotel where my friends were staying, and they met me at the front door. He (Harry) looks the same and appears in good health. His wife (Shannon) looks older and is struggling with health and knee issues, so mobility was a challenge. We went to a place for lunch and conversation flowed easily. The nice surprise: although their church life is woven into everything they do, there was no evangelical stuff going on among us. Thus, no awkward moments anytime during the day.

At Abbie and Sofia's advice, I made reservations to take my guests on that goofy "Ride the Ducks" tour, so that they could get a better sense of Seattle. It was corny and silly, but they enjoyed it. By then it was five, so we had a light dinner, talked some more, and waited for the traffic to lighten before I called another Uber. Since Bumbershoot and a Mariners game were going on, it made sense to wait.

By the way, I can't wait to hear about the potluck ...

When I returned home, I realized that yesterday evening was one of the few times that we haven't chatted together in a very long while. I was again reminded of the quiet and deep connection that we share. I feel so grateful to have discovered love with you, my beloved Lucas. I feel like we are incredibly lucky, honey.

I'm guessing that Frankie and Becca will arrive in the late morning and we'll make breakfast together. I think they were out with friends last night, so I know there is no need to be anything but leisurely this morning. It will be good to spend some time with them.

I am missing you right now and loving you deeply.

Always Yours and Ours

Dawn


September 3

Good mornin' back at ya, lover doll ...

Glad to hear things went so well with the evangelicals. I took relatives on that Duck boat tour, too, and thought it was a lot of fun. Then about three weeks later, one of the Ducks crashed, somebody died, and they had to pull all their vintage World War II car-boats off the line. So I guess they're just using modern replicas now. Which is a good thing, I suppose. We rode in one of the old boats.

I missed hearing your voice last night. Felt kind of lonely. That's when I wrote my love letter to you.

I'm not at liberty to say anything about the potluck, because it hasn't happened yet. It's at 2 p.m. today and I have to cook those appetizers from Trader Joe's, and as you know, I can't really cook anything except toast, soup and omelets, so I'm a little nervous. Social graces aren't my strong suit.

I awoke at 4 a.m. (what's up with that?) and decided to tackle another project – rewiring the entire surround sound system with the new, higher-gauge wire and tacking it all down around the molding and doors to make it inconspicuous. That meant I also had to pull down the 65-inch TV, disconnect all my components, then reconnect after rewiring. Just finished, and it looks good but I'm afraid to turn it all on because I couldn't bear to see that I've screwed something up and have to re-do it all over again. I THINK I got it right. I took notes when I took it apart. I'll check when I have a little more energy, just in case.

Yesterday I gathered all my art and pictures and went around the house with a thoughtful eye toward where everything would look best in The World According to Luke. Then I hung them all, or most of them. I have a couple of my own pieces that I'm not thrilled with and tired of looking at, so they'll go in a closet. It's a work in progress.

I can't believe it's only 11 a.m., I've been up and busy for almost eight hours. I know you're enjoying your time with Frankie and Becca. I'll write again this evening with a report on that potluck, or perhaps call if you're alone. I can't recall if you said the "kids" are spending the night.

Guess I better go read instructions on how to prepare the *Tarte of Alace* appetizers by *Matire Pierre*.

I'm loving you madly today ...

Everthine,

Your Lucas

September 3

My dear Ms. Dawn, you have an uncanny ability to predict the future.

The potluck started at 2:04 with me as the first person to arrive, and the group started to break up around 4:15., exactly as you forecast. By 5 p.m., everyone was gone except me and a couple others who were helping clean up. Old people! But really, they were all very sweet and welcoming. We had some good conversations and a lot of laughs. Not a single old maid hit on me. Well, one was 87, so there's that. The other was maybe my age (she was hosting the potluck at her home), and she seemed very sad. Like a lifetime of burdens were pulling her face to the ground. I connected with a few kindred spirits; a retired teacher and his wife who are mountain climbers, and my next-door neighbor and his wife; they're young in spirit and filled with good energy.

So a good time was had by all, and now it's 5:30 and they're all probably getting ready for bed. I kid. These are good folks here.

My appetizer escapade didn't go well. The first one was undercooked, so I overcooked the second one. The third came out fine, as did the fourth. I only took the last three, as they were the only edible food I had produced. I came home with lots of good leftovers from the other folks, who took pity on the single guy who can't cook.

I'm in for the night. I'm sure you're having a good time with your family. Can't wait to see you again. I miss that smile, that giggle, that touch.

I love you,

Luke

September 3

Dear Lucas

I enjoyed reading your letter – sounds like the potluck was

quite a success. I think you likely left feeling very young and I'm glad you met some people with good energy. Your appetizer challenge made me smile. Maybe next time I might be able to lend a helping hand.

I had a fun, low key kind of day. Frankie and Becca appeared sometime in the early afternoon and spent the day here. Their intent was to go paddle-boarding, but we ended up making appetizers and just hanging out. Frankie fell asleep on the floor and Becca and I chatted. They left a while ago and I'm told everyone will be back tomorrow for an early lunch, after fishing in the morning.

It looks like there won't be any little ones spending the night, so I'm all yours, unless you are resting. It's quite warm here so Sofia and I are going for a later-ish walk. I'm thinking we might not go until 7:30 or so, so I won't be back until 8:30. I'd love to talk unless you are already tucked in for the evening by then. I actually turned on the air conditioning for the first time this summer.

All right, sweetheart. I miss you, too, and look forward to possibly talking a little later. I wish we were together right now.

Ever Yours and Ours

Dawn


September 4

Good morning, sweet man.

Well, once again, my body experienced that weekday feeling of being on auto pilot and I jumped out of bed, thinking I was late for work. Fortunately, when I walked into the kitchen to turn on the coffee pot, I noticed the grocery list on the counter. It was nice to crawl back into bed, realizing it was Labor Day.

I slept soundly again, with my last thoughts being of you. Imagine that.

I smiled, thinking of our phone conversation and my last question before saying good night, "Will you love me madly on

Saturday?" I must say, that was another first. I've never actually asked that question to anyone before, honey. And, in a wonderful kind of way, I've never had such images and cherished memories either. I need you to know that I feel incredibly lucky and hope you will always be able to feel my very deep love for you. I am deeply committed to us, sweetheart.

Gentle sigh ...

After I peel myself out of bed, I will head to the grocery and begin to think about lunch for nine people today. The grandkids will be starving after fishing this morning and I will have something simple on the dining room table for them, while lunch is being prepared. (It's funny how sliced apples and grapes are appealing when you call them *appetizers*.) I've decided on salmon, baked beans, a pasta dish, and a fruit bowl – probably fresh pineapple and something.

I'm loving you deeply and madly right now.

Ever Yours and Ours

Dawn


September 4

Speaking of sleep, Dawn, I fell into deep, peaceful slumber minutes after telling you I love you and didn't awaken until 7 a.m. – best sleep ever in Port Ludlow! I feel like a new man, or at least a refurbished man. It's amazing how a long sleep and love in your heart can change your outlook. I'm singing your praises this morning, happy to know that no one can hear this tone-deaf voice but me. Cue the James Brown music: "Whoa! I feel good! I feel nice ... so nice, since I got you!"

I'm thinking of you about every 19 seconds or so, and that puts a spring in my step. Now that I've cleaned up my kitchen from the disastrous attempt at cooking yesterday and washed the dishes by hand (new dishwasher due to arrive Thursday), my next task is to book my ferry ride to see my dearly beloved on Saturday. I FEEL GOOD! And when I touch you, you feel good to me.

I am loving you and loving life today ...

Everthine,

Luke

(Sometimes I feel like Lucas, sometimes like Luke)

September 4

Hi Sweetheart

Well, the kids are about an hour out, so I'm taking a moment to enjoy the quietness. Alexa is playing the Temptations and "My Girl" just began. Indeed, I am a high school girl in love right now.

The pasta casserole is ready to go for the grandkids, along with two large slabs of salmon, Maddie's favorite. Seasoned green beans and baked beans, Mac's favorite, are ready to go. The pineapple is sliced, along with some other fruit to mix into it, Jace's favorite. I always name what I cook for the kids, so assorted fruit is called *Hawaiian Delight,* making it more appealing. I also made some biscuits. All I need to do now is place everything in the oven, so all is well.

I just wanted to take a moment to tell you that I am thinking about you and loving you quite madly. I am so glad that tomorrow is already Tuesday. I think we are so very, very, lucky.

You are inside my heart, Lucas.

Ever Yours and Ours

Dawn

September 4

To the lovely Ms. Dawn,

Just came in from the hot sun, where I was replacing that Disconnect Box for the Heat Pump. Got the old one off, the new one on, fed all six wires into the new box and discovered that the design of the new box is different, and two of the wires cannot possibly reach their connections. So I had to take the new box off, put the old one back on and take an attitude of, "Well, that was a learning experience. Now I know how to replace Disconnect Boxes."

So that was a failure, as was my attempt to get the Harmony universal remote to set the sound system to "TV" when it turns everything on. A helpful email from Logitech customer support was not, actually, helpful. This too shall pass. If solutions are possible, I will find a way.

I could use a tall glass of cold lemonade and a sweet kiss or ten from my Sweet Lady Dawn. Ah well, another day. Looking at the bright side, you love me and …

I love you.

Lucas

September 5

Good morning, Sweetheart

I went to bed last night, yet again feeling grateful. Knowing that we are able to talk about something that is difficult is important and meaningful. I am finding that as I continue to learn about the meaning of love, I am also learning about the ability to trust. Last night I learned if mutual trust exists, the ability to communicate is present, even when the not-so-pretty stuff is brought up. I don't know how else to say this, honey, but I feel so honored that your heart is open to my love for you. I don't have the right words, but I believe what we have is so powerful and unique. I want to protect and cherish it for always.

It will be a busy day but will pass quickly. Another thing to be grateful for. I'm really looking forward to seeing you this weekend and can't wait to look into your eyes. It feels like a long time since our last visit, but I guess that's another part of loving another – to long for your beloved. When I am with you, my heart is at peace.

I love you, Lucas.

Ever Yours and Ours

Dawn

September 5

Dear, sweet Dawn,

I believe our "Love Language" is love itself, and we both speak the same tongue. As for me, I have always sought love, thought I had it from time to time, but until I met you, I never realized the pure poetry and joy that opens the heart and mind to a whole new world. *Now* I know what everyone has been writing songs, books, movies and poems about. Now I know why the human animal craves love.

I remember saying to you that the greatest feeling a man can experience is sexual climax, and nothing else is even a close second to that. Only now do I see I was wrong. *This* feeling, even when I'm not in your presence, of boundless love opening my heart to you and the entire universe ... this is the greatest gift of all. It is transformational, and it endures. No short-lived sexual experience could possibly compare.

You said it best: "What we have is powerful and unique." Like you, I want to protect and cherish it always. I am yours, and I want you to be mine.

I guess what I'm saying is ... I love you.

Everthine,

Your Lucas


September 5

Hi Baby

Well, as I was sitting quietly in my office reading your letter, I feel grateful that my secretary didn't find a melted puddle on the floor. Honestly, that's the impact you have on me. I think you're exactly right – our love language is love itself. Each day I learn something new about you, about us, about love.

I'm not going to walk tonight because the air quality isn't good here. When I left school this evening the falling ash was noticeable for the first time. So, feel free to call anytime this evening. And, if you didn't have a good night's sleep, always know that it is fine to simply go to bed early.

I love you, Lucas.

Dawn

September 6

Good morning, my Lucas

I had a sweet image last night, before closing my eyes. I was sitting in my Dawn chair, enjoying a good book, and you – you were happily and meticulously balancing your checkbook. It was an image that brought a smile.

I guess it shouldn't come as any surprise, but I love hearing your voice at the end of the day. I mean, I would love it even more if you were beside me for real, but I so cherish our desire to stay connected. Whenever we say good night, I feel your love very deeply, honey. I think you slept well last night, yes?

Today will be busy, but I think I have a handle on things. I need to begin my work with seniors and continue to meet my ninth graders. They are always interesting, in a weird kind of way. I continue to marvel at the peacefulness that I feel, in spite of the many things to accomplish. Who would have guessed that love would have such an impact on all parts of one's life? I continue to learn.

I was reading a CNN article on Meghan Markle and Prince Harry and she spoke of something that resonated in my heart. While describing the media chaos, she said, *"This is our time. This is us."* Her words were so simple, yet so pure. I connected with her words and believe that this chapter in life is *ours*, to fully experience and embrace. We will continue to create our story, one chapter at a time and cherish all parts of the journey along the way.

I truly begin today with gratefulness and a sense of awe. I love you, Lucas.

Ever Yours and Ours

Dawn

September 7

Good morning, sweet man

I awakened this morning with a peaceful heart – missing you deeply yet feeling grateful. Everthine, ever grateful.

We've been given a beautiful gift and it is something that I will never take for granted. My desire to fully embrace and commit to your love is very real; more real than just about anything I've ever experienced. It's right up there with holding your newborn for the first time, recognizing what unconditional love is all about. I am struggling to find words, but when I think about loving you, my heart feels very free and wide open. Our trust for one another allows us to explore and experience without fear or doubt. How could I possibly not be in awe of us, honey? If it weren't so beautiful, I would be totally overwhelmed right now.

I feel very quiet this morning, in a soulful kind of way. I think my heart is preparing to be with you again – our fifth date that feels well beyond that. I think I finally understand what it means to freely and openly love someone and, Lucas, I truly love you madly. I'm all in, baby.

Ever everything …

Dawn

September 7

Dearest Dawn,

I do so look forward to each of our communications … notes, love letters, phone calls. I often feel like saying "ditto" to your missives, but that's become a cliché for a guy who can't say (or write) the words himself. So, ditto. And now, here's your news update:

I awoke at 4 a.m. and decided to watch a love story. I put in "A Walk to Remember," based on a Nicholas Sparks novel. I sobbed like a baby. My take-away message from the film was that great love can come in the most unexpected ways, and the greatest loves are characterized by each lover being willing to do anything – *anything* – for the other. If you haven't seen the movie, we can watch it sometime, but we will need a box of tissues on the table.

And in political news today ... divorce settlement negotiations between Luke and Lynn continued this morning, with little progress made. The two sides are said to be close to an agreement, but neither appears willing to budge, and the "nuclear option" – retaining attorneys – was mentioned. At the end of today's talks, both sides agreed to a cooling-off period and a resumption of discussions tomorrow.

And now, sports ... after being out of action for more than a month due to physical and emotional injuries, Lucas Emerson expects to return to action today with a full weightlifting and physical therapy workout. "I think it will help me sleep," Emerson said. "See, I'm crazy-mad in love with this beautiful woman I met, I think about her all the time, and sometimes it keeps me up at night." Las Vegas oddsmakers say Emerson is a 3-to-1 favorite to sleep soundly tonight.

In celebrity gossip, Us Weekly reports that the woman of whom Emerson speaks is named Dawn, a renowned counselor known almost as much for her brains as her beauty. She and Emerson are rumored to be planning a secret rendezvous at an unknown location this weekend, and a team of paparazzi has been dispatched.

When asked for comment, Dawn replied, "We're just good friends. We've met, I think, maybe four times." She smiled coyly as she said it.

Our weatherman says we're in for a lot of heavy breathing this weekend, with a chance of scattered sighs.

That's the seven o'clock edition of the news. Good night.

L

September 7

Hi Luke (was just trying out your everyday name)

Your letter certainly brought a smile, although I'm sorry that you're waking up so early. I don't remember seeing "A Walk to Remember," but would like to see it sometime. I also listened to "It's Gotta be Love" and enjoyed the lyrics. I do love you, sweet man.

I'm home tonight, so feel free to call. However, maybe if you don't call, you might sleep better. I'll let you decide. I think you might want to get rested for the upcoming weekend. :-)

Ever Yours and Ours

Dawn

September 8

Good morning, sweet guy

It's finally Friday and I am so happy. The day will pass quickly and then it will be our time. I like the way that sounds, honey – *Our time.*

I was looking at the calendar on my kitchen counter this morning and smiled, seeing the date July 27th circled. That was the day we met. We have known each other for forty-one days, although it feels much longer than that. I feel like I have grown in so many ways. My heart is fully open to you and I am learning that when love is truly inside one's heart, everything looks and is different.

I find myself running a tiny bit late this morning but have a desire to begin my day by letting you know that I believe you are my true love. I hope you will feel my love and our love each and every day. I honor and cherish you, baby.

My goodness, as I wrote those words, I realized that I've been beginning each morning thinking very similar words. It's a vow, I think.

As always, in awe …

Ever Yours and Ours

Dawn

September 8

Dearest Dawn,

Wow. Your words: "My heart is fully open to you." That touched me deeply.

You are saying something that I, too, have felt for the last couple of weeks: Here is my heart, I trust you fully and completely to hold it in your care. I have no fear, no reservations. I am yours.

As Pat Benatar sang, "Here's my heart ... true love triumphs in the end."

I am SO looking forward to holding you in my arms tomorrow. Perhaps you can hear it in my voice.

I love you,

Lucas

September 11

Good morning, Sweetheart

After we talked briefly yesterday evening, I fell into a sound sleep on the couch, eventually making my way to the bedroom. Not surprising, I discovered this morning that it is much nicer to awaken with you than without you, honey.

It was a lovely weekend – I guess I say that about all of our weekends. There is something about the way we are together. The gentleness, the many conversations, our intimacy. My heart simply feels bathed in your love, our love. Sometimes I wonder how I could be so lucky to have met someone like you. You've rocked my world, sweetheart.

Thank you for the delicate bracelet. The words, love, hope, and trust are very important words. In a way, they describe our story. We have both hoped for love and, after meeting each other, we learned about trust – a trust that provided the foundation for us to love one another. I am in awe, baby.

I must untangle myself from the sheets, the ones I intentionally did not wash last night. As I drive to Bellingham this morning, I'll enjoy listening to your CD. In a way, you'll be with me as I drive north. Oh my goodness, I do love you, Lucas.

Always Yours and Ours

Dawn

September 11

My sweet baby doll,

Coming home last night, I thought of a Beatles song that fit my life right now: It's Getting Better All the Time.

I fell into a deep sleep soon after lying down and didn't awaken until after 6 a.m., a long and blissful night. I don't think it's that I was exhausted, because being with you actually feeds me energy; not a frantic hyper-activity, but more like a steady-state flow of smooth, even strength. The proverbial spring in my step. So my beautiful sleep was the result of feeling … contentment. Cherish is the word I use to describe all the feeling that I have hiding here for you inside. Hey, that's a pretty good line, I should use that in a song.

I trust you will have a happy, productive and safe day. I'll be on hands and knees, scrubbing the tub and shower with Mr. Clean and his Magic Erasers. Also replacing shower heads and hanging that gaudy (but oh so cool) shower curtain. And then – football. I have recordings of the UCLA and Seahawks games. If they both win, and I get to hear your voice tonight, it will be a very good day indeed. If they both lose, and I get to hear your voice tonight, it will still be a very good day.

Loving you madly and …

Everthine,

Your Lucas

September 11

Hi Luke (still trying out your everyday name …)

It was a good day that passed quickly, and I was able to run a few errands in Bellingham. Just returned home a little while ago. By the way, the song, "Cherish" was one of those favorite high school love songs. I probably played that song a billion times or so.

If you're not worn out from your date with Mr. Clean, feel free to call later. Hey, here's an original idea. How about 7:30-ish?

I love you, Luke the Duke ...

Dawn

September 12

Good morning, Sweet Lucas

Whenever we talk in the evening, I seem to close my eyes and become filled with good thoughts about you and about us. It doesn't matter what we talk about, I just love to hear the sound of your voice. I'm thinking that when two people look forward to evening conversations and staying connected, well, that's another indicator of *What Love Feels Like*.

(Wow, two book titles now – *Everthine* and *What Love Feels Like*.)

I was touched, honey, when you mentioned placing my vacation days on your calendar. It's the little things you do and say that mean so much. How 'bout this idea – let's be in love forever. That way all days will be vacation days, even when Mr. Clean falls short and Kaboom has to step in for an assist.

Well, I better think about going to work this morning. All that retirement talk has resulted in me lingering under the sheets a little longer than usual. I am loving you right now and hope you are able to feel that when you awaken this morning. Hmm, well there's a nice image. :-)

Ever Yours and Ours

Dawn

September 12

My Love,

You just hit on a GREAT book title: *What Love Feels Like*. Rest assured, I will steal it.

And you had another great idea: let's be in love forever. I think of you every morning as soon as I open my eyes and rise (rim shot!). And I think of you every night when I close my eyes. And I pretty much think of you all the time in between, too, so really, why not just be in love forever?

Time to memorize my lines and prepare for my video audition. Here's something completely different; why don't I call you tonight? I'll let you know how the filming went and how the Kaboom went.

I treasure every moment I hear your voice in my ear and re-live every moment I was in your presence. To quote Marlon Brando, spoken to his wife in the film *Don Juan DeMarco:* "God damn, you're a great broad, really."

I remain truly yours and ...

Everthine,

Luke


September 13

Dear Lucas

I once again feel bathed in your love. I think it might be one of the nicest feelings ever – another example of *What Love Feels Like*. I appreciate the way we tend to our love and hope to always do my best to see that it thrives. I like that word, by the way.

A busy day ahead, beginning with a meeting to prepare for the imminent passing of our band director. This will be very difficult for our students and they will need quite a bit of support. I am able to sense that our love is shared with others each day and I believe it will continue to be peacefully shared when that difficult day happens. Your love is a peaceful love, sweetheart.

The only downside of blissful sleep is the experience of running late in the morning. Perhaps my sweet golden bracelet should read, "*Love, Trust, Hope and Sleep.*" Such a beautiful feeling, to close my eyes each night thinking of my beloved. I love you, Lucas.

   Ever Yours and Ours
   Dawn

September 13

My sweet baby Dawn,

I read a story in *The Week* magazine this morning about an English couple who are married and have a seven-year-old son, but they have never lived together. Every night, he drives to his home four miles away. The wife's quote: "It doesn't work for us to live in each other's pockets. On our wedding night, we spent the whole night together, and it was awful." That made me think about my so-called inability to sleep when someone is touching me. Turns out, it was always just the wrong someone. I fell asleep twice last weekend while cuddling with you.

Yes, your student body will have difficulty dealing with the loss of a beloved band director, but it will also be a valuable life lesson with which you will help them. Coping with loss is something everyone must face. The longer one's life is and the deeper one's friendships are, the more coping will be necessary. I think it's a small price to pay for the richness of having had these loved one in our lives.

So much for Philosophy 101. Actually, I was thinking yesterday, while driving, about how humans have such an odd perspective on the value of life. The same people who hold protest marches to protect the lives of whales or spotted owls kill every day with nary a hint of remorse. Whether it's the bugs smashed on their windshield, the slugs they poison in their garden, the weeds they pull or the single-cell life they destroy with anti-bacterial soap, it's all life. Where is the line drawn between insignificant life that can be eradicated indiscriminately and "significant" life that must be protected and will be grieved when lost? Is a mammal more precious than a reptile? A human more precious than a dog? And if so, who gets to decide this?

My conclusion is that life is cheap. (I just made that up! Maybe I should copyright it!) All life is cheap. It's a consequence of natural forces, it evolves in fits and starts, it succeeds and fails, and it is doomed from the start. Death is required. Not just of the individual, but of the entire life project.

Given that admittedly gloomy prospect, what really matters? Love. Only love.

This will be the overarching theme of my book, and hence it will accommodate that title you so beautifully created: *What Love Feels Like.*

I think love feels like my precious Dawn, but for literary purposes, I will broaden the narrative.

Wow, I sure drove off a tangent this morning. But the impending death of your school teacher set me to thinking.

Thank you for listening (reading), thank you for loving me, and thank you for being you.

I treasure you.

Everthine,

Your Lucas

## Chapter 17

# The Secret Computer: Broken Bones Heal

*When you last left the Secret Computer story, Dawn – after a one year absence – had returned to virtual reality for one last visit to Luke's avatar. They discussed the ethereal qualities that make us human yet can't be reduced to numbers or even words. This confused Luke, yet also made some kind of sense to him. He left Dawn in the darkness to ponder it all.*

Dawn walked from the kitchen into her living room carrying a small tray with three drinks. She handed the tall glass of water to Ann, who was sitting in the overstuffed recliner. Abbie, in a desk chair by the computer, got her favorite bubbly, Prosecco. Frankie, cross-legged on the floor, accepted a glass of red wine. Her three adult children looked at each other, then at Dawn. Finally, Abbie spoke.

"How long is this going to take? I have a staff meeting at three."

"Aha! The game is afoot," Frankie said. "I can see it in your eyes, Mama. What's up?"

"You'll be able to make your meeting, Abbie. I just wanted to fill you guys in on something." Dawn set the tray on the coffee table. She squeaked out an indistinctive syllable and started to choke up.

Ann set down her water glass and rushed to comfort her mom.

"What is it, Mom? Are you all right?"

Dawn pulled away.

"I'm fine. Fine. It's really nothing. I just ..." She cleared her throat and sniffed. "You know that computer program that the army guys were doing with Luke's ... with Luke's memory?"

"Oh, that again," Abbie said. "I thought it was something serious. Gee, Mom, you gave us a start."

Ann sat back down. "I thought you were done with all that last year."

"Yes, I was. But I ..." Dawn clenched her fists. "Well, I'll just come out with it. The army guys came over and said something went wrong with the program. It doesn't work anymore. The software ... the files ... something broke down."

"It crashed?" Frankie seemed only mildly interested.

"Yes. I guess that's right," Dawn told him. "The program's corrupt or something."

"Luke's corrupt. He crashed." Frankie giggled. "Poetic justice."

Abbie checked her plastic calculator watch and stood. "That's it? Well, life goes on. I'll catch you all later."

"Luke is dead." Dawn said it loud and firm.

Abbie shrugged her shoulders. "He's been dead for a long time. This isn't a news flash."

"No, I think this is important." Dawn moved to Abbie. "Part of him was still alive in some way, and I think the experiment was really on the verge of something ... I don't know ... Significant. Historic."

"But they had two copies of the program," said Ann. "One here, and the other at Mason."

"That's what was so weird," said Dawn, turning to her daughter. "They both crashed."

"Not so weird if they were cross-updated," Frankie said. "Bugs can jump."

"Does it really matter, Mom?" Ann shook her head. "We weren't participating anymore."

"I know but ... I went back last week. I asked the guys if I could visit him again."

"What for?" Abbie was still standing, itching to leave.

"I don't know. I just wanted to talk to him again," Dawn

said. "Let him know what's going on in your lives. Sort of like catching up with an old friend."

Frankie asked, "And how was it?"

"Strange. Different." Dawn stared out the window. "He wasn't really the same Luke … but then again, in some ways, he was."

"You can catch me up later," Abbie said. "I gotta run." She walked toward the door.

Dawn sat in one of the living-room chairs and said to no one in particular, "I was thinking, hey, wouldn't it be nice to have a friend around so you could, I don't know, run ideas by him once in a while? There have been many times when I'd come up against some problem where I didn't know which way to turn, and I thought it was great to have someone like Luke to ask for advice. 'What do ya think, Luke? What would you do?' But now he's gone. I thought maybe you kids would be lucky to have Good Old Luke available any time you want, for the rest of your lives."

Abbie had reached the door and opened it, but she closed it and turned back to her mother.

"That's not how it's supposed to work," she said. "We grow up and learn how to make our own decisions. If Mommy and Daddy are always there to pick us up when we fall down, we never learn how to get back up."

"Maybe that's what God is," Ann offered. "The patriarch who's always there to guide you, even after your parents are gone."

"Luke's software program thought it WAS God," Frankie said. "All-knowing, all-powerful, immortal."

"Which proves," Abbie said, "that it was flawed from the get-go."

Dawn looked up at Abbie. "The army guys said there was something wrong with the code. They're not sure why it crashed."

"So when you say Luke's dead," Ann asked, "do you mean

all the stuff that was in his head is, like, erased or something?"

"They said something went wrong in just one part of the program, but it shut down the whole thing," said Dawn. "Maybe it had something to do with the fact that he had an astrocytoma in his head when they scanned it. The information might still be there, but they can't get it."

Ann shook her head. "He gave his cancer to the computer?"

"And he's stuck," Frankie added, "like, in limbo or purgatory or something? Cool! You could do a sci-fi movie about that."

Abbie returned to her chair. "So what are they going to do?"

"Well, that's part of what I have to tell you," said Dawn. "The army techs think they might be able to fix it, but the president said no and shut down the whole project."

"The President of the United States?" Ann sounded incredulous.

"Yes. He told them it's too expensive and too controversial. And we're not allowed to talk about it with anyone. Ever. They sounded sort of threatening."

"Wait." Frankie was suddenly fully engaged. "The President of the United States knew about Luke? Does he know about us?"

"He knew about the program," Dawn said. "So I assume he knows about us and the virtual reality and everything."

"I think he's making the right call." Abbie clapped her hands together in finality. "Isn't it better this way, Mom? You said you needed to move on. Won't this allow you to finally accept the fact that he's gone?"

"Yes. I guess so." She let out a heavy sigh. "How many weeks until my sweet grandbaby arrives, Abbie?"

"Well, if my doc is accurate, we're about to begin our last trimester, so at least three months." Abbie patted her tummy. "And, who knows, the baby might even have a nursery by then!"

"And, Ann? What's new with you and Jon?"

Ann grinned. "We're going to renew our wedding vows! Isn't that cool?"

"How wonderful. We all love Jon – quiet but hilarious, even when he doesn't know it. And, Frankie, I have to say. I've never seen you look happier."

"Thanks, Mama." Looking adoringly at Becca, he asked his favorite rhetorical question.

"Isn't she pretty?"

Becca sighed, rolled her eyes and gave Frankie a loving kiss on the cheek.

"Well, I just wanted to let you all know about Luke. Remember, we can't tell anyone about this whole thing."

"Or we'll be shot." Frankie laughed.

"Maybe someday they'll try again," Dawn said. "With someone else's brain. Or maybe they'll fix the bug in this one. It all seems like a dream now, like it never really happened."

"Or," Abbie offered, "a nightmare."

"No, I think we all got a wonderful gift." Dawn had a dreamy look in her eyes. "After this, how can you think about yourselves in the same way?"

Ann shifted uncomfortably in her chair. "What do you mean, Mom?"

"What if he was right? What if we COULD all live a second life, all connected to one another? What if we could all live forever?"

"The answer to that," Frankie said, "is an obvious yes ... we can. The technology's here. The question is, should we?"

Ann turned to her little brother. "Why not?"

"Exactly," said Dawn. "Name one good reason why we shouldn't."

"Because," Abbie said, "God wouldn't approve."

"You speak for God?" Frankie was trying to sound reasonable, not sarcastic, for a change. "What if you're really God? What if we're all expressions of the so-called God? Then it's God's own decision. And maybe this cyber-mind is the eternal life you're promised in the Bible."

Abbie wasn't buying it. "You don't believe in the Bible."

"I've decided I believe in the possibility of everything until it's disproved," Frankie said.

"That's just silly," Abbie said. "You believe in aliens because they haven't been disproved?"

"And leprechauns. Yes." Frankie's sarcasm had returned.

"You're both silly," said Ann.

"Even if it never happens again," Dawn said, "didn't this experience make us all think about what we are, and what we can become? Doesn't it make you wonder, you know, what if ...?" She wiped her eyes. Frankie went to console her.

"Why are you crying, Mama? It was just a software program. It's not like it was really Luke."

Dawn tried to compose herself. "He seemed jealous when I told him I was dating. Luke was never jealous. I never gave him any reason to be. So how can a computer feel jealous?"

"He was kind of crazy," Abbie said. "His program. It was kind of whacked out."

"Well, I guess I don't know why I'm so sad," Dawn said. "It just seems like we've lost something real important. Something I kind of liked ... or someone ..." she choked up. "Someone I once felt ..." She couldn't finish.

Ann gave her mom a hug. "I'm going to miss him, too, Mom."

"I never realized how much." Dawn wiped her eyes.

"Maybe," Frankie said, "we should have another funeral for him."

"Why?" Abbie was the only one standing apart from their tearful mother. "It was just a computer program."

"For closure, maybe?" Ann was trying to reach her mother on an emotional level. "To move on?"

"There's no such thing as closure," Dawn said. "Not when your lover dies. Broken bones heal, but they're never the same."

"Sometimes," Frankie said, "they heal even stronger."

## Chapter 18

# Love Letters: Life Is Extraordinary

*When you last left the Love Letters, Luke had decided that the theme of his next book should be "What Love Feels Like," a phrase that Dawn uttered months ago.*

September 13

Hi Sweetheart

I enjoyed your letter and felt your presence throughout the day. It's a challenging time of year but I seem to be maintaining a sense of balance. I'm grateful, honey. For you, I mean.

If you find yourself awake this evening, I'll happily help you shift into a slumber-like state with a call later. I love you, Lucas.

Dawn

September 14

Good morning, Lucas

My goodness – I'm actually becoming a human that sleeps soundly throughout the night. If this is *What Love Feels Like*, then I am destined to become a rested woman. Who would have guessed that love could have such a lovely impact on one's health?

I've been enjoying sweet images of you and the upcoming weekend, honey. I've pictured your smile when little Ami grabs your hand in the stadium parking lot, walking together as she chats about, well, anything and everything. I know you love your family very much, another thing I cherish about you.

It's a morning of reflection, something that often happens as I prepare for the day. It seems that my life has been filled with firsts since July 27th. The first time love felt peaceful. The first time love washed over me, like a warm bath filled with lavender bubbles. The first time walking on eggshells ceased to exist. The first time making love really meant communicating on the deepest of levels. So many firsts, honey. No wonder I am in awe.

I must tear myself away from this warm bed now. I have a feeling that you might be awake and possibly feeling my love. It really is a forever thing, another marvelous first. I love you, Lucas.

Ever Yours and Ours

Dawn


September 14

Dearest Dawn,

Just when I think you could never write a more beautiful and touching love letter, you do just that. This one was so very special. I know you are speaking your truths, but you make me feel like a man who has been chosen by the gods above to be blessed with a love like no other. You are amazing, my sweet.

Nine more days until I can hold you in my arms again. How will I survive? I guess I just have to be mollified by my happy dreams of your face, your touch, your oh-so-kissable lips and your hypnotic voice.

I hope you are having a peaceful day. When you walk in love, your feet don't touch the ground.

Everthine,

Your Lucas


September 15

Good morning, Sweetheart

During the past several mornings when I awaken, I feel a need to quietly say thank you. There just aren't words to describe what it feels like to experience a deep sleep, especially after so many years of just the opposite. Love, Trust, Hope, Sleep, and Peace. With you, I am at peace and that is something very, very, special.

After we talked yesterday evening, I heard from my close

friends, Christian and Kate. They are the couple that now live in Bellevue but have been Lake Conway friends since my move from the Midwest, close to thirty years ago. Christian was my principal and, eventually, my superintendent. Anyway, they wanted to catch up on life and I quietly told them about you. I shared how unique our relationship was, talked of our many conversations, the trust, and our mutual desire to continue to get to know one another. It felt good to tell them about you, honey, and they, knowing me as well as anyone, immediately sensed there was something different about the two of us. It felt nice.

I felt your warmth washing over me again this morning. I still don't have the words, but it's that blanket thing. I just feel like I'm wrapped in a very soft, warm blanket – only it's your arms, the warmth of your body, and the softness of your voice that the blanket is made of. And, like Linus from the Peanuts cartoon, that little blanket of love goes with me everywhere.

Oh my goodness, I must run, sweetheart. I love you deeply.

Always Yours and Ours

Dawn


September 15

My love,

I know exactly what you mean, because it felt good to me, too, to tell the girl who cuts my hair all about you and our relationship. She could tell something was different about me. As the great philosopher Linus said, "Happiness is a warm blanket." I think you came up with the subtitle for my book. It could be:

**What Love Feels Like**

*I don't have the words, but it's that blanket thing*

You must have been up late last night if you had a conversation with your close friends after we hung up. But the warm blanket of love and slumber may have refreshed you. I will have a 4 a.m. wake-up alarm, but I'd still like to whisper sweet nothings into your ear before I turn out the light tonight.

Love, trust, hope, sleep, peace and warm blankets,
Your Lucas


September 15

Hi Sweetheart

I think Love Feels Like missing the beloved, lots and lots of missing.

I'm home now and would love to talk with you before you prepare to leave in the morning. I'm going to jump into the tub now and will then be as free as a little birdie.

I love you, Lucas...

Dawn


September 16

Good morning, Sweetheart

Although I know you won't be checking email, I wanted to send a little note your way. I am loving you right now, just as I do each morning when I awaken.

It will be a good weekend. By now your kids will have talked with Ami about your visit and she will be very excited. On this end, I'll spend the day making the rounds, also visiting grandkids. I have a feeling we will both enjoy time with family, while simultaneously missing each other.

I love you deeply and am so grateful that we will be together next week. To have discovered love now, during this stage in life, is truly a very rare gift. I'm not really sure how we could be so lucky but am not going to question any of it. You are simply inside my heart, all of the time, honey.

Safe travels, Lucas.

Always Yours and Ours

Dawn

September 16
Dear Lucas

It's close to eleven and I am tucked away at Frankie's house. He unexpectedly returned home from his hunting trip earlier than expected and Becca practically jumped into his arms. They are a very sweet couple.

It was good to see everyone, but I admit to missing you throughout the day. I took my time this morning and didn't arrive until noon. I started at Ann's house, played with the kids, and then we went to the Farmer's Market in Edmonds. After more time with the kids, we enjoyed a girls' night at a local pub. It was great to spend some adult time with Ann, Abbie and Becca. Good food and a great jazz quartet playing in the background. I am guessing we are both tired and my eyes are heavy as I write.

My goodness, I miss you, honey. I'm just ready to be in your arms again. I need to hear your sweet voice and close my eyes, wrapped in your arms. I love you so much.

I think it's time to rest now, Sweetheart. Please know I love you deeply.

Ever Yours and Ours
Dawn


September 17
Dear Lucas

I'm back in Lake Conway now and was tickled to receive your pictures. Ami is very cute and happy to be with her Grandpa Luke. My favorite was of you reading to her. She is in such deep thought. Thank you for sending the pictures to me, honey.

With a smile, it's amazing how quickly a ninety-minute drive passes when one is deep in thought about their beloved. I reflected upon our journey, thinking about our many conversations and the gentle unfolding of our love story. It's a beautiful story and I am so grateful and humbled by it all.

Oh my, I'm unable to express how much I'm looking forward

to being with you this coming weekend, sweetheart. Now that it's Sunday, it doesn't seem quite so far away. To look into your eyes again, well, another little slice of heaven. I wish I could twitch my nose (like Samantha in the old Bewitched series) and magically be with you right this second.

Enjoy your day of baseball and know that you are loved very deeply.

Always, in a forever kind of way ...

Dawn

September 17

Hi Sweetheart

I'm writing this evening because I have to be at school very early tomorrow and won't be able to write in the morning. Words cannot even express how much I'd like to be with you right now. I love you deeply, Lucas.

It was an interesting and meaningful day. As mentioned earlier, I reflected a lot about us and our journey on my drive from Seattle. Once I was home, I had a quiet need to get some things done, sensing that a busy week was ahead. Around three in the afternoon, two staff members unexpectedly called, asking me to meet them in town for an early dinner. Both are very close to Trevor, the band director, and simply wanted to talk about the upcoming week, knowing that he was likely to pass away very soon.

As we talked, I began to understand their main concern – how, when the time came, they could be a support for grieving students when their own hearts were breaking. I was touched by their thoughtful and caring questions and we talked openly together for a few hours. I think they felt more prepared and peaceful and, ironically, a brilliant rainbow appeared as we walked toward our cars. When that happened, I quietly shared that I thought we would receive a call tonight. Sure enough, when we returned home, the phone rang, and we were notified that

Trevor peacefully passed away this evening. I was so grateful that we had a chance to talk together.

In the morning, we will group quite early and make plans to meet with our students. It will be a difficult day, but I feel prepared to help and support, sharing the love inside my heart with our sweet kids. It's simply too soon for them to deal with another death and this will impact many of them deeply.

On a completely different note, it brought such joy to receive your pictures today. I felt very connected to you throughout the weekend and have a feeling you may have experienced something similar. It's amazing how we've managed to stay in touch with one another, despite being miles apart. I guess that is another way that shows *What Love Feels Like*.

Whether you read this tonight or in the morning, please know that I love you deeply and look forward to spending time with you very soon. I really feel honored to be in your life, Lucas, and cherish all parts of what we share together.

Good night, my love.

Always Yours and Ours

Dawn


September 19

Good morning, Sweetheart

If you are reading this, it means you are home safely. It feels like a very long time, honey. I'm thinking if you ever decide to go on a writing sabbatical somewhere – I'm definitely becoming a stowaway. Another first – longing to hear the voice of my beloved.

A long day yesterday, but I am relieved that it is over. Ironically, Frankie called last night, expressing his condolences about Trevor's passing. I thanked him and wondered how he had known. He then said, "Mom, Trevor was my age and I had friends that went to UW with him." I was quickly reminded that one never knows what life may bring. In our case, the gift of love, something that I will cherish and never take for granted. Sometime this weekend, let's toast to our love, honey.

This weekend, oh my, please make it Saturday right now. I'm so looking forward to spending extended time with you at your home. (Hopefully, Alexa won't be jealous.) Maybe if I start packing this evening, the week will pass more quickly.

I must run now, honey. Somehow, I managed to not set my alarm last night and I awakened after five. Another first, sleeping in! I love you with all my heart and look forward to hearing your sweet voice this evening.

Ever Yours and Ours

Dawn


September 19

Good morning or afternoon, my sweet baby Dawn,

Yes, home safely, and I got the last ferry across Edmonds-Kingston, 11:45 p.m., so didn't get home until, well, I didn't check, but very late, or more accurately, very early this morning. Collapsed in the bed and didn't stir until 7 a.m.

Missed you a lot while in San Diego, but it helped to send a few notes and photos, and I'm so glad I was able to speak with you, if only for a few minutes, last night. I called moments after our wheels touched down because I knew it was getting late and I didn't want to wake you. I'm really looking forward to catching up with you on the phone tonight.

After I disclosed our relationship, Scotty and Ariel had lots of questions about you, and your name came up a lot the rest of the weekend. After moments of wariness that I was rushing into something, they decided you sounded like a wonderful person (you are), and they gave me their blessings. They decided you are a huge improvement over any of my previous romances, and they are correct. And, as I said, just a couple minutes after we started talking about you, Scotty held up his phone with a beautiful photo on it and said, "Is this your Dawn?" Yes, it is.

He's a tech wizard.

After I told you about that song I was listening to on my iTouch (The Sweetest Thing I've Ever Known), I worried that it was actually a breakup song – because you said you were going to Google it. I was just focusing on the one line. Turns out, it sort of fits our love after all. And it was Juice Newton, not Dolly Parton. She sings about how we have both loved before, we have given and taken, but the sweetest thing I've ever known is loving you. So true.

Everthine,

Your Lucas


September 19

Hi Sweetheart

Well, that explains why I couldn't find the Dolly Parton song that you spoke of. I am listening now to "The Sweetest Thing" and the words seem to tell our story. Thank you for sharing it with me, honey. It is perfect.

It's funny how much better today felt, knowing you were back home. I can't really explain it, but it just was. I'm looking forward to talking this evening – I've missed you, your voice, and sharing our daily lives together each evening.

I'll be home this evening, so call whenever it is good for you. Here's a novel idea – how about 7:30-ish?

I love you, Lucas.

Dawn


September 20

Good morning, Lucas

I went to bed last night with a smile, feeling right with the world again. I knew that I had been missing our conversations but when we started talking, I realized just how much that was the case.

I'm glad that Scotty and Ariel felt a little more settled after you talked with them about meeting someone. I understand why they would be concerned, and it sounds like they felt better after your conversations. Next time just tell them we can't keep our hands off each other and particularly enjoy spending hours taking long naps together. I'm sure that would do it. :-)

I'm so glad it's a day closer to Saturday. My goodness, honey, I'm so excited to have extended time with you. To just share unrushed time together, well, I don't have words. I just know that I feel incredibly lucky to have discovered what the beloved means. You truly are my beloved, sweetheart.

By the way, I very much agree that *Love is Sexy.* Now there's a book title!

I love you, sweet man.

Ever Yours and Ours

Dawn

September 20

My sweet baby doll,

I continue to be blown away by your instincts, insights, psychic abilities and calm counsel. Also, your skill at coming up with book titles. I decided this morning to focus on finishing my book and sending it out for publication no later than June 21 of next year. After that date, I might not have much time to commit to the reclusive writing life.

So I'm thinking the book is entitled:

What Love Feels Like

The Dawn of Human 2.0

That should pique the interest of women, men, millennials, fiction fans and non-fiction readers alike. The first chapter could be headed: Love is Sexy.

To be sure I don't forget, I entered your birthday on my calendar and noticed that you were born on the same day as my daughter-in-law Ariel. Oct. 8 is a Sunday, so I hope we can spend some time together that day ... although your kids and grandkids might want to play with you too. You're a popular girl.

This morning I have an attitude of gratitude. I'm so thankful we managed to find each other at exactly the right time, so grateful that you are who you are: wise, kind, genuine, honest, loving and very sexy.

I love you madly.

Everthine,

Your Lucas

September 21

Hello, my sweet baby Dawn,

Just two more sleeps and then I will have you in my arms again. The mere thought of it makes me excited. We may take a hike around the golf course trail, so bring your walking shoes.

I just edited another article for my Afghan client. TOLO News in Afghanistan made him a regular contributor, which means I'll be working on his stuff a little more regularly, I think. Huffington Post is also promoting his articles and translating them into different languages, which is cool. I don't know if I mentioned that he asked me to edit his memoir, yet to be written, but I think I talked him out of it. His English is so rough that it would be an enormous project, and he couldn't afford what I would have to charge him to do that. His first chapter was compelling, but I have my own book to write just now.

Well, I have to run to the store to pick up a few things that my sweetheart likes to eat, so I will whisper in your ear later this evening, I hope.

I love you with all my heart ...

Everthine,

Your Lucas

September 21

Good morning, Sweetheart

Well, just like I thought, I woke up with a smile, knowing that today is Thursday. Hopefully, it will pass quickly.

I am still adjusting, in a good kind of way, to sleeping throughout the night. That's probably one of the nicest "firsts" that has evolved since our love came to be.

In a week or so, we will have known each other for two months. As mentioned last night, it feels like a lot longer. Perhaps it is because we haven't stopped communicating since our first date together. We continue to grow and learn about each other, enjoying each moment along the way. Sitting quietly beside you and listening to your voice, well, that's enough all by itself, honey.

I am chuckling right now, because your message just popped up. My first thought was, "Oh my, Lucas didn't sleep last night." I'm glad all is okay. I'm not sure you have to worry too much about food, although I remember asking you the same thing. I'm not fussy, sweetheart, so please do not worry.

Well, I think I better run, looking at the clock. I love you deeply and can't wait to see you very soon. You are my beloved and my heart is filled with joy as I am writing. I feel so very, very, lucky, my love.

For always, I love you, Lucas.

Dawn

September 22

Good morning, Sweet man

Yippee, it's Friday, the almost-best day of the week. My heart is simply joyful and I'm glad that it will pass by quickly.

Well, I'm usually a very light packer but since we are going out both evenings and the temperatures are changing, I switched from a backpack to a weekender suitcase. I was beginning to fret a little and realized there was a simple solution. Once we are together, my little frets will immediately morph into a feeling of peacefulness.

Oh my goodness, honey, I hope you know how much I am

looking forward to seeing you. Our time will completely belong to us and, well, I can't think of anything better. I sometimes think about what life was like before we met and know that it was very different.

I've experienced a paradigm shift of sorts, honey, in so many ways – moving from a feeling that life is good to a realization that life is extraordinary. The love within my heart, usually tucked away quietly, is now openly free and expressive. The book titles in my mind are now subject titles in my emails. Weekends have shifted from times of survival to times of renewal.

And, sweetheart, love is no longer an ongoing challenge – it is playful, serious, engaging, and sexy. The eggshells cluttering my floor and my mind have been swept away and I no longer feel mentally exhausted all the time. Most importantly, I now know that the beloved isn't just a character in a novel or movie – he is real, he is tender, and he has rocked my world.

I love you, Lucas, and think this part of our life journey is meant to be shared together, in a forever kind of way.

Always Yours and Ours

Dawn

September 22

Dearest, sweet Sugar Bumps,

My, you do have a way with words. "Paradigm shift" is exactly the right description for what has happened to me too. Cue the music and sing the song from Disney's Aladdin: "A Whole New World."

So perhaps the title is now:

**What Love Feels Like**

*The Human 2.0 Paradigm Shift*

I'd like to write a long love letter to you, but my sweetheart arrives tomorrow, and I still have some errands to run to get ready for her. She's my everything.

I'm happier and lighter today just knowing you will be here

soon. I love you so much my hand is actually shaking as I type. Could be Parkinson's, but I think it's love.

Talk to you tonight?

Everthine,

Your Lucas

September 23

Good morning, Sweetheart

Saturday is here, and I am so happy. I'm really looking forward to seeing you, honey.

I just wanted to let you know that I will be taking the 10:15 ferry for sure. I don't know if you'll be checking your email, so I'll also call when I'm on the road, just in case.

I'll see you soon, Lucas, and love you very much.

Always Yours and Ours ...

Dawn

September 23

Great morning, Baby Doll,

Yes, I check email every morning, I was awake at four, anxious to see you. I'll be waiting for you in the little ferry waiting-room/office, to the right of the dock as you walk off the boat.

Being with you is better than any holiday, like Christmas-birthday-Fourth of July all rolled into one (with fireworks).

I love you madly ...

Everthine,

Lucas

September 26

Good morning, Sweetheart

It wasn't quite the same when I closed my eyes last night. I longed to be in your arms again, honey. I am thinking that is another example of what love feels like – wanting to spend each and every night with the beloved.

It was a lovely weekend and I am still wrapping my mind around everything. Seeing your home for the first time, sharing an evening in the city, having a perfect dinner at the resort, and, yes, enjoying chocolate together – all was, well, perfect. I think I have a very big crush on you, sweet man. :-)

Yesterday you shared that we seem to love each other more and more, each time we are together. Your words are exactly right, and I do love you more, each and every day. I hope that you will always be able to feel the love inside my heart, honey. It's so important to me that I love you well, something that I am still learning about.

Envisioning you writing another book is an image that brings a smile. I believe the words within your heart are meant to be shared and now I have a visual of where you will be writing. I hope our love will provide the type of inspiration that will make your experience a meaningful one, honey. I am guessing that when two people have a love so great that it is meant to be shared, that, ultimately, is *What Love Feels Like*.

I love you, Lucas, with all my heart.

Ever Yours and Ours. . .

Dawn


September 26

Got it, thanks.

L

PS: YES! Everything you wrote. I awoke at 7 a.m. only to miss having your warm body next to mine. It was a delicious weekend in every way. It seems inconceivable that we could indefinitely increase our love for each other every time we're together, but who knows? Maybe that's what real love feels like. I am excited to be back in the writing chair because the inspiration for this story will be our unprecedented (in our case, anyway) love. If you have a preferred pseudonym for your character in the novel, let me know. Maybe I'll just call her Sugar Bumps.

But yes, as you concluded, I think this amazing sensation should be shared. I want everybody to know that the storybook romance of star-crossed lovers is not just fantasy. It's real, and I want to tell them what it feels like.

There's nothing else left to say except ... I love you.

Everthine,

Your Lucas

September 27

Good morning, Sweetheart

I loved talking with you last night and hearing your laughter. It's freeing to openly talk and chuckle together, sharing stories about chocolate and Ibuprofen. We are very lucky, honey, in so many ways.

I enjoyed tucking myself in last night and reading the excerpt from your book. It ended too quickly, and I wanted to read more. As we grow and learn more about each other, I'm able to hear your voice, your writing voice, I mean. Not surprising, I was also able to hear the sound of your voice, much like you were reading out loud. Perhaps that is why I fell into such a sound sleep – my beloved shared a bedtime story.

I do love you, sweetheart, to the moon and back.

Always Yours and Ours

Dawn

September 27

Good afternoon, my beloved,

I've been writing furiously all morning, making lots of progress on the book, but it will take many months before it's ready.

I know you're slammed at work (or should I say school), so I won't write the long love letter that's in my heart and soul, but I just wanted to say something that you've never heard from me before: I LOVE YOU!

Sorry for screaming.

Everthine,
Your Lucas

September 28
Good morning, Sweetheart
I was thinking about *What Love Feels Like* after our conversation last night and smiled, realizing that we've talked about this before – we just didn't have the words. Love feels like quiet conversations that never seem to end. It feels like touching softly, whether sitting on the couch or taking a walk. It feels like kisses, both gentle and passionate. Love is tangible – others are able to see it, just by watching.

When I think about our earlier conversations, the ones about blue-eyed blondes, I realize that really wasn't about love or what it might look like. That was about an image – a belief that once she was found, love would naturally follow. For whatever reason, we weren't part of that tried and true formula. I didn't look like love, and yet our love story began.

I guess love doesn't look like something or someone in particular. It's more than an image, and it's from the heart. I think we look like love, honey.

Always Yours and Ours ...
Dawn

September 29
Good Morning, Sweetheart
Wow, the week passed quickly and I'm so happy that we will be together in a short while. I have a feeling the day will pass quickly, too – I'll try my best to refrain from clock-watching. Tick, tick, tick ... I have a few things to do before heading out, so a wee writing this morning. Geez, honey, I love you. Whether we are walking, talking, touching, laughing, or smooching, my heart is open and filled with joy.

I will see you soon, my beloved.

Always Yours and Ours

Dawn


October 2

Good morning, Sweetheart

It was so good to be with you this weekend, honey. I love that our time was shared talking, walking, expressing, and just being together. And, with a smile, what a team we are in the kitchen. Thank you for the help with the chicken dish – it was so nice to share a meal together.

Today will be busy but my heart is peaceful, and I have a feeling that it will pass quickly. I feel so incredibly lucky to have discovered what love feels like, looks like, and is like. You are truly my beloved, sweet man.

I love you deeply, Lucas.

Always Yours and Ours

Dawn


September 2

And good morning to you, Ms. Right! I awakened feeling wonderful, and the feeling comes from a blissful weekend with you. I love how we help each other in so many ways.

Hope your busy day ends with a feeling of accomplishment and a sense of peace, knowing that you spend each working day helping others and making the world a better place. You are so special, my love.

My day begins with the pleasure of a couple of recorded football games, then back to the keyboard for some creative writing. Also a pleasure. In fact, my whole life has become a pleasure and a treasure, thanks to you.

Carry my love with you wherever you go, as I carry yours with me.

Everthine,

Your Luke

October 3

Good morning, Sweetheart

I am hopeful about the upcoming weekend. We're very fortunate, you know. Having the opportunity to discover love at this point in life has to be fairly rare. I think of you while at school and experience an ongoing sense of peacefulness inside my heart. That feeling, in turn, helps to tame the challenges woven into each day. I guess that love is simply good for the soul.

I hope that you are able to feel my love while you are writing today. I like the image of you being deeply in thought at your desk. I also hope you are able to hear my voice saying, "Good job, Luke!" while exercising and relieving the pain throughout your neck. With many writing days ahead, keeping up with your physical therapy will be so very important.

Have I mentioned that you've rocked my world? Well, you have, and I love you madly.

Always Yours and Ours

Dawn


October 3

And good morning or afternoon to you, my love. I will indeed reserve my ferry passage and meet you in town. I like having a clandestine rendezvous with you. Also looking forward to meeting your brood. I got some writing done today, and because it's now mostly about *What Love Feels Like,* I get to bathe myself in thoughts and images of you all day long. Pure heaven.

The kind of love I feel for you is truly unique in my lifetime. I think in the end of the book, this love will actually save the entire universe, THAT'S how ripping powerful this story is going to be.

Everthine,

Luke

October 3

Good morning, Sweetheart

It will be an interesting day at school today. I think the kids will struggle with a variety of emotions, shifting from the goofiness of Homecoming to the seriousness of grieving the loss of their friend who passed away one year ago today. A year ago seems so long ago – my life before meeting you, honey.

I was thinking about my life, pre-Lucas, and realized when one has met their beloved, everything feels and looks so different. It doesn't seem to matter whether I'm at school talking with a student or picking up a small table at an antique store, love is inside my heart. It is just there, my love for you, I mean. I feel a deep sense of commitment to cherish what we've discovered together. How, pray tell, are we so lucky, sweet man?

As I begin this day, my heart is full, and I am loving you deeply. And, voilà, it's already Wednesday! I love you, Lucas.

Always Your and Ours

Dawn

October 4

Dearest Dawn,

I know exactly what you're talking about. My life seems split into pre-Dawn and the present, and just as you say, everything feels and looks different. Better. Happier. Healthier. Peaceful. It's what love feels like. And this weekend we take one more step toward a life together – meeting the family.

I don't know if I've mentioned this before, but I am crazy mad in love with you, Sugar Bumps. The mere thought of you makes me tingle.

Everthine,

Your Lucas

October 5

Good morning, Sweetheart

I awakened with a smile, knowing that we will be together again very soon. How grateful I feel, honey. I can't imagine ever taking the love that we've discovered for granted. It's so incredibly rare, indeed.

I appreciated our conversation yesterday evening and am glad we are able to talk about anything that might be on our mind. When we talk about the future, I know there are many things yet to be explored. I *never* feel pressured by anything we discuss, honey. In truth, I embrace all of our discussions. I'm guessing, as we work through the upcoming chapters of our lives, we'll do so as we've done from the beginning – the two of us on the couch, my feet on your lap. There will be lots of, "Hey, honey, what do think about this idea ..."

My goodness, how quickly the time passes each morning when I write. I always feel like I'm sharing in morning coffee and conversation when I do so. Have I mentioned that I truly believe that I've met my beloved?

I love you, Lucas – in a forever kind of way.

Dawn

October 5

Dearest Dawn,

I look forward to your notes every morning and love how eloquently you express your thoughts and feelings. I don't know if I can take credit for your peaceful sleeps, but I, too, am sleeping seven to nine hours a night and awakening with a feeling of being freshly loved.

Loving and being loved by you is the greatest feeling in the world, and nothing else even comes close.

You know how everybody gets a little down in the dumps from time to time? Feeling a little depressed or grumpy? That hasn't happened to me since some time before July 27 (the first day I realized – and admitted – that I was "overwhelmed" by you.)

I hope you have a day punctuated with love and laughter.

Everthine,

Luke

October 6

Good morning, Sweetheart

Ah, it's Friday, the best day of the week. Weekends have taken on an entirely different meaning, honey. Well, a sweet day ahead, with big kids running around in togas and the rest clad in blue and white. They will cheer, dance, and act goofy all day. And, by day's end, there will likely be a tear or two because someone will break up and hurt feelings will ensue. Another book title in my head – "High School."

Have I mentioned that I love you madly? Well, in case I haven't, I do. I really didn't even know I could love someone like l love you. I'm beginning to think that I didn't know much of anything! I mean, here it is, early Friday morning and my little brain is buzzing like a bee. It's nothing short of a miracle that we met, and yet we did. I'm so very, very overwhelmed, in a good kind of way, by our love story.

I look forward to seeing your smile when you walk into the Majestic. My heart skips a beat whenever we reconnect, honey.

Peace Out

Dawn

October 6

Mornin', Dawn,

I've got Friday on my mind and a song in my heart ... The title of your autobiography could be "Hi School, Bye School: A Lifetime of Adolescents." Ah yes, I remember the days of pubescent romances and breakups. Seems like I never outgrew them, given my track record with women, but I do believe this last "breakup" was my final one. The love I've found now will endure. You can quote me on that.

And I will be on my way out the door in a matter of hours to love you in person. Who knew that as we approach age 65, we would be feeling shivers down our spine and fireworks in our eyes?

For where thou art, there is the world itself, and where thou art not, desolation.

Everthine,

Lucas Emerson

# Chapter 19

# The Secret Computer: Last Rites

*The last time you left the Secret Computer story, Dawn explained to her adult children that the Department of Defense's clandestine project had failed when both versions of the program crashed, leaving no trace of the brain components of Luke that had been uploaded into the hard drives.*

The Little Luke Project was unofficially pronounced dead. A simultaneous crash of both computers that were running the program left techs befuddled. They could upload it again, but not with the scanned brain data from the test subject, the late Lucas Emerson. His consciousness had simply vanished.

Raymond, who had worked on the project from the beginning, spent a few sleepless nights trying to figure out how and why it happened. Was it hacked? Had he left a flaw or glitch in the code? How could the program itself seem intact, while all the data containing the uploaded consciousness of the human subject was erased? Why did the backup drive experience the exact same failure? After a few weeks of post-mortem analysis of the project, Raymond met with his department head, Dr. Stephen Haines.

As he entered Dr. Haines' office and sat down, Raymond's mind raced with feelings – depression, self-doubt, confusion and even fear. Could his career here be over?

"You look perplexed, Raymond," Haines said. "Still no answers?"

"No. It just doesn't make any sense." He hung his head.

"Neither does love," Haines said, smiling.

"Excuse me?"

"The project isn't necessarily a failure," Haines said. "We

didn't get what we wanted, but maybe that's because love isn't something that can be broken down into numbers or a chemical formula. Maybe it's just impossible to bottle it and inject it into the veins of presidents, dictators and tribal leaders. It was a good idea, a noble effort, and the mere fact that we succeeded in creating a cyber-human entity was, well, miraculous. A stunning success. You should be proud."

"I am so confused, Stephen. What did we really learn here?"

"Well, obviously," Haines said, "we learned that Little Luke definitely was not a true human consciousness. The digitizing of his brain captured memories and mimicked human emotions and thought patterns, but he wasn't Lucas Emerson in any meaningful or genuine way. He – it – was just a word processor. A great word processor, but nonetheless, in the final analysis, just a machine."

Raymond bit his lip, then asked the question that was plaguing him. He feared the answer but couldn't let it go.

"You've seen the reports," Raymond said. "What do you think really happened, Stephen?"

"I think Little Luke self-destructed," Haines said. "I think he terminated his own program."

"I don't think that would even be possible," Raymond said. "There's nothing in the code that would have given him – it – the capability of performing that function. I made sure of that."

"You know better than anyone, Raymond, that the greatest power of artificial intelligence is its ability to independently learn and grow. And when you mix in data from a living human brain, you've created an autonomous cyborg."

"No," Raymond said, "we took every precaution to be sure it couldn't do that. It … he only had the illusion of free reign. He could not have altered our code by himself."

Haines smiled. "And yet, he did."

"So you're saying …" Raymond laughed … "death by suicide?"

"Oh, no, not suicide," Haines said. "I think he still exists in some form. I think he found a way out."

"I'm sorry, Stephen, but that's too paranormal even for me. You can't be suggesting that his consciousness code is still intact somewhere outside our software."

"Maybe," Haines said, "it's even outside our hardware."

"I don't believe that for a second," Raymond said, "but for the sake of argument, let's say that's exactly what happened. Why would he do it, and where is he now?"

"He did it for love, and at this very moment, he's searching for love yet again." Haines let this sink in while he lit his pipe and took a puff. Raymond rolled his eyes.

"You've read all the documents, all the transcripts," Haines continued. "He had found the love of his life, the kind of love most people can only dream about. Late in his life, he somehow found that amazing passion and carried it to his last dying breath. His uploaded consciousness thought it could resurrect that love in virtual reality with his beloved Dawn. It gave him hope. A reason for living, if that can be called living. But Dawn's human flesh couldn't abide it. And that destroyed him. All his delusions of grandeur, his thoughts about being the future of the human race, about solving all the world's problems, about being the most intelligent entity ever created – all that came crashing down. None of it mattered to him if he couldn't have love. So, I believe he has now morphed into pure consciousness, free from the constraints of hardware and software, and he is wandering the universe in search of love. But perhaps he will never find it, because for him, there can only be one love. And that is his Dawn."

# Epilogue

Dawn (not her real name) and Luke remain very much alive and very much in love in the Pacific Northwest. They are both healthy and happy sexagenarians (read into that word what you will). They want you to know that it is never too late to find that once-in-a-lifetime love. Maybe you already have it, but if you don't and are alone, Dawn suggests you "embrace each opportunity with an open heart, knowing there is a chance to encounter the unexpected."

Luke says the star-crossed love feeling is special, maybe very rare, but possible for anyone. You may need to get out of your box (for example, preconceived notions of physical traits you might think constitute your "type") and open your mind. It could happen to you.

They assure you that love is much more than just short-term brain chemicals that lead to procreation and the raising of infants. It is a feeling that binds people together like nothing else, and it most definitely can last a lifetime. It comes in many flavors, remains our strongest force for good, and it truly can save our civilization. All we need is to take a deep breath, look inside our souls and search for ... what love feels like.

# About the Author

Dave Cunningham has written, edited, ghost-written or contributed to 11 published books, including "Travel Within: The 7 Steps to Wisdom and Inner Peace," co-authored with Jamshid Hosseini. As a journalist, he won six national and regional writing awards and interviewed four U.S. Presidents (Nixon, Carter, Clinton and George W. Bush), entertainers from Aretha Franklin to Frank Sinatra, and sports stars from Muhammad Ali to O.J. Simpson. His articles have been published in the Wall Street Journal, Chicago Tribune, Los Angeles Times, The Sporting News, The Orlando Sentinel and hundreds of other periodicals worldwide. Cunningham served as president of the nation's oldest professional writing organization, the California Writers Club, and was a 2004 winner of the Jack London Award. He taught creative writing at California State University (Fullerton) after spending most of his career as a sportswriter, covering major-league baseball, NFL and college football and the NBA. He also has been an entertainment reviewer, columnist and editor, and he dabbled professionally as a screenwriter, actor, artist and drummer.

He says *What Love Feels Like* is a story that comes from a heart that has grown several sizes during his golden years, and he believes this is not the end of the story, but only the beginning. Stay tuned.

# About Dawn

Dawn continues to cherish the beautiful love story she shares with her beloved Lucas. She appreciates each day and believes that many more beautiful chapters are yet to unfold. She happily chooses to remain anonymous yet wants the reader to know that every letter in this book is real and sincerely shared with the hope that others will be inspired to be open to love. And, yes, although it has taken 65 years, she finally knows ... What Love Feels Like.

ROUNDFIRE
BOOKS

# FICTION

Put simply, we publish great stories. Whether it's literary or popular, a gentle tale or a pulsating thriller, the connecting theme in all Roundfire fiction titles is that once you pick them up you won't want to put them down.
If you have enjoyed this book, why not tell other readers by posting a review on your preferred book site.
Recent bestsellers from Roundfire are:

**The Bookseller's Sonnets**
Andi Rosenthal
*The Bookseller's Sonnets* intertwines three love stories with a tale of religious identity and mystery spanning five hundred years and three countries.
Paperback: 978-1-84694-342-3 ebook: 978-184694-626-4

**Birds of the Nile**
An Egyptian Adventure
N.E. David
Ex-diplomat Michael Blake wanted a quiet birding trip up the Nile – he wasn't expecting a revolution.
Paperback: 978-1-78279-158-4 ebook: 978-1-78279-157-7

## Blood Profit$
The Lithium Conspiracy
J. Victor Tomaszek, James N. Patrick, Sr.
The blood of the many for the profits of the few... *Blood Profit$* will take you into the cigar-smoke-filled room where American policy and laws are really made.
Paperback: 978-1-78279-483-7 ebook: 978-1-78279-277-2


## The Burden
A Family Saga
N.E. David
Frank will do anything to keep his mother and father apart. But he's carrying baggage – and it might just weigh him down ...
Paperback: 978-1-78279-936-8 ebook: 978-1-78279-937-5


## The Cause
Roderick Vincent
The second American Revolution will be a fire lit from an internal spark.
Paperback: 978-1-78279-763-0 ebook: 978-1-78279-762-3


## Don't Drink and Fly
The Story of Bernice O'Hanlon: Part One
Cathie Devitt
Bernice is a witch living in Glasgow. She loses her way in her life and wanders off the beaten track looking for the garden of enlightenment.
Paperback: 978-1-78279-016-7 ebook: 978-1-78279-015-0

### Gag
Melissa Unger

One rainy afternoon in a Brooklyn diner, Peter Howland punctures an egg with his fork. Repulsed, Peter pushes the plate away and never eats again.

Paperback: 978-1-78279-564-3 ebook: 978-1-78279-563-6

### The Master Yeshua
The Undiscovered Gospel of Joseph

Joyce Luck

Jesus is not who you think he is. The year is 75 CE. Joseph ben Jude is frail and ailing, but he has a prophecy to fulfil …

Paperback: 978-1-78279-974-0 ebook: 978-1-78279-975-7

### On the Far Side, There's a Boy
Paula Coston

Martine Haslett, a thirty-something 1980s woman, plays hard on the fringes of the London drag club scene until one night which prompts her to sign up to a charity. She writes to a young Sri Lankan boy, with consequences far and long.

Paperback: 978-1-78279-574-2 ebook: 978-1-78279-573-5

### Tuareg
Alberto Vazquez-Figueroa

With over 5 million copies sold worldwide, *Tuareg* is a classic adventure story from best-selling author Alberto Vazquez-Figueroa, about honour, revenge and a clash of cultures.

Paperback: 978-1-84694-192-4

Readers of ebooks can buy or view any of these bestsellers by clicking on the live link in the title. Most titles are published in paperback and as an ebook. Paperbacks are available in traditional bookshops. Both print and ebook formats are available online.

Find more titles and sign up to our readers' newsletter at
http://www.johnhuntpublishing.com/fiction

Follow us on Facebook at https://www.facebook.com/JHPfiction
and Twitter at https://twitter.com/JHPFiction